THE CASE OF THE PRINCESS AND THE INTERSTELLAR BOUNTY HUNTER

NOVELS BY COLIN ALEXANDER

LEIF THE LUCKY

Starman's Saga: The Long, Strange Journey of Leif the Lucky
Murder Under Another Sun
The Lucky Starman
A Planet of Wrath and Tears
The Secret of the Martian Girl

THE INTERSTELLAR REACH OF HUMANITY (THE REACH)

Complicated: The Interstellar Life and Times of Saoirse Kenneally
The Case of the Princess and the Interstellar Bounty Hunter

OTHER SCIENCE FICTION AND FANTASY

Princess of Shadows: The Girl Who Would Be King
Accidental Warrior: The Unlikely Tale of Bloody Hal
My Life: An Ex-Quarterback's Adventures in the Galactic Empire

MYSTERIES

Lady of Ice and Fire
God's Adamantine Fate

A Novel of the Interstellar Reach

The CASE of the PRINCESS and the INTERSTELLAR BOUNTY HUNTER

COLIN ALEXANDER

afictionado
FICTION BY COLIN ALEXANDER

*For Mom and Dad, who usually
figured out what I was up to*

PREFACE

Understand something: I am going to lie to you. Oh, not all the time, of course, and not about every little detail. It's not that I wouldn't do that; it's more that it's too hard to make up every piece of a story so that it holds together and reads as true. You would realize you were reading fiction, I'm afraid, and I would lose you. A good lie must be inserted unobtrusively amid the truth, concealed within statements that can be verified, like a trace of poison hidden in an otherwise tasty meal. Then you would swallow it. CenSec—our slang for Central Security—could probably create a complete fiction that you would swear was verifiable, but I am not that good a liar. I'd be lying if I claimed otherwise.

That was a joke. I'm told my sense of humor isn't that good either.

How did I become so conversant with lies? It goes with my job, in a way. I am a librarian. I have the privilege to hold the position of third assistant librarian, History and Historical Fiction Section of the Planetary Library of the Directorate in the capital city of New Edinburgh on the planet Offyonder. I feel compelled to note that, for

a planet so far out in the Interstellar Reach of Humanity, our library and databases rival even those of planets near Earth that are members of the Assembly of Worlds.

In fact, we are an unusual world. For all the men and women who flew starships through wormhole after wormhole to settle new planets, we are among the very few worlds where people actually established a better, more peaceful society. We have civic justice, with equality for our people, and we have civic order. Oh yes, there have been a few issues—call them hiccups—but we did what we set out to do, and perhaps none have done it better.

Enough of pride. You can look up all of that, including my role in our society, even though it is not a position of any grandeur. What matters for this particular topic is that I deal extensively with books of both fiction and history; and history, let me assure you, is heavily laced with lies. Truth is determined by the winner.

I have often wondered if it was my comfort and familiarity with fiction and with lies that led CenSec to pluck me from my comfortable and obscure position for a job that the man who said he was to be my handler told me was of utmost importance to the Director himself. Once the mission was explained, its importance was immediately obvious to me, as it will be to you. Of course, another factor might have recommended me to a security service. That is, of the loyal retainers of the Directorate, I was as unknown to others as it was possible to be. I was, and am, a modest man of modest abilities and ambition, a man of no importance.

ACT I

W. S. Gilbert, *H.M.S. Pinafore*

CHAPTER ONE

Sᴴᴱ ᴡᴀs ɴᴏᴛ ᴜɴᴀᴛᴛʀᴀᴄᴛɪᴠᴇ.

This is the wrong way to begin. I know that. I can only plead that, after a more-than-thirteen-hour flight from New Edinburgh to the Susan Anthony Airport on the subcontinent of Serendipity, followed by a three-hour drive into smog-smothered Bannion, the sight of my first objective made an immediate and indelible impression.

I could tell she wasn't unattractive even through the smoky haze that passed for atmosphere in Donovan Black's Wormhole, the bar where my inadequate information package said I could find her. The bar might have been named for the wormholes that allowed starships to reach planets across the Interstellar Reach of Humanity, including Offyonder, where it stood, but I would have called the place a different type of hole. The only bright and polished object in sight was the double-barreled shotgun on a rack behind the bartender. Tables of wrought iron painted black were ranked across a poured concrete floor, maybe half of them occupied in the late afternoon.

The customers filled the place with a babel of conversation along

with the smoke from our native broadleaf joints, which contained nicotine, and from Earth-derived cannabis. A row of radiator pipes along one wall was the heat source during the winter; there was no hearth. The pipes were quiet now, although the spring weather outside kept enough chill for me to wear a jacket. Inside, the bodies added warmth, although not enough of those bodies had been bathed recently, so they added more than warmth. My nose wrinkled. It was time to do what I had come to do. Standing where I was wouldn't accomplish anything.

My favorite leather boots kept sticking to the floor as I walked over to her table, courtesy of a variety of liquids that had been spilled and partially dried without mopping. She did not look up from the glass in front of her, as though she was debating whether to drink the dark brown contents. Three identical empties sat next to the full glass and a black knit cap.

"You're Solly?" I asked.

"Who's asking?" She looked up at me.

Up close, I saw nothing to revise my initial estimate. She had high cheekbones and a strong jaw—a proud face, I thought. Wide eyes of light brown, with darkness below them, framed a straight nose. Her mouth was small, set hard, with thin, chapped lips. The smooth skin of her face said she could not be even thirty years by Earth standards, but that skin was drawn taut over cheekbones and hollowed cheeks in a way that said her eyes had seen more than they should have. A shaggy mass of brown hair had been hacked into a semblance of a bob, except on the right, where it was shaved back from the temple to past the ear, showcasing a wide, jagged scar that split her scalp. A tattoo of two intertwined stems rose from behind her right ear to bloom in small flowers at the tip of the scar. The thorns on the stems were as large as the petals.

"Martin Allgeier, third assistant librarian of the Offyonder Planetary Library," I said by way of introduction. "I would like to discuss a business proposition."

"Whose business?"

"The Directorate." I confess I was proud to offer a business relationship on behalf of the planetary government of Offyonder. I held out my holographic identification card—absent a combined facial and retinal scanner, the closest you can come to a guarantee of identity on Offyonder—as proof of my bona fides.

Her eyes narrowed as she scanned my card. Then she leaned back in her chair. She wore a false-leather duster styled in large brown-and-black geometric patterns. It was at least two sizes too large, so that even though it was open down the front, I couldn't discern her figure. For the same reason, the jacket could have concealed a variety of objects. "I've worked for local Bannion police and the gray-and-blacks—CenSec, that is—here. Never heard of you."

"I'm from New Edinburgh. There is no reason you should have heard of me." Indeed, the same could be said for the vast majority of the population. And, of course, I am not an individual who stands out in any way.

I could tell from the way her eyes flicked up and down that she was measuring me. I have a narrow, rather standard, white face with only enough melanin to make it not pale and no scars or birthmarks to make it interesting. My brown hair is neither shiny nor curly. It merely lies there to cover my head and fall partway across my forehead. My eyes are brown and soft, my nose thin in proportion to my face, which is also consistent with the rest of my frame. She was not impressed, probably because I am not an impressive physical specimen.

"All right, Martin Allgeier. I am Sol. Why don't you take a seat and tell me first who you are, beyond a title and this card, and second, what business the Directorate wants me to attend to." Her voice, rough and raspy, could have come from too much alcohol and smoke, but it did fit her. "Hey, Donovan!" She waved at the bartender. "Bring us another of your special mash."

I wondered what variety a place like this would call "special." Offyonder has many species of wild grasses that can be cultivated, then fermented in a mash and distilled to produce liquors with flavors ranging from sweet and sour to hot and spicy. Our mashes are famous across much of the Reach and probably could have rivaled our exports of doped diamonds—diamonds co-crystallized around microscopic veins of lithium, rhodium, and other rare earths that are crucial in the generators starships used to make wormholes—except that we drink so much of them ourselves.

The barkeep, a tall man with a broad, round face, full lips, and skin as black as the depths of space, with an expression as friendly, brought over a glass of special mash while I settled in a chair. *Settled* is the wrong word. My frame was tense, and I leaned forward from the edge of the seat.

"I had a comm message from Grandma Toby that she was coming to see me," Sol said to Donovan. "Not someone from the Directorate. Did you know about him?"

They both looked me over.

"No. I know Toby is coming," Donovan said. "She just moves a little slower nowadays." His voice was softer than his face predicted.

"Hah. Not when it's something she wants. She's only slow with money in advance." Sol ignored my existence.

"Toby will be here. You know about her and money."

Sol shrugged and looked back at me. "For now, you can talk."

She took the glass from Donovan and pushed the one that had been in front of her over to me. I acknowledged the gesture that it was safe to drink by taking a gulp. This mash was sour enough to pucker a drainage pipe, never mind a mouth. The taste hid the alcohol until the drink reached my stomach. I grimaced and introduced myself again.

"A third assistant librarian." She took a slow drink. "You sound proud of that."

"I am," I assured her.

"You do understand, Mx Allgeier, that the Bannion police and the gray-and-blacks and … other people here pay me to find and catch people they want. Sometimes they do not care about the condition of those people when I turn them over."

"Yes. A bounty hunter. That's what I was told." That was nearly the limit of the information on her I had been given. It was one of life's ironies, I thought, that my library in the capital had extensive databases about people and events on Earth and many other planets—even if somewhat out of date, as they were updated only when ships came in-system—while information about people across the ocean on this subcontinent was almost nonexistent.

"Then I do not understand why a third assistant librarian is here to see me. I do not retrieve overdue library books."

"The Princess Claire is missing," I said. "CenSec believes she was kidnapped by Spartacist rebels."

Sol arched one eyebrow. "Claire Montaigne is not a princess and our Director is not a king, though I have heard some call him that," she said.

Might as well be, I thought but did not say. "You need to understand some of the background. Claire is the Director's niece, and he … has no children of his own. He treats her as if she were his own daughter and … indulges her. Her mother died a few months before the Riots, that's ten years ago now. Her father, Geoffrey Montaigne, was the middle Montaigne brother, between the Director and Joshua. He was the amiable and popular one, but for all of that, the insurrectionists broke into his house and murdered him during the peak of the Riots. Claire was fifteen. She had, well, a breakdown. She has not been … right since. If calling herself and being called 'princess' helps her, who are we to deny her that little pleasure?"

Sol's gaze could be intense. "*Princess* and *king* are words that set a few people above others. That would violate the Good Speech Guidelines, no? As a librarian, you should be more skilled with words."

When I did not respond immediately, Sol continued. "Ah yes. Our GSG are voluntary guidelines, so we can permit the use of the word *princess* but dance around calling a person crazy."

She might be toying with me, daring me to acknowledge a violative word that could be coupled to a violative thought. I liked that spark, however. To be as honest as I'm willing to be, I've had plenty of those thoughts, but I'm skilled enough to keep them to myself.

"It is mandatory to use the voluntary guidelines. How else can we be sure they are used? It is the enthusiasm with which they are used that is up to each citizen."

Sol found this perplexing. "Does your library have a book to explain this?"

"The *Citizen's Manual* would be best," I said. "Everyone gets a copy when they turn fourteen, and they have to pass a test at eighteen to earn full citizenship and university eligibility." I paused to consider the one additional item of information on Sol in that minimal dossier I had. "You came from off-world about five years ago, so you might not have this manual or even know about it. In fact, I don't think we distribute to Bannion at all, and you can't make an electronic connection to the library from here. The Serendipity subcontinent is a bit outside of civilization."

Sol's grin was pleasant to see. "Someone from Earth would say any planet as far out in the Reach as Offyonder is a bit outside of civilization, you know. In Bannion, you'll find people use whatever words they please and don't care about your GSG."

She might have had sarcasm in her words, but I still liked the way the lines curved in her cheeks. We had relaxed the GSG after the Riots anyway, and I even make a point of using gendered pronouns. I had not been sent here, however, to debate the finer points of GSG or discuss why control of speech led to proper thought and thus maintained civic justice and order.

"Maybe we should return to the business at hand." I hoped she would keep her smile.

Sadly, her features hardened. "If Claire—whatever we wish to call her—has been kidnapped by Spartacus and the ragtag remnants of his rebel band, why hasn't the Directorate sent its overwhelming armed force to inflict yet another annihilating defeat on them and save your 'princess'?" She paused while I flushed, then added, "Let's leave off the sarcasm for now. Why not the ArmedSec battalion? Why me? And why you?"

My handler had, of course, anticipated these questions and coached me on the response. "She flew here to dedicate the new hospital, so the Spartacists could be holding her either in the Uplands or Bannion. Transporting ArmedSec by air is restricted by the planes we have with the necessary range, and sea transport would take too long. Also, they have missions on the mainland that cannot be neglected. Even for Claire." That was perhaps the most delicate way to put the situation. "You are known among the people here, and your reputation is that you earn your pay. The Prin— Claire will be more comfortable with a woman. I am a nobody and will not be noticed."

Sol regarded me for a moment, then finished her drink. "Whatever the Directorate chooses to say about them, the Spartacists are not to be trifled with. This will be expensive."

"I am prepared to transfer this amount of Directorate Markers to your account immediately on acceptance, with an equal amount of DMs when Claire's plane takes off with her on it." I held the face of my comm out for her to see. That opened her eyes. Literally.

"Plus expenses," she said. "Plus any bribes I need to give—and I decide on the size of the bribe. Plus immunity for any … collateral damage. And CenSec stays away from me. If you believe in DeepSec, them too."

"Agreed, except that I can't say anything about DeepSec. I don't think they even exist outside of stories people tell, and I work in the Directorate."

That was the truth too. There were rumors all across Offyonder about a "deep security" apparatus, a security service buried deep inside the Directorate, responsible only to the Director himself. Those rumors say that DeepSec watches the watchers, culls whoever needs culling, and does whatever the Director deems necessary. However, no member of DeepSec had ever come forward or been outed. Sol obviously knew all that because she extended her hand to me across the table.

"Done," she said. "Make the transfer of my upfront."

I extended my comm to touch the one she held out and tapped in the coded sequence. That way, the payment did not require waiting for a connection back to New Edinburgh, a detail anyone with her background would expect. That done, I took her hand, paying attention to the scars across her knuckles as I did. Grip strength is not an indicator of character or bravery. I fervently believe this, as my hand is rather soft. Hers was hard and rough. It felt like I had been gripped by an assembly of steel struts and cables.

"Solly!" The shout from the entrance to Donovan Black's Wormhole carried more force than I would have expected from the small gray-haired woman in pants and a loose shirt who was quickly limping to our table. This had to be Grandma Toby.

"Solly, this time you need to do something. You, not me." It was a voice that would not accept refusal, a parent telling a child to attend to chores. Sol's eyes left me at once, as if I were an uninteresting piece of furniture. "They've taken Lizzie Quickfingers! I would have been here sooner, but I had to be sure I had the information correct before I spoke to you."

Sol was on her feet in an instant. I rose as well, even if no one noticed. Standing, she was even with my height, but I am only five-six. It was hard to be sure with that oversized jacket of hers, but her shoulders were probably broader than mine.

"This is not possible, Toby. Her mother pays protection for her." The words were delivered as an announcement to anyone in the bar who was listening. Anger flashed in Sol's voice and on her face.

"It's the truth. Her mother died of the wheezes two days ago, in case you hadn't heard. Maybe people figure there's no more money for protection."

"Who took her, Toby?" Sol demanded.

"Dobson's boys from Castlegate Street. Nicky and two others," Toby said.

"They're out of their territory," Sol said.

"Word is they have protection on this." Toby's eyes were dry and hard. "Word is they're going to auction her."

"Who is Lizzie?" I asked, taking another look at Toby. "Your grand-daughter?"

Sol blinked, possibly surprised I was still there, but she answered.

"She's a streetdancer. Not Toby's anything. A fourteen-year-old street kid who's a liar and a thief when she's not dancing for solid DMs. For all of that, she reminds me of someone I used to know."

"Call the police," I said. "Or CenSec. They will stop this."

"No. You didn't listen to Toby." Sol's voice was harsh. "They are going to auction her for sex. They will also charge for people to watch. If they have protection, and they must, that means the police and the gray-and-black captain are getting a cut."

That was not possible. The police would not do that. CenSec would not tolerate it. Except, apparently, they did. One glance at Sol's face told me that. This was not New Edinburgh.

"She's a damned little thief and she's stole from me and from people I put her with when she ran off from that excuse for a mother, but she doesn't deserve this. You need to do something, Solly. This time it's beyond 'Toby finds a way.' I will pay for your services." Toby brandished an e-voucher so everyone could see it, then damned near shoved the card in Sol's face.

Sol pushed the card to one side. "Stop it, Toby. No fee."

I felt sorry for this Lizzie, whoever she was. Truly. She did not deserve what was happening to her. But I also felt sorry for Claire, who was not a liar and not a thief, and who had no control over who her family was. More important, there was a clear connection between what happened to Claire and my future.

"Wait," I said. "You're working for me. We have a job to do."

"I'll do that job," Sol said. "But there is nothing in the agreement we just made that says I cannot do other things. This one afternoon will not matter. They are auctioning her, not hiding her. It will not be hard to find them."

Sol waved off two more attempts by Toby to give her the card. She grabbed the knit cap off the table and yanked it down on her head, hiding the scar. Then, without so much as a glance at me, she strode past Toby to the exit. I hustled to keep up with her. We were outside before she realized I was still with her.

"This is not your concern," she said. "I will meet you here tomorrow morning. I will be at the same table. We can begin the search for your … *princess* then."

I summoned up such fortitude as I have. "Our business engagement has already started," I said. "My instructions are to remain with you during its term."

Sol drew back a step and looked me over again. Possibly, the sum of money she had accepted only moments before had an effect on her assessment. "Very well," she said. "Maybe you can be useful. Are you armed?"

I reached under my jacket and drew my Directorate-issued weapon.

What I held was a classic nine-millimeter semiautomatic. It was a Peacer-grade weapon with an electronic sight. I have always been amazed that, despite all the advances in technology that have taken us to the stars, for killing we still rely on bullets blasted out by chemical explosive from guns that would be easily recognizable to a man from hundreds of years ago. The reasons, I suppose, are obvious. These weapons can be produced by simple printer manufacture on many planets, they are immune to electronic trickery, and they kill very efficiently. I released the magazine and showed her the loads.

"Armor-piercing," Sol said. "I have the same. Suitable for even Peacer body armor at short range."

I slid the magazine back in. "I've had the fundamental training for anyone with a position in the Directorate. I know which end to point at someone I want to shoot."

She grunted. "Remind me not to be overdue on my library books. Come on."

CHAPTER TWO

SOL TOOK A LONG STEP TO CLEAR A BATCH OF REFUSE THAT HAD NOT BEEN outside the door when I arrived. Then she plunged into the pedestrian traffic along the street. I managed to avoid getting the trash on my boots and hurried to stay with her. Many of the people we passed greeted her with the show of a hand or nod of their head. Those who did not, regardless of the expression their face might wear, stepped out of her way.

It was a decent day in Bannion, which is to say that the gray cloud that routinely smothered the city only obscured any floor of a building above the fourth. That wasn't bad. It could have been right down to the ground. Bannion's geography was partly the culprit. The city sat in a bowl surrounded by mountains on three sides, and it fronted the ocean on the fourth. Those mountains, and the Uplands past them, were the reason the city was there at all. They held rich deposits of doped diamonds, a rare find on any planet. The naturally occurring doped diamonds might not be as perfect as the ones created in the labs on Earth and a few other advanced planets, but they would

work in the wormhole generators. Ours were sufficiently less costly than the ones from Earth to make shipping them on interstellars an attractive proposition. They served as the basis of our profitable trade across the Reach.

Those same mountains created the perfect conditions for thermal inversions. The Uplands were also excellent sources of coal, so Bannion relied on cheap coal for heat and power. Since the population of Bannion was there to get the products of the mines shipped out to the real cities and towns of the Directorate on the mainland, no one cared if the people here rotted their lungs in the foul air. There were always more who were glad to take the pay. Bannion was truly the armpit of Offyonder.

We forged our way through the tangled, garbage-strewn streets, every breath a reminder of the grime in the air that also dimmed the light. As if to emphasize what we were breathing, the concrete and bricks of the buildings and streets were streaked with black and gray from pollution that washed down in the frequent rains. Yet Bannion needed those rains—not for the water but to clear the refuse from its streets.

Rats scrabbled across every street we went down, picking and choosing among the leavings. The sight brought to mind a saying: The rat is second only to the human as a successful interstellar invasive species. How rats found their way into starship stores to cross the light-years was beyond my understanding, but they managed it. Wherever humans ventured, rats almost always came along. That observation does not include the fact that a single individual some-times represents both species. I did not intend that as a joke.

The citizenry on the streets, whether selling, buying, or on their way from one point to another, appeared as feral as the rats and as grimy as the buildings. Most of them wore the blue button-up-the-front coveralls we produced in quantity to guarantee people an outer garment at a fair price. On the mainland, people hated them, and they served as the root of many a snide comment about Good Clothing Guidelines, so they were shipped over to Bannion and given away. Here, the populace—gratefully or otherwise—wore them. The only contrast was a teenage girl in a short white dress—well, it had once been white, but on these streets, it stood out despite its dirt. She was dancing barefoot, earning an occasional tossed DM. I felt in my pocket and threw the ones I found to her. I should not have done that when I was on Directorate business, but she made me think of this Lizzie. I should not have allowed that to bother me.

Sol knew her way, which was fortunate. Bannion was nothing like New Edinburgh, or even our smaller towns across the sea on the mainland. Those places were laid out in neat grids, if they were large enough for multiple cross streets, and carefully mapped, with the maps updated as the towns grew. Bannion was a maze. No GPS satellite was positioned over it, and I doubted the streets had been digitized even if the Directorate had spent money on a satellite. The city had simply grown in organic bursts along with the output and importance of the mines—although that did not mean its denizens were important.

Sol stopped at a roadside vendor of grilled meats here and a storefront there to ask about a girl being auctioned. Sometimes she tipped a coin for the response. On one street, we passed a pair of Bannion police in dull blue uniforms, accompanied by a CenSeccer, immaculate in her gray shirt, black pants, and black jacket with its Unity shoulder patch of two hands clasping, one white and one black. No, she was not immaculate. One end of an epaulet had come loose so that it flapped as she walked, an odd bit of slovenliness for a CenSec officer and even odder for her commander to tolerate. Their hands hovered near their holsters if anyone came close. For them, Sol had only a nod, not a word.

Sol turned to me after six or seven brief conversations and said, "As you have no doubt heard, I have a location and time. This is not a secret. Not with bids and not with an audience planned, and there is no need for secrecy when protection is bought. Protection!" She spat into the street. "The only protection they need is from someone else trying to steal her to do the same. No one will come to save her. Well, they didn't buy protection from me." Her face matched the grimness of her words.

From the last vendor Sol spoke with—a woman selling pans of roasted vegetables she claimed were authentic gene-modded Earth stock—we took a short additional walk to an unprepossessing two-story building of badly mortared brick. Garbage was scattered liberally across the street in front of it. Two stone steps led up from the street to the front door. That doorway lacked any kind of electronic lock or video screening, which was not surprising. Those systems came from off-world and were still uncommon even in New Edinburgh, although our library had one at the main entrance. A crudely handwritten sign gave a comm number to call.

"They're making enough money at what they do to afford a comm," I said.

"This bunch mostly deals drugs. Some good stuff. They make money. And for this, they want a clientele with enough money for a comm." Sol tapped the number into her unit. I couldn't make out what the voice on the other end said, but I heard, "This is Sol," from her. "You know me, know the number on your screen. I've got a friend here. You might as well let us in."

There was no audible reply, only the sound of a latch being pulled back on the other side of the door. Footsteps retreated and the door stayed closed. Sol looked at me, then pushed the door open. I followed her in.

Behind the door was a small bare vestibule. Whoever had pulled the latch had not stayed to greet us. Beyond was a large room, curiously arranged. Most of the furniture had been pushed to the walls. A mattress lay on the floor in the center of the room, and I could guess its intended use. On the other side of the mattress were a couch and end table. Two large men in dirty work pants and T-shirts lounged on the couch. Each had a pistol holstered on his belt, the handle pressed outward by similar paunches. A third man stood behind the couch, one hand resting on its back, the other holding a pistol. It wasn't aimed at us, only casually held, pointing off to the side. That man had to be six-five, with a short black beard and receding hairline framing a hard, square face. The three men in the room accounted for the men Toby said had taken Lizzie.

"So, Solly," said the tall man, "I didn't know you liked these kinds of games. Or maybe you're introducing your friend to them." He grinned at me, which I did not appreciate. "The fun doesn't start until nine. Or maybe you want some different fun first." He gestured with the pistol to a glass jar on the end table. It was filled with pills and capsules and transdermal tear-offs. From the expressions of the men on the couch, they had been enjoying some of their own wares.

"I'm not here for your party, Nicky," Sol said. "My job is the girl. What does it take to get her out—intact?"

Nicky laughed. His eyes went to his right. That drew my eyes in that direction as well. A short hall led off the room we were in, a door at the end of it and another one midway down one side. Nicky's eyes came back to us.

"You don't have that kind of money," he said. "If you did, you wouldn't spend it on street trash like her."

"Tell me the price."

Did Sol think she could charge this as an expense on my mission? One look at the set of her jaw made me drop the question. Not that I would have brought it up anyway.

Nicky's eyes narrowed. "You're serious. I'll tell you how much and why. This one is a virgin. We examined her. She is. Streetdancer at her age, but she is. We're auctioning each of her holes. You gotta cover that. Then there's plenty of people who are payin' to watch. Gotta cover those. And Captain Campbell—you know Captain Campbell of CenSec, and I know he knows you. He's covering us, and the C-sucker gets his cut. And we were gonna have our own fun after, and you gotta cover that." Nicky gave a number that would have bought the Princess Claire. "You got that?"

"I have a card that will cover it." Sol tapped a small surface pocket on her jacket.

"One hand moves," Nicky said. "Only to that pocket."

Sol brought her right hand slowly to the pocket and unsealed it. Only her fingers went into it and worked out an object that her hand screened from all of us.

She flipped it at Nicky and dropped down to her left as it flew from her hand. A shuriken buried one of its points in Nicky's left eye.

Nicky had fired one shot as the shuriken flew, but it went through where Sol had been and struck in the vestibule.

Screaming, Nicky clapped a hand to his eye, which only buried the point deeper. The two on the couch tried to leap up and draw their weapons simultaneously, but their coordination was affected by whatever vice they had indulged in. Sol was faster. Both hands had gone under her jacket as she dropped to the floor. They came out with weapons that blazed and filled the room with thunderclaps.

I'd dropped to one knee myself the instant Sol moved, having no desire to stand there and be shot. My attention went to the door at the end of the hall as it cracked open. A light in the hall ceiling glinted off metal in the opening. I fired in that direction. Twice. Rounds designed to punch through even Peacer body armor treated the door like tissue paper. A yell sounded behind the door. Then a thud.

It was over that fast. Nothing continued except the ringing in my ears. Sol was in a low squat, one leg straight out, the other bent so her ass was nearly down to the floor. She straightened up, and that gave me a look at her armament. Her right hand held a pistol like the one I had. In her left was a chopped-down double-barrel. She walked across the mattress to look at the two on the couch. Both were dead, one with a bullet wound over his heart, the other flayed open in multiple places from the flechettes out of the double-barrel. Nicky was writhing on his back on the floor behind the couch, screaming and cursing. Sol fired one shot into his head. She retrieved the shuriken, wiped off its point, and replaced it in its pocket.

"The room at the end of the hall," Sol said to me. She advanced down the hall, pressed tightly against one wall. I copied her, although the lack of activity from the room made me think it would stay quiet. We passed the side door and went to the end one—a cheap drywall sheet with two chest-high bullet holes in it. Sol kicked the door open and swept both weapons across the small bedroom beyond. A body lay on the floor, hit twice in the left chest.

"Not only will I never be late with a library book again," Sol said, "I'll never even borrow one to begin with. You ever shoot a man before?"

I told her, "No. Of course not."

Her gaze spoke of disbelief. "It doesn't seem to bother you much."

"Not at all," I said. "He was an evil man."

"Hmm. How did you know it wasn't the girl?"

"I … well …" I stammered a bit. "She wouldn't be loose to go to the door. And no fourteen-year-old is going to open a door into a gun battle."

"Maybe," Sol said.

CHAPTER THREE

LIZZIE WAS IN THE ROOM DOWN THE CORRIDOR, BOUND, GAGGED, AND NAKED on the floor. I was ashamed that this had happened in our Directorate. Granted that the Directorate was not perfect—and Bannion was not a real city of the Directorate—but civic justice and order on a young world around a far star were among our prized accomplishments. We taught in our schools that what we had done on Offyonder was special. I felt shame to be looking at the bare body of a teenage girl. This was not something our society condoned. I could not bring myself to touch the girl, so Sol had to undo the bonds.

Once freed, Lizzie clung to Sol like moss on a rock. No words came, only sobs. We needed to get her away from the building—but for that, she needed clothes. There were none in the tiny room and it was hard to start searching because of the way she clutched at Sol.

"Snap out of it," Sol said at last. "Half the neighborhood either heard the gunfire or has heard about it by now. The locals won't get involved where there's shooting, but Campbell is as crooked as they

come, and he may be doing more than just looking the other way. We need to leave, and that means you need something to wear."

Lizzie was still crying and shaking, but she did stand and begin to move on her own.

We found pants she could wear in the other room, where the man I'd killed lay sprawled on the floor. We never found her underclothes. Sol stripped a shirt off one of the dead men on the couch and then pulled it over Lizzie's head the way she might dress a doll. She had to tie a knot in the shirt at the waist because it was so large. Before we left, Sol grabbed the jar of drugs from the table and stuffed in into a pocket of her coat.

"Bonus dividend for us," she said.

I assumed she meant to sell them. I said nothing.

When we were outside, with Lizzie in between us, the girl's shirt billowed in the wind like a schooner in a stiff breeze, showing off its bloodstains to everyone in the street. People gave us plenty of space and found other places to look.

"Listen to me!" Sol hissed at Lizzie. When there was no sign of comprehension, she grabbed Lizzie's shoulder and gave the girl a hard shake. "Are you listening to me?" It took two repetitions before Lizzie nodded. "I'll get you to Grandma Toby. She'll give you clothes, a little moncy, help you get out of Bannion to the Uplands. What you do there is up to you, but go. There's nobody to buy you protection here anymore, and what happened today can happen again. You go! Understand me?"

I think the response was a genuine nod of Lizzie's head and not simply the way her body was shaking.

AFTER A SERIES OF COMM MESSAGES WITH GRANDMA TOBY, WE LOCATED HER AT THE waterfront in the harbor. She was sitting on an overturned crate and smoking a broadleaf joint, as though she spent all her days that way. Sol made clear that her conversation with Toby was private by walking with Toby another dozen paces along the water's edge and turning her back to us. Lizzie sat on the paving stones with her arms wrapped around her knees and her head down, while I stayed apart and gazed out at the water.

Beyond the harbor, the sea stretched out to the horizon. The view made me wonder what it had been like to come live in Bannion when it was first settled, cut off from civilization by that infinite sheet of sea, dependent for supplies and any new human contact on ships that appeared only irregularly on the horizon. Of course, this was not very different from a newly settled planet dependent on starships dropping through a wormhole. The analogy to what was commonplace put the concept of a subcontinent isolated by ocean back in perspective.

Sol's return from speaking with Toby put an end to my musing and brought me back to where Lizzie sat. "Lizzie," she said, "Grandma Toby has spoken with Donovan Black; you probably know who he is. He has someone with a car who will take you out of Bannion to the Uplands. You go with Toby now. Go, no questions."

Prisoners walked to the gallows with more energy than Lizzie showed, but she did not look around. Sol stared at her back until Toby put an arm around the girl and they walked off into the mists curling up from the water.

By this time the light, such as it was, was fading fast. Sol made no attempt to sell any of the drugs as we left the harbor. She brought them home with her. She brought me as well. My urging that we had to begin our search for Princess Claire was fruitless. It was too late in the day to start, she said. My protests that lodging had been arranged for me in Bannion, and that was where my driver had taken my baggage, were also to no avail. Sol insisted. A rumble of thunder with an increasing drizzle may have helped decide me against wandering around in search of the place I was supposed to stay.

Her home proved to be a tenement building in the section called Harborside, not far from the river that bisected Bannion and also near the harbor at the river's mouth, where we had met Grandma Toby. There was little to distinguish it from any other building in that block.

Poured concrete decorated only by streaks of soot faced the street. It lacked any street number or indicator of an address. It did have a robust metal door with a lock. Sol produced a metal key from one of her pockets and opened it.

A short hallway led from the entrance to a room that was probably a good size, but Sol's place felt cramped the moment I stepped inside. It was packed with furniture: an overstuffed couch, with some of the stuffing escaping a cushion in white tufts; four armchairs, two in a fake leather and two in some sort of fabric, none of them matching; tables covered in bottles and empty food containers; shelving along the walls crammed with all manner of bric-a-brac; and more of the same strewn around the floor. A pair of narrow windows set high in the opposite wall would have let light in during the day, although how much light was questionable—they were partially blocked by blankets and towels stashed in front of them. As I looked at the windows, a flash of light lit up the glass, followed by a blast of thunder and torrents of water splattering against them.

I turned back to the contents of the room. Here and there I saw weapons. A shotgun leaned against one wall, while three pistols competed with empty bottles for table space. Two nunchakus hung over the arm of a floor lamp, while a pair of shuriken were embedded in the edge of a shelf across from the couch. Based on the other punctures that ran along the shelf, it served as a frequent target.

I took all of this in quickly. I am good at that. A plaintive yowl sounded from somewhere, but I saw no physical part of a cat or other creature to go with it.

Sol pulled out the bottle of drugs she had taken and stirred around in it with three fingers. She pulled out a trio of ovoid gray pills.

"These are good ones." She popped them in her mouth and swallowed dry.

She held the bottle out to me. I declined with a shake of my head and held my empty palms out to her.

"Suit yourself," she said. "I'll be right back. Make yourself comfortable." She retreated to a hallway at the rear of the room.

The couch was the only surface for seating that did not need to be cleaned off. I elected not to use it, because if I did, when she returned from that other corridor, she would be at my back. I'm a bit odd that way.

If I wasn't going to sit, I was going to take a closer look at more of what was in the room. A small statue that stood in a cleared space on the beat-up coffee table in front of the couch caught my eye. No. It wasn't a statue. It was a trophy, a figure frozen atop a pedestal in the middle of a whirling dance move. Draped over the figure was a red ribbon with a golden medal attached. Along the ribbon, I read: LONDON FREESTYLE DANCE COMPETITION. GOLD MEDAL. The date was about a dozen Earth years ago, although I'm not precise about keeping track of the year on Earth.

I picked up the trophy with the ribbon and medal dangling from it. The inscription on the trophy and medal was the same as on the ribbon. Underneath those words on the trophy was an engraved name: SOLANGE MARIE-LOUISE VALERIE DE GILBERT ET DE MONTMICHEL.

Sol came back into the room while I was studying the engraving. Her coat was gone and she wore a loose flowered shirt that left her midriff bare. Its two top buttons were open. That shirt and her close-fitting pants revealed a figure that still could have been a dancer's. She was not moving as smoothly as a dancer, though. Whatever she had taken, on top of the earlier alcohol, was having an effect.

"This is your name, your real name?" I asked. "You were on Earth."

"I'm Sol," she said. "Old history. No meaning." Her words slurred.

She plucked the trophy from my hand and placed it on a shelf next to a mounted pic. Then she made her way back to the couch and sat down. *Dropped down* would be a more accurate description. She opened another button on the shirt. It was now open past her xyphoid, with only one button holding it closed.

"You could sit with me," she said, smiling. But almost immediately, her eyes rolled up. Her head tipped back and to one side. Her body followed, slumping over on the couch cushions. The shirt hung open and down, exposing one breast.

I stood where I was, frozen. The invitation Sol—or Solange—had made was obvious. The way she was now passed out on the couch, well, I could have done whatever I wanted, and in the morning, told her whatever story I decided to concoct. I didn't want to do that. Possibly it was because she had risked herself in a gunfight for a girl who was nothing and meant nothing. Possibly I could say I am simply timid. Regardless, I was not going to touch her.

Another yowl sounded. I turned and this time spotted a creature perched in one of the window recesses on top of a folded blanket. It was a three-tail kit, fifteen pounds' worth from its size, cloaked in black fur. Catlike green eyes blinked at me, and it wound its three tails together. The kits were native to the Offyonder mainland. Earth rats ate Offyonder vegetables and fruit and human garbage. The three-tail kits, although not obligate carnivores like Earth cats, ate the Earth rats and made themselves at home in human dwellings. When the rats who had journeyed by starship to Offyonder made their way by seagoing vessel to the Serendipity subcontinent, humans imported the kits from the mainland to control the rats. It was a tribute, in a way, to the beauty of our hybrid ecology.

The kit leaped away as I pulled the blanket down. The blanket was large enough to cover Sol. I lifted her feet onto the couch so that she would be more comfortable. Then I spread the blanket over her and tucked it under Solange Marie-Louise Valerie de Gilbert et de Montmichel's chin.

That done, I turned back to the trophy and took the pic next to it off the shelf. It showed a young couple in front of a fountain landmark I did not recognize. One of the two was a younger Sol, her face more rounded, her hair short, neat, and even. She wore an open black leather jacket over a white pullover, the grip of a pistol in a shoulder holster protruding from under the jacket. She gazed up at the man next to her with what I could only call adoration.

He was several inches taller, with slicked-back black hair in a widow's peak and a trim goatee. His white skin was a stark contrast to the hair, and I would say his face was hard. I couldn't tell where he was looking, but it was not at Sol or the cam. His black shirt was open almost to his navel, showing off sharply defined muscles and dark chest hair. A thick coat of hair is a sign of health in a dog, but in my opinion, it is superfluous on a man. I didn't like him.

I returned the pic to its place, cleared off one of the armchairs, and removed the kit that hopped up there before I could sit down. From the chair, I watched Sol for a few minutes. She was breathing easily; no risk there. The tautness had gone from her face, leaving it softer. I doubted she was more than a year or two older than the Director's mentally challenged Claire. I wondered how she had come to be on Offyonder, nearly seven hundred light-years from Earth, where she had won a dance competition. How had she come to be what she was? In fact, I wondered about the man in the pic.

I shook my head and checked the timer on my comm. Out in the Reach, Offyonder is a fairly modern place as worlds go, but we can't afford a fleet of geosynchronous communication satellites that would allow communication with any part of our globe at any time. We don't even need those satellites, since New Edinburgh and most major settlements are on the Hastings Peninsula and microwave towers suffice. What we have is a pair of medium-orbit satellites that can be used to reach out-of-the-way places, and Bannion was as out of the way as it got. The communications window these satellites offered was open now, and for this mission I had been issued a comm that could contact a satellite.

I called my handler in New Edinburgh to report. I was able to say that I had made contact as planned and the mission was proceeding. I found a reason why nothing else had happened in the rest of the day. I did mention the corruption of Captain Campbell.

CHAPTER FOUR

I WOKE TO THE SOUND OF GREASE SPATTERING AND THE SMELL OF BACON COOKING. I was still in the armchair in Sol's front room, where I had fallen asleep. Wan gray light filtered through the narrow windows and outlined the crouching black kit and its tails. I sat forward and regretted it. I am not old, not nearly old enough to be stiff in the mornings—yes, I am past thirty Earth years of age, but only by a couple—but the back cushion was below the level of my head, so my head had tilted back. To make things worse, the chair lacked any support in the lumbar region. I would blame the state of my musculature on the poor design of the chair.

I stood up, stretched, touched the floor between my feet, and rotated my hips through a few circular motions. I would do.

The couch Sol had occupied was empty, the blanket piled at one end. I followed the signals of breakfast to the corridor at the back of the room. An opening in a short hall revealed a tiny kitchen.

Sol shut the stove off as I appeared. She grabbed a plate from a sideboard, turned, and extended it to me. I saw four strips of bacon,

burned black, and a pair of eggs fried to yellow stones on a white field as hard as plastic.

"For you," she said. No residue from the previous night's intoxication showed on her face or in her eyes. She had mostly combed out her hair so that it fell across her head in a gentle wave to be tucked behind one ear. The side with the scar and tattoo had been shaved smooth so that both stood out.

"I did not expect you to make breakfast for me."

Her lips twitched in what did not become a smile. "Call it a thank-you for what you did last night."

"I didn't do anything last night."

"That's my point."

The meaning of her statement was clear; it did not need a reply. I bit into the bacon. While the brittle stick snapped and crunched between my teeth, Sol poured herself a glass of what looked like Donovan's special mash. I looked askance at it as she took a drink.

"I ate already," she said. "I allow myself one in the morning to get started. Sometimes more." She gulped down half of it. "Old behavior … expectations … you know …" She mumbled words into the glass. Only some were audible.

Sol focused on drinking the mash rather than expanding on what she had said, and I chose to ignore the cryptic part. While she drank the rest of it, I worked my way quickly through the breakfast she had made for me. Chicken and pigs thrive on Offyonder, so bacon and eggs could be considered the planetary breakfast. In all but the poorest households, a girl would know how to cook bacon and eggs by the age of six. That thought took my mind back to the trophy and the picture. To the conversation we had not had. To how little information I possessed about the person I had been told to rely on for a job of such importance.

"You are from Earth originally," I said. "Regardless of what might be old history, you are from Earth." I had never met such a person before. Obviously, all humans came from Earth initially, but Offyonder is about as far from Earth as the Reach goes.

"I pretty much told you that," Sol said. "You are looking at me as though you expect tentacles to sprout from somewhere."

"No, no." I made myself laugh. "I am only surprised you came here. Where was that pic taken, the one on the shelf where you put the trophy? On Earth somewhere, I assume."

Sol tipped her glass back to get the last drop of mash. "It's a place called Trafalgar Square. In the city of London, if you've heard of that."

"And who is the man?"

Sol shot me a sharp look over the top of her glass. "That's Gilbert Mortimer." She collected my plate and put it, along with her glass, into the kitchen's tiny sink, turning her back to me in the process. "I was his partner," she said in the direction of the sink. "I loved him very much. He is a true celebrity among interstellar bounty hunters."

I made note of the past tense in her first two sentences, filed that for another time. "I am surprised you describe a bounty hunter as a celebrity. Especially on Earth. That makes no sense."

"Oh, but it does." She put both hands on the edge of the sink, bracing herself there while she looked up to where the ceiling joined the wall. In a sudden move, she spun around to face me again. Her eyes darted to the egress, but it was a very small kitchen, and I was in the way. "This is all in the books and databases in that library you pride yourself on. Even if that library is updated only when a ship comes into the system, this isn't like a new development on a world that sees only an occasional starship. This information has to be in your system. How come you haven't read it?"

The question was delivered as an accusation. I admit that I flushed. I do that easily. "My expertise, as I told you, is history and historical fiction. I could discourse all morning on the emperors of Rome or offer quotations from the meditations of Marcus Aurelius. I don't know anything about interstellar bounty hunters. You are probably the only one who has ever come to Offyonder."

I could, in fact, have discoursed at length on numerous other topics, as I read widely; however, it was not safe to go into many of those areas. What I said about bounty hunters had the virtue of being true in the sense that I had no need to know about bounty hunters on Earth. Only this particular bounty hunter who had come to Offyonder.

"You should broaden your horizons," Sol said dryly. "We are celebrities. On Earth, and probably on most planets belonging to the Assembly of Worlds. And Gil achieved super-celebrity status." She paused. "Listen. The Reach is how big? Fifteen hundred light-years across by now. Probably more. I doubt anyone knows. Even on Earth, all databases are out of date. A ship through a wormhole is pretty much instantaneous, while a radio signal is limited by the speed of light. So, it's only when a ship comes in from somewhere that new information from that somewhere can be entered.

"There are always people who have done things that make them want to disappear into the Reach. Sometimes what they have done is significant enough that authorities want them back. Who's going to get them? The Solar Council Peacers are spread so thin, have always been so undermanned, they're not going to do it. They only care about wars and planetary societies in collapse; that's where their orders send them. No police force from any world is going to go. Even among the Assembly of Worlds, no planetary authority would let police from another world operate. It's us! We go get them. That's why we're celebrities. And Gil, well, like I said: super-celebrity."

In the course of that short speech, Sol had changed. Her eyes shone; her whole face lit up. She stood taller.

"So how do you go from a dance competition on Earth to being a celebrity as an interstellar bounty hunter?" It was a reasonable question. "And how did you wind up here? Offyonder is not where celebrities go."

The light in her eyes dimmed. "For all your Directorate's vaunted civic justice and civic order, in Bannion and the Uplands there's a lot of money to be made. Plenty of business for me." She held my eyes for a moment, then truly deflated, a tire that has run over a spike in the road. Her shoulders sagged downward. "The rest is my story," she said. "That's … another time."

I did want to hear her story, but judging from the droop at the corners of her mouth and the overall slump of her body, it was probably a long one. What might interest me could not take precedence over what I needed to accomplish, and it could certainly have no place in what I reported to my handler. "Let's start on our job, then. What we did not start yesterday."

Her face and posture signaled relief at my direction even with the reminder about our dereliction of duty yesterday. The kitchen was too small for that sort of conversation, so we returned to the crowded front room, where she reseated herself on the couch. I went back to the uncomfortable armchair after scooping the kit off the seat. I was, obviously, not going to sit next to Sol. I made a point of not looking at the picture or the trophy, since she clearly did not want them brought up again. At least, not now.

"What do we know?" Sol asked. "It has to be more than her name, famous as that is for this world."

It was embarrassing how little we did know about the situation. "I told you that the Princess Claire was here to dedicate the hospital, which makes sense since it is the Claire Montaigne Medical Center and Clinic of Bannion."

"Everyone in Bannion knows about that hospital," Sol said. "The Directorate has told everyone since construction started, whether they listen or not, that it was being built so that people in Bannion would finally have modern health care. But it is so far up the mountain road that most people, the people who need it most, can't get to it. And can we avoid calling her 'the Princess' all the time? It's a waste of breath."

There was truth in what she said, but I did not need to acknowledge it. "That kind of talk about the hospital, a major investment of the Directorate in Bannion, is verging on a breach of GSG," I said. "I would like us to avoid that. Even the third assistant librarian needs to be an advocate for our civic justice and order."

"Of course."

I had meant my words to be gentle. Her tone left me feeling chastised. I ignored the sensation. "What we know is that *Claire* reached the hospital. Her activities there were brief because they were limited to what she can handle. She presided over a short ceremony, made an announcement on behalf of our Director, and greeted the chief hospital administrator along with some of the employees. Then she left for the airfield, where her plane was waiting to take her back. She never arrived at the airport."

"The airfield is in the Uplands, through the pass on the mountain road," Sol said. "Since it is the only airfield on Serendipity, its use is solely transoceanic transport, and that only for high-priority travel. Its use is restricted to Directorate business and a few of your privileged people." She leaned forward on the cushion to peer at me. "*You* would have come through there."

"Well, yes. This is important Directorate business, and it can't wait three and a half weeks for me to sail to Bannion from Port Gandhi. I mean, the airfield is not officially restricted. It is only that, with the cost of a transoceanic flight in terms of resources, we can't have flights on a regular basis."

"Of course." A short pause followed. "How was Claire traveling to and from the hospital?"

"Three-car motorcade," I said. "She would have been in the middle car, with a driver and a CenSec guard. CenSec driver and a CenSec guard in each of the other two cars as well."

"Three cars filled with gray-and-blacks do not typically vanish into thin air," Sol said. "Usually, making them vanish would need an explosion big enough to be obvious. Has the Directorate received any demand? Ransom or otherwise?"

"No."

"And you, the Directorate, are sure this was done by the Spartacists?"

"Who else would it be?"

"That was my question." Sol fixed me with an unblinking stare. I found it uncomfortable. I thought she could be a difficult interrogator to deal with.

"If you are asking if there are factions within CenSec, or even ArmedSec, that would do this as part of some power struggle, I do not believe it. Our Director and Joshua Montaigne have the complete loyalty of their services."

"Until the day they don't," Sol said. "I'm not suggesting you would know. Only that we cannot ignore the possibility and go running around the Uplands chasing Spartacus without some evidence that he is behind this. The Directorate did send *you* to hire *me*."

I had to admit that she made sense. If there was a question about the loyalty of personnel in CenSec, using a nobody librarian and a bounty hunter might be a good plan. "I will keep that in mind," I said. "I even will not discount the possible involvement of the fabled DeepSec."

That was rewarded with a smile. "Do you have images of Claire?" Sol asked. "Authentic ones, I mean. Not the sort of pic they put up that is manipulated to make her look like the second coming of Helen of Troy."

I blinked once. "Yes. You're from Earth. The Trojan War. The face that launched a thousand ships." She smiled again. I had passed a test. "I do. Here." I made sure my comm was locked to allow examination of only the file I brought up. Then I handed it over. Sol took her time swiping through the images.

In truth, as much as I ever tell it, Claire did not need her images manipulated for beauty. She had the blond hair and pale blue eyes of the Montaigne family, with soft curves that made her face more oval than angular. Her pale white skin never had a blemish. The tight-fitting gowns or athletic wear—depending on the setting of the image—showed off a trim figure with good muscle definition. I had seen her in person during some functions at the library, so I knew this was all true.

"She could have been an athlete, or even a dancer," Sol said. "She has the build for it. Maybe a distance runner or a martial artist. Her eyes are funny, though, in these images."

I knew what Sol meant. I had noticed it myself when I had seen her in person, that odd vacant expression of hers. In anything that reached the public, Claire's eyes were fierce, a touch narrowed, as if intent on whatever was in front of them. In these unaltered images, her eyes were wide, almost unfocused, as though some fairy creature in the distance was more interesting than the world around her. There was scuttlebutt, never said where it could be heard by anyone who would report it, that the eyes were a window on the soul and the mind, and that Claire's were empty because she had neither a soul nor a mind behind them. I could not speak to that, but I had seen those eyes.

The library had images, as well, of the Director, his brothers Geoffrey and Joshua, and their wives from years ago. The Director and Geoffrey were instantaneously recognizable, adult male versions of Claire: blond, blue eyed, and pale skinned. Joshua stood out starkly, with the same skin color but coal-black hair and piercing black eyes. The images were from long enough ago that the Director had still been referred to by his name, before he became only Director or the Director, an appellation now enshrined in GSG. That was back when Geoffrey, Claire's father, had referred to the Montaigne brothers as the Three Musketeers, a reference I knew, even if no one else understood it. Claire was the only child in that family. Her eyes had not been odd when she was young.

"It doesn't mean anything," I said. "It can't matter for what we need to do."

"On that, I agree," Sol said. "I think we should visit the hospital."

CHAPTER FIVE

"I'll arrange a car," Sol said. She vanished out the door before I could follow.

I suspected that she did the arranging with Grandma Toby, who I imagined arranged a great deal in Harborside. I suspected as well that the arrangement was made at an inflated price, which is why Sol had me stay behind. I would not have minded. It was not my money. She also arranged, when I gave her the name of the lodging where I was supposed to stay, to have my baggage delivered to her place so that I could change clothes while she was out.

The vehicle Sol returned with was a four-seater with a cargo bay in the rear. It was dented and every surface was scratched, but the electric engine was silent even if the rest of it rattled loudly as we cruised through the streets, forcing bikers and pedestrians to the side. Battered as it was, this vehicle was another symbol of triumph for the Directorate. Most of the structural components were printed from multipurpose polymer at plants outside New Edinburgh, and the lithium for the batteries came from the mines in the Uplands. It

was easy to see why our Director said we had no need of the Assembly of Worlds.

Our route was the reverse of the one I had arrived by yesterday. The northern end of Bannion was almost empty, the road lined by a long string of derelict buildings. The damned Bannion smog had been so thick I had not noticed them on the way in. With better visibility, this vacant slum did not create a positive impression. I reminded myself that Bannion was across the world from the center of civilization. Some rough edges could be expected.

The storm of the previous night had sent water cascading down the tributaries into the river that led to Bannion's harbor. It had caused flooding up in this north end, now mostly receded to large puddles. The water swept the open sewers clean, which was a positive effect, but one that would lead to an awful reek in the harbor come low tide, which was not such a good result.

The mountain highway was steep and winding as it rose from sea level to the pass. About halfway up, we drove out of the smog and fog layer into blinding sunlight. The storm of the night before had blown out completely, leaving—up here, anyway—a crystalline blue sky. It was a welcome sight to my eyes. I sorely missed it after only one day in the Bannion soup.

Curiously, there was no traffic coming down the road from the pass. I would have expected haulers bringing the raw material from the mines and produce from the Upland farms down to Bannion. That produce was what fed Bannion. Of the mine output, almost all of it went across the sea to Port Gandhi, where the doped diamonds were sent to the spaceport for the starships to take into the Reach and trade for the modern tech our Directorate enjoyed. The rest, the routine lithium and rare earths, we used for ourselves on the mainland. I filed the absence of vehicles for later consideration.

The entrance to the hospital was down a narrow, one-lane road that cut away from the mountain highway and ended in a mostly empty parking lot. Sol and I sat in the car and looked at the hospital for a few minutes in silence. The Claire Montaigne Medical Center and Clinic was one of the structures that made me proud of what our Directorate had accomplished in our time on Offyonder. Set on a broad shelf of land high on the road to the pass above Bannion, the hospital was a four-story building of shining steel from the electric forges outside New Edinburgh framing wide walls of glass from the works at Barstow. All of it had been shipped across the ocean at a substantial expense and then constructed well above the foothills by skilled teams, some of whom had been flown in, so that the people of Bannion, half a world away from the center of the Directorate, would have modern medical care. Well, as modern as you could have seven hundred light-years out into the Reach.

"First time here?" I asked Sol.

"Yes. Been to the Uplands plenty, but never had a reason to come here."

"Beautiful, isn't it?"

"Most monuments are," she said.

I wasn't quite sure what to make of her comment, so I let it pass. We got out of the car and walked along the path to the entrance. It was a long path that wove between banks of red and yellow flowers native to the Uplands—plants we have brought to the mainland to use as decorative ground cover. The walk made me realize that the air was thin this far up. It occurred to me that for inhabitants of Bannion with wheezes caused by the smog, the location of the hospital, beautiful as it was, might not be salubrious.

Inside, the polished stone floors of the reception area and the corridors that led from it shone in the light coming through the glass walls. Once we passed the information attendant at the front desk, the only person I saw was a middle-aged man in blue coveralls wielding a long-handled rubber tool. His job appeared to be ensuring that neither dirt nor scuffs marred that stone flooring. The echoes from our footfalls made me think of Sol's comment that the people who needed the hospital could not reach it. And the ones who really needed it would not breathe so well here if they did reach it. This was not an observation I intended to discuss with my handler.

Dr. Samuel Lomell was the chief administrator and physician-in-chief of the hospital. A secretary guarding his office door insisted his calendar was full. When Sol commented on the contrast between the emptiness of the hospital corridors and the fullness of Dr. Lomell's calendar, the secretary made an audible sniff.

"Any openings in Dr. Lomell's calendar are reserved for doctors and for important meetings that arise in the course of the day," he said.

My title of third assistant librarian did not impress him as implying that one of those important meetings had arrived. A substantial number of solid DMs that appeared from a pocket of Sol's duster, however, was sufficient to make our meeting important enough. It took a brief call on the secretary's comm to confirm that Dr. Lomell would meet with us in his office.

When Dr. Lomell appeared, he proved to be a tall man who wore blue work pants and a shirt manufactured from the same wool as the custodian's coverall. What distinguished him, in fact, from the custodial crew was his fitted white jacket, the attire that since time immemorial has meant "doctor." His dark brown face wore a genial smile under a broad nose. The fringe of mostly gray hair that ran from a little above his ears to the back of his head marked him as someone well into his middle years. He ushered us into his office, which took up an entire side of the building, the floor covered with woven carpets that must have come from New Edinburgh. He gestured for us to take two chairs on one side of a massive desk made of polished red wood from the forests of the Hastings Peninsula. He seated himself behind the desk in a chair that was probably real leather.

Lomell leaned back in his chair and interlaced his fingers across his stomach. "I am curious to hear what brings such an unusual pair to see me, although anything to fill my empty day is welcome."

"Empty?" I asked. "Your secretary made it clear your schedule was packed."

"I'm sure," Lomell said. "How much did you have to bribe him?"

Sol chopped the figure in half. I asked Lomell if he was going to take a cut or confiscate it.

"Neither," he said. "He needs the money. Most of them do. This hospital was ostensibly built to care for Bannion's poor, of which we have plenty, but as I am sure you have already figured out, the only poor that we have here are the staff."

"This verges on breaking GSG, Doctor," I said. "Dangerous speech makes me uncomfortable."

"Then I apologize for your discomfort," Lomell said. "The Directorate is clear that we need to follow GSG to avoid dangerous speech or thought that could upset our civic justice and order, although I will note that each new version of GSG appears more concerned with words that would injure the Directorate than individuals or groups of individuals."

"The Directorate did relax the guideline having to do with individuals on matters such as pronouns and intended humor." I did not want to spend my time defending what Lomell should understand.

Lomell gave me a smile that said he was accustomed to people defending GSG, regardless of how they felt. The smile did not last long. "Yes, that loosening is greatly appreciated. However, when it comes to aspects of civic justice and order, I would say that Captain Campbell's murder is more of an issue than any words of mine."

"What!" The word burst out of Sol. She sounded surprised.

"Yes," Lomell said. "Two of his CenSeccers brought him in very early this morning. Partially disemboweled. As though someone had used one of those barbed spears the deep-sea boats catch armorfish with."

"The man was corrupt," I said. "A corrupt CenSec officer."

"One of his men said he thought it was about a payoff." Lomell shrugged in his seat. "I'm sure it was. Down there, if someone's hand isn't out, it's because it's already in someone else's pocket." He blew out a sigh. "We have strayed from the intent of your visit. Which you never told me."

"We are here about Claire Montaigne's visit to this hospital," Sol said. "Can you tell us what went on? What did she do? Where did she go?"

The questions brought Lomell upright. He leaned forward, elbows on his desktop. "Now I am interested. Your reputation, Sol, is known to me. And some bureaucrat from New Edinburgh. About Claire Montaigne. Why?"

"My questions first," Sol said. I heard again a tone that would brook no disobedience.

"Damned little," Lomell said. "And nothing that hadn't been scripted. She came with a troupe of eight CenSeccers. Was introduced to me up here. Cut a ribbon that had been strung across the main entrance. Read a short speech in the main reception area, which she did not do very well. Then she met with a group of our lower-level workers. She was pleasant; they were appreciative. Not that the CenSeccers let more than a couple of them actually approach her. That was it. CenSec took her back to their cars, and away they went."

"You said the speech did not go very well," I said. "What do you mean? What didn't go well? Was she interrupted?"

"No, no," Lomell said. "Nothing like that. But it was a problem even getting started. Apparently, her favorite guard, a CenSeccer named Gregr, had been ill and did not accompany her. She wanted to talk to me about that instead of giving the speech. As if I could diagnose and cure him from here. Then, we finally got her to start, and it wasn't a long speech, but multiple times she just went off it completely. She'd say something and jump to something else. One of the CenSeccers would have to direct her to the script, actually make her look at it."

Sol leaned toward him, although the width of his desk kept them far apart. "What did you think of Claire?" she asked. "You did meet her personally as part of the schedule."

Lomell looked at me before he answered. "To avoid any question of breaching GSG, I am going to keep this clinical. Her eyes never focused on me. I don't think her attention did either. It was as though something else, something I couldn't see, was occupying her. When she spoke, I won't call it flight of ideas, but her associations were loose. I must tell you that I'd seen her before, on a consultation two years ago when I was still in New Edinburgh. She is significantly worse now. Much worse."

"You saw her before. Do you know what is wrong with her?" I asked.

I used the word *wrong* myself specifically to put him at ease in the conversation. It was a breach of GSG to say that there was something *wrong* with someone. That implied inferior status and applied shame. You would say that a person had a *condition*, the same as they had a particular hair color or secondary sex characteristics. In the case of Claire Montaigne, however, it was widely understood that even saying she had a condition would be a breach of GSG. I had never spoken with a physician who had consulted on Claire Montaigne, and I wanted him to speak freely.

"No." Lomell was emphatic. He drummed his fingers on the desktop while he regarded us, doubtless assessing the likelihood that his words would be reported. "Something occurred at the time of the Riots," he said at last. "People who had any contact with her before and after know this, even if they will never say it. But … what was it? Did the stress from the Riots and the deaths of her parents cause her to have a breakdown? Did she coincidentally have a psychotic break? Did she, again coincidentally, have some form of encephalitis and then a strange postencephalitic syndrome? I do not know. What I can say, because I have said it, is that there are elements of psychosis and of early dementia, and it is progressive."

He sighed. "I already made the mistake of saying that to Joshua Montaigne and suggesting that, even without being a member of the Assembly of Worlds, it ought to be possible to obtain a more accurate diagnosis and, possibly, treatment on a more sophisticated planet, even Earth. Offyonder is rich enough, although we could also join and simplify the process."

"You are implying that Joshua Montaigne did not like your suggestion about treating Claire," I said.

"He did not." Lomell slumped back in his seat and steepled his fingers. "He said that Claire did not believe she had a condition that required treatment, and she did not want any treatment. He reminded me of our pillars of civic justice."

"This makes no sense," Sol said.

I waved a hand for her to stop. It did make sense. It was part of civic justice that an individual had the right to decline treatment—any treatment, for anything. True, if this had been any ordinary individual, they would have been told that exercising that right would harm our society by depriving the Directorate of their useful work and that they and their family would have consequences. One way or another, people did what was good for them. This, however, was Claire Montaigne.

"I take it that was the end of the consultation and the matter," I said.

"Not quite," Lomell said. "Within a week, I was transferred from New Edinburgh to here. I suppose, given that Joshua was involved, I should be grateful. You know the rhyme."

I did know the rhyme: *Cross a Montaigne, never again!* People said it nervously and under their breath when they thought no one important was listening. It was not because people who crossed Joshua Montaigne disappeared. It was because pieces of those people then appeared in public places.

"Thank you for your candor," I said. "This is as far as it is safe to go in that direction. As far as the Assembly of Worlds is concerned, if we joined, we would need to accept scholars and travelers here. More important, we would need to contribute our people to the Peacers, meet their enlistment quotas. Their return to Offyonder after service would bring unwelcome speech and attitudes and would threaten our civic justice. Can we return to the original question of what happened here and move away from the medical diagnosis?"

Lomell gave me a sharp look, as if surprised that I had reversed course so fast and equally surprised that the third assistant librarian would be offering an opinion on the question of joining the Assembly of Worlds. I was, though, only repeating the position of Directorate officials, especially on the point of having our people serve in the Peacers.

It was Sol who pulled his focus back to where it needed to be. "Could we meet with the workers who met her?" she asked. "Only briefly."

———

Our meet and greet with the workers was structured in an entirely unsatisfactory way. Alternatively, it was entirely satisfactory, depending on whether any genuine conversation was expected to take place. The workers were brought to the front reception area and placed in what could have served as a receiving line. Sol and I walked along that line and were given time to learn each worker's name, their job, and their quick impression of Claire's visit. They told us how nice Claire had been, how she had greeted each of them by name, and how thrilled they had been to meet her. The fact that their performances were taking place under the watchful eyes of two CenSec officers may have had something to do with their behavior.

We did have one exception. Midway down the line was a grizzled old man. His back bent forward when he was standing up straight. The knuckles of his hands were swollen. When Sol came in front of him, he grabbed one of her hands between his and pulled her close.

"My family lives in Harborside, Solly," he said. "We respect you."

"Thank you," she said. "Tell me who you are."

"Johnston McGwire," he replied. "I take care of the outside grounds."

"And the parking area?" Sol asked. McGwire nodded. "And what did you think of the visit?"

"The Princess Claire, she thought she was somewhere else." McGwire's eyes kept darting in the direction of one of the CenSeccers. "She was having a conversation, but I couldn't tell who she thought she was speaking to or what she was saying. In the middle of it, she did something odd."

"Odder than speaking to someone who wasn't there?" I asked.

He looked at me, then again at the CenSeccer.

"It's okay," Sol said.

"All of a sudden, she hugged me," McGwire said. "Kissed me on the cheek." His voice was down to a whisper. "Said, 'It's good to see you, Uncle. Share my kisses with your coworkers. You're my favorite uncle.' I thought I would die. My whole face was hot. That gray-and-black"— his eyes went back to the same one—"was staring at me. But then she let go and clapped her hands and said something to the air beside her and went on to the next one of us. But there was a purse in the pocket of my coverall. A lot of money. I did split it with everyone."

Sol was smiling, although it was an odd smile. "You take care of the grounds. Did you see her leave?"

"Yes."

"Which way did they go?"

"The driveways coming in and out of here are only wide enough for one vehicle in each direction. They took the one that would go back up the mountain road. Toward the pass."

Sol moved on after that. From the corner of my eye, I could see the CenSeccer McGwire had watched start to come over. I broke away from Sol to intercept him.

I should be clear that I am not the sort of man who can put the fear of God, or any other deity, into anyone. I did intimate to that CenSec officer, however, that if any harm came to Johnston McGwire, he should know I made regular reports to my handler in New Edinburgh and that my previous report had mentioned Captain Campbell's corruption. I am sure he drew the appropriate conclusion. It is good to report to powerful people.

***

I RESERVED ANY FURTHER DISCUSSION WITH SOL UNTIL WE WERE SEATED IN OUR vehicle. Then I asked, "Why were you interested in the direction they went when they left the hospital? The airport is in the Uplands, she was only here to dedicate this hospital, and she left with her CenSeccer escort. Nothing untoward happened here."

Sol did not start the engine. Instead, she fixed me with a hard stare. "You were told that she was here for the hospital. Is it possible there was another agenda they might not have told a third assistant librarian?"

I was forced to admit the possibility.

"And you told me that there was a gray-and-black driver and guard in each car. That makes six. Lomell said eight gray-and-blacks came in with her. I am not going to discount the possibility that there are factions within the Directorate, even within your most loyal CenSec, that might have different objectives. Let me do the job you hired me to do."

I wanted to protest, as I had before, that CenSec served the Director and the Directorate; however, the person CenSec reported to directly was Joshua Montaigne, and there was always talk that CenSeccers had been "pruned" by him. There was likely more reality to that than the whispers of culling by the rumored DeepSec. Officially, there was only the occasional case of corruption, but the library did have some interesting records. I decided that if I protested, Sol would think I knew how to do her job better than she did. She would not appreciate that.

"Do you think she is demented or just crazy?" Sol's question came while I was organizing my thoughts.

"The Princess Claire, you mean?"

"Claire. Yes."

"You mean because of what Lomell said?"

"And because of the way McGwire said she acted."

"I don't know. Something is wrong, very wrong."

"Yeah." Sol tapped out a brief rhythm on the steering mechanism with her fingers. "If this has to do with CenSec factions, it is going to be difficult. Even if we are talking about retrieving a person from the Spartacists, it will be touchy. When the person is out of touch with reality, the degree of difficulty skyrockets."

"Is that your way of saying the price goes up?" I had no authority to pay more, but I did not want Sol to say she was out. I would not want to explain that in New Edinburgh. Besides, our agreement about expenses offered plenty of leeway in hiding extras.

"I didn't say that. Yet." Sol started the car. "Let's talk to CenSec at the airfield. I want to know why we have different numbers of gray-and-blacks and whether they know why there is no traffic on the road going down."

Above the hospital, the road slanted upward at a steep grade. In places, it was dug into the side of the mountain and wound higher in a series of switchbacks. Below us, sometimes uncomfortably close to the edge of the road, was the sharp drop-off down to the bowl of smog that concealed Bannion. At this elevation, we were above the tree line. The only vegetation was a thin green ground cover that coated the slopes. It grew out rapidly in response to moisture, then shriveled up when the ground dried. Its current lushness was a reminder of the thunderous rainstorm we had heard from Sol's apartment.

We had not gone far from the hospital when the road leveled out for a short stretch and ran through a man-made cut in the mountainside. Then it dipped, the first real decline since we'd left the foothills, before resuming its twisty climb to the pass. At the bottom of this dip, where the road was tightly bound by the sides of the cut, a large pool of water had collected. Sol stopped the car before the pool.

"This explains why there's no traffic coming down," I said. "Nobody is going to drive one of these electrics through that. The first hauler to find this must have turned back and reported it." I peered up the road but saw nothing. "They've halted traffic, but nobody has done anything about clearing it."

"Yeah." Sol was studying the water. "This is odd, though. I can't count the number of times I've been on this road, but I don't make a point of studying the engineering. Still"—she pointed across the water to the upslope side—"there has to be a culvert under this road to take the runoff. The ground up here doesn't hold water well. You can see the drainage ditch coming down."

"If the drainage was blocked, would you get this?" I asked.

"Maybe. That was a heavy storm last night. You saw the flooding in Bannion along the road out. Let's take a look."

We left the car and walked down to the water's edge. The pool was turgid. Whatever was below was obscured.

"Shit," Sol said. "No help for it. I'll bet something is down there."

Disgust evident both on her face and in her voice, she returned to the car, took off her duster, and laid it carefully on the driver's seat. Without the coat on, I could see one pistol in a shoulder holster, a larger hand weapon holstered at her hip, and a sizable knife sheathed at her belt. When she headed back to the water, the hilt of another knife projected above her waistband at her back.

She edged into the pond, cursing again as the water came up around her boots. "Ow! Kicked something."

She bent over and stuck her hand into the water. "It feels like the edge of a grate here. Not where it should be. It feels like it's on top of ground."

She waded in until the water was halfway up her calves. "I think there is something on the bottom here, but so much dirt has washed down, I can't see." She pushed one sleeve up her arm, bent over, and thrust the arm into the water. She fished around for a minute.

"Got it. Hang on."

Sol gave a tug and her hand broke the surface, holding an object. It was dripping and covered with dirt, but it was definitely a low-rise boot.

"I would say this goes with a CenSec gray-and-black uniform," Sol said. "Would you agree?"

She came back to dry ground, holding out her prize. The tread was typical of CenSec boots. "Yes," I said. "I see those a lot."

"Then I would say the drainage is blocked because the body—or bodies, more likely—of gray-and-blacks were shoved into it. No one would notice, because they're under the road, not until all the rain came and the water backed up. I'll guess the grating was pulled off and left at the roadside. If anybody saw that, they would assume a road crew was lazy and didn't replace it properly. The floodwater pushed it to where it is now."

"Are you saying Spartacus staged an ambush here?" I surveyed the landscape around us. There were no trees or bushes, but there were enough irregular rocks and boulders to provide concealment.

"It could have been Spartacus or one of his commanders," Sol said. "Nobody knows how many of those groups exist, or how all of them tie into Spartacus."

"But how could they have figured the timing?" I asked her. "Unless they had an informer at the hospital."

Sol shielded her eyes with one hand as she gauged the available cover. "If they were waiting away from the road and knew when Claire's motorcade was coming, they would have been able to get into position. Traffic isn't heavy on this road. If someone came at the wrong time, maybe they're in the culvert too. Either that, or this is where one CenSec faction found it convenient to get rid of the other."

"And do what with … Claire?" We had heard no demand from anyone. Of course, I might not have been told of any demand, or Claire might have been killed by mistake and also be in the culvert. If Claire was dead, it would have to be a mistake. She had no authority, no following, and, quite possibly, no knowledge of what day it was.

Sol held her comm out and stared at it. "This is a good spot for an ambush. No room to maneuver, enough cover, and no signal here for the comms." She slapped her hands against her thighs. "We should turn back to Bannion."

"Why? What good does that do?"

Sol laughed. "The first reason is that, like you, I know the electrical systems on the cars made on this world. We're not going to drive this thing through that water for the same reason drivers aren't coming down this road—the vehicle would short out and, maybe, we'd get electrocuted. Once we get back to where we have a signal, we can call the airport and tell them to send a crew to clear the drainage. Let them have the pleasure of opening that culvert. And I want an internal combustion vehicle. If we're going beyond the airfield, charging stations are not always where you want them. IC is more reliable. Finally, I want to get cleaned up." She wrinkled her nose at the gooey residue the water had left on her boots, clothes, and skin.

Knowing the source of the residue, I had to concur.

CHAPTER SIX

IT WAS LATE AFTERNOON BY THE TIME WE WERE BACK IN BANNION. SOL DROVE down to Harborside to find the man who had provided the car. I could already catch the rising smell as the tide went out and hoped this chore would go swiftly. Fortunately, she located him without difficulty. Money changed hands and we were left with the understanding that an IC vehicle would be available for our use the next morning. With that arranged, Sol headed not for her apartment but for the Wormhole.

Donovan Black's Wormhole was crowded when we arrived, but the table where I had found Sol the previous day was vacant. Sol walked straight to it amid calls of "Hello, Solly," and "Good evening, Solly," from all across the room. Apparently, Donovan reserved that table for her, and the entire clientele knew it.

Donovan's face was no friendlier than on the first night, but he brought over two dishes of food: chunks of chicken baked in a dough, with a fried egg on top. He also brought two glasses of his special sour mash. The food was good, I will admit, if not up to the standards of a

top New Edinburgh restaurant—not that I eat in such establishments. The crust was brown and flaky, the chicken tender. I ate all of mine, along with sips of the potent mash. Sol, on the other hand, only nibbled at her food while she finished one glass of mash and started a second.

That table was Sol's not only for eating and drinking; it also served as her office. She pulled out her comm as soon as we were seated and began making a series of calls while she took the occasional bite of her food and drank her mash. I could hear most of the conversations. She made arrangements for us to have passes that would allow us access to the airport buildings and the airfield, if we wanted it. She made arrangements to meet certain people, including some from CenSec, and to speak with workers. Promises of money were involved in most.

I, of course, had not had any difficulty moving through the airport when I arrived, but I was coming from New Edinburgh, not Bannion, and my travel had been arranged by CenSec. Had it been a mistake not to have made arrangements for Sol, given that she would face a different situation, particularly given the current circumstances? I hoped she was not annoyed that I had not obtained passes in advance. I told myself that the third assistant librarian could not have done that. More to the point, my handler would expect Sol to be able to manage it, if she were as capable as she was supposed to be, and Sol would know which people we should meet. It was not for me to impress her, although I did think I would enjoy it if I could.

At last, the conclusion of one conversation did not lead to another call and the start of yet another discussion. She clicked off her comm and slipped it into her duster. "I think that is the best I can do for now." She looked over to the bar. "Too early to go home, though."

"You said you would tell me more about yourself when there was time," I said. "If it is too early to leave, then there is time to do that." I did need to supplement the meager knowledge we had about her background.

"I did say that, didn't I?" Sol sighed. "Buy me another mash, and I will."

"You've already had four." I pointed to the line of empties.

"Then you will be buying my fifth. And sixth, I would imagine."

I was paying anyway, so I signaled to Donovan. She took the glass from his hand and drained half of it.

"My real name is fake." Sol grinned. A loud belch followed. "Oh, it's authentic, but it's phony at the same time."

"How is that possible?"

"My parents are wealthy and their parents were wealthy," she said. "Quite some Earth years ago, the government of France needed to raise more money and couldn't raise taxes further. France is a country on Earth. A country is a little like a separate world, except it's only a part of a world even though it can have its own customs, and language, and even military."

"History is my specialty," I said. "I know about the countries of Earth, and there are other worlds in the Reach that have separate nations too. It's not a good arrangement for civic justice and order."

"Never mind your civic order. You asked for my story." She drained the remaining liquid from that glass. "In France, having the *de* in front of the last part of your name means you are part of the old nobility. It doesn't mean anything, except for snobbery, but that means plenty. To some people. The government of France set up a system where, if you paid enough money, you could be a de Something. They used up all the old names, where the families had gone extinct, and then started making up new ones. All authenticated by the government. That was my parents. Because they were rich and could now claim they had social status as well as money, they sent me to a famous school in London. That's in a different country. It was the type of school where you live at the school, which meant I didn't have to live with them. Suited all of us, I guess." She signaled for another drink.

"I wasn't a very decorous student. No friends. Always in trouble. Fights. I joined the Junior Peacemaker Training Unit. You know what that is?"

"No." I really didn't.

"Well, you know the Peacers, the armed force of the Solar Council Off-Planet Personnel? You must."

"By reputation only," I said. "They've never been based here, and the Directorate certainly does not want them."

"Reputation is good enough." She chugged down more mash and blocked the resulting burp with the back of her hand. "It's for teens who want to join the Peacers when they finish school and are old enough, which is eighteen on Earth. I had to join a unit at a common-people school in the city because nobody at a school like mine would ever go into the Peacers. My parents were horrified. My school was horrified. Do you know why I joined?"

"To horrify your parents and the school?"

"No. Well, that was a side benefit." Her grin was directed to the bottom of her glass. Some of the long hair on top had fallen across the shaved side of her head. She pushed it back, working her fingers through a tangle as she did. "On Earth, the only way you can learn to use weapons or learn martial arts is to be in a national military or the Peacers. That's why I joined. I was good at all of it. I wanted to compete in martial arts, but my parents had to agree and they wouldn't. All they would let me compete in was dance. You saw the trophy.

"I like to compete. I like to win. Everybody at school made fun of me for joining the Junior Peacers. I didn't care. Except for some fights. Then it was in the news that Gilbert Mortimer was on Earth. He was actually in London. I heard through the Peacer group that he was going to be at a particular shooteasy." She stopped because her glass was empty.

Gilbert Mortimer. That was the celebrity bounty hunter in the pic on Sol's shelf. "What's a shooteasy?" I waved to Donovan for more mash.

"Anytime you tell people they can't do something or have something, they find a way around it." She accepted the new glass, stifled most of another burp that came on the heels of her first gulp, and resumed talking. "Shooteasys are private clubs where people go to shoot weapons they're not allowed to have in the first place. It's illegal, of course, but the police don't mind. Unless someone gets shot somewhere, and then they crack down for a while to show they mean business, but never mind that. I knew where Gil was going to be!

"The most famous, the most glamorous interstellar bounty hunter, and he was only thirty. And I was going to meet him! All you needed to get in was to have the right person to vouch for you. I was only sixteen, but they don't check. Somebody started a shooting contest. I won. And I got to shoot with him! All different weapons. Oh God, he was so gorgeous. And the stories of where he'd been and what he'd done. It was heaven on Earth. He gave me his comm code." She stopped. The joy that had been bubbling in her voice fled. "I need another."

After I got it for her, she cradled the drink with both hands. She contemplated the surface of the liquid before she spoke. "Of course, I was ratted out. Marybeth Carnivale, may she rot in hell. I broke her nose and several of her ribs. It didn't matter. I was already done. The headmaster called me in, notified my parents. I was expelled. My parents said I was a disgrace. I couldn't go home; they threw me out. They said I had better figure out how to support myself. I told them to fuck off. I'd show them. I called Gil.

"We met in London. He said all the right things, all the things I needed to hear. He said he could use a new partner. He'd been solo for a few years, but someone who could shoot as good as me, he was okay with that. That's when we took that pic. It's Trafalgar Square in London. I think I told you that.

"He said he had a hotel room two blocks away. We should go there, have sex for the night, so he could be sure we would be good together. I was *sixteen*. I hadn't thought it through that way. I said I wasn't sure. He laughed. He said I obviously was sure. He said I'd made up my mind, I just didn't recognize what making up my mind was like. 'Solange, if you're still a little girl, you let me know. I'll see you get back to your parents.' That's what he said."

The contents of the whole glass went down at once. "So, I slept with him. He was rough and it hurt and I cried, but he told me that I obviously loved him and I told myself that I loved him and it was okay."

Right at that moment, I would have liked to inflict a slow and painful death on Mx Gilbert Mortimer. "There's more to your story, isn't there?"

"Oh, there's more. So, so, so much more. But not now. Not even with another glass."

Tears were starting to make their way down cheeks I would have sworn had been dry for eternity. I couldn't ask her to say more. Not here. Maybe not anywhere.

"I think you should be back at your own place," I said.

She nodded. When she stood, she wobbled.

"You can lean on me, if you want," I said.

"I can walk on my own." Her words would have been resolute if they hadn't been slurred a little. "Just catch me if I … stumble."

The Wormhole was the kind of place where people make sure they don't see or notice what they should not see or notice. We were able to reach the exit without a word or a glance from anyone, including Donovan. From there, we made our way slowly to Sol's apartment. I gave thanks that despite the hour and the reputation of Harborside, no one accosted us.

"Just put me on the couch," Sol said when we were in the mess of her front room. "That's where I sleep anyway. I don't use the bed."

I helped her out of her duster but did not touch any of the weaponry she was wearing. She paid no attention to it. She did fumble for that bottle of drugs we had taken, but her coordination was no longer able to manage it, so she left it alone. She allowed me to help her lie down on the couch and put her feet up as I had done before. I found the same blanket I had used the previous night and covered her with it. The black kit waved its three tails and supervised my work from its position on the back of the couch. It found no cause to disapprove.

I sat down in the same armchair and watched her for a little while. There had been a few instances, as I was helping her onto the couch, where my hands had touched her skin: her hands, her legs just above her ankles as I brought her feet up, once between her neck and shoulder as I positioned the blanket. There was no question in my mind that she had flinched each time.

It is the truth, to the extent I ever tell it, that I am a man who enjoys the company of women, despite being a man of few social graces or skills. Even so, within the broad range of human interactions, I would say that the physical act of fucking is the most over-romanticized and overrated. It was better for me to sit on Sol's chair and create in my mind conversations between us and shared experiences that we would never have. From the moment I laid the blanket over her, I did not touch her. That is a sworn statement.

CHAPTER SEVEN

THE NEXT MORNING, WE WERE BACK AT THE SPOT ON THE MOUNTAIN ROAD where the culvert had been blocked. A work crew was there, four of them in coveralls with gloves over their hands and masks over their faces, under the supervision of a CenSeccer in gray and black. Her only concession to the work being done was a mask over her face.

By the time we arrived, the pool of water was gone. The crew had piled six filled plastic bags at the side of the road where the cut widened. A sole with the typical CenSec tread stuck out of one of the bags, revealing its contents. A small truck with an open cargo bay was parked near the bodies, a car a little farther up the road. Both vehicles were white with CenSec markings in red.

The CenSeccer waved for us to keep going, but Sol stopped the car, letting its IC engine idle roughly. That brought the CenSeccer over to Sol's window.

"What part of *move on* don't you understand?" The CenSeccer sounded irritated. I suppose, having spent her morning pulling decomposing bodies out of a culvert, she had a right to that.

"I'm working for CenSec," Sol said. "Contract from New Edinburgh, from HQ. You pulled out six, I see. Were all of them CenSec? Was there anyone or anything else in there?"

The woman's eyes narrowed, although the mask blocked the rest of her expression. She had to be wondering if Sol was telling the truth, if she really did report to someone in New Edinburgh who would be upset if Sol's questions were not answered. In the end, no part of the answer was a secret she had to keep. "They were all CenSec. There's nothing else in there. You're welcome to crawl in yourself and check."

"I'll take your word for it," Sol said. "Were any of them from your unit at the airport?"

"No, I'd assume they're the ones who flew in. Don't know any of them beyond uniform and identification."

"So, you don't know anything about two more gray-and-blacks who joined this group?" Sol asked.

The officer jutted her masked chin forward into the window opening. "What the fuck are you implying? I don't know anything about that. It's not my job to know everybody's assignment, or to be telling you if I did." CenSec officers, in general, are accustomed to interrogating rather than being interrogated. This one's voice said she had reached the limit of the tolerance induced by Sol's mention of HQ.

"We'll only be here a few more minutes," Sol said.

She drove past where the crew was working and halted where a switchback turn began. Sol cut the engine, stepped out, and walked to the outer edge of that hairpin. She stopped there, looking out. I had no option but to join her.

The mountainside fell away below us in a sheer drop, damn near vertical. Sol's feet were mere inches from the edge and she was looking down, yet her stance was relaxed. It was an effort to make myself stand as close to the drop-off as she was. I never had the grace or balance of a champion dancer.

"The level of the soup is lower today," Sol said, giving the smog the name used by those who lived in it. "It's pretty much only in the

Bannion Bowl. The mountain valleys up here, not even much haze. Do you see what I'm looking at?"

A long way below us, the mountainside and valley were clothed in trees. We were far enough out of the Bowl that the smog had not killed them. The most common tree on the subcontinent was one found on the mainland as well. It grew a single trunk that shot up straight, easily reaching 150 or 200 feet at maturity, with numerous branches beginning at about fifty feet. Its leaves were bright green, the center of each leaf about the size of the palm of an adult man, with three to six lobules coming off the edges. Each leaf bore a vague resemblance to a hand, hence the name of handtree given by the original settlers. Those leaves created a dense canopy, which made it easy to see what Sol was talking about. A gash had been cut into the canopy of leaves covering the slope. A bright spot of sunlight reflected from the opening.

"There's metal or glass down there," I said. "After the ambush, they sent the cars over the edge."

"Yes." Sol was shading her eyes and scanning the area below. "There's enough road before this turn that an electric could accelerate to a speed that would launch it out for a good fall. They could have packed the bodies in them, but maybe the culvert was easier. No one would have figured on there being enough rain to block the road."

I tried to summon outrage over the wanton destruction of those vehicles. We do make our own vehicles on Offyonder, but this was a meaningful loss of resource on a still thinly settled world—especially on the Serendipity subcontinent, where shipping cars over the sea took almost the same effort as sending interstellar cargo. Still, the vehicles were replaceable. Not all people were.

"The numbers don't match, though." I turned to Sol, glad of an excuse to stop gazing into what felt like infinity.

"The gray-and-blacks, you mean." Sol came away from the edge and I followed her back to the car. "Yeah. Lomell said there were eight at the hospital. Unless he miscounted, where are the other two?"

"In the cars?" I suggested.

Sol shook her head. "No. No reason to split them up. Whatever you're going to do with the bodies, you do it with all of them. This makes a fight between CenSec factions unlikely. We know the eight were split up among three cars. Two are not going to take out six, unless they had help from ambushers. Maybe we've got two gray-and-blacks working with Spartacists."

I have read enough history that nothing about betrayal could surprise me. "Maybe we should find out about the two CenSeccers from the airport who joined up with the ones who came with Claire."

"Yeah," Sol said. "Let's do that."

———

THE PERSON THE SUSAN ANTHONY AIRPORT WAS NAMED FOR WAS OBSCURE ENOUGH that even I had to query our library database before departing New Edinburgh, but when I had looked her up, I had to concede that she was an appropriate selection to illustrate civic justice. The Directorate always paid close attention to the details of civic justice, and this helped a great deal in maintaining our civic order.

The airport itself was not impressive. That may have been a factor in choosing an obscure historical figure for the name. It was carved out of a rocky plain well over a mile high. The location had probably been chosen because this was the first sufficiently level ground on the other side of the mountains. It certainly was not convenient to the mines or the farms, but it was the closest available location to Bannion, which supplied all the construction equipment and personnel for the airport, and the already barren land did not need to be cleared. Closest to the road was a cuboidal brick building with a steeply pitched roof that sported a tall antenna. Signs carrying the red-and-white CenSec logo—GSG GIVES RESPECT. CENSEC PROTECTS RESPECT—were fastened between windows of the first floor. Across a short open space from the brick building stood the terminal building, a two-story rectangle of concrete. The grounds were nothing but rock and dirt, without any attempt to decorate the place with flowers or greenery. The sign proclaiming Susan Anthony Airport was metal painted black where it was not rusted—about as elegant as the brand for some enormous farm animal. Sol's preparations the previous day saw us ushered through the door marked CENSEC ONLY on the second floor.

Gerd Willoughby had not been the captain of the CenSec unit at the airport when I came out from New Edinburgh only two days ago. He was not happy to see us.

"Arrived yesterday," he said as we walked into his office past the nameplate by the door, which had not yet been changed. "Told Bradford he was relieved and sent him back on the plane that brought me." He pushed out a snort. "I'm sure if he'd had any advance warning, he would have thought about running to the Spartacists in one of the hill camps. As it is, though, I have no briefing, almost no resources, and now the two of you." He fixed us with a stony stare from close-set eyes. "We have records on you." He indicated Sol with a nod. "A bounty hunter. Who has done jobs for us. There's a nice price on Spartacus's head. I'd think you'd be going for that."

Sol smiled and tilted her head so Willoughby could not miss the scar. "Good reasons for not doing that. Nobody can tell me what his head looks like. In fact, nobody I know of, and that includes CenSec, has a way to confirm identification of him at all. Too easy for you to deny I got the right man. Or can you give me that information now?"

I could hear Willoughby's teeth grind. "No, I can't. Beyond the fact that Spartacus is a man, nobody can give you more. Word is, he's this well protected because he's a Peacer agent sent to destabilize the Directorate, give the Peacers an excuse to send a force here, take control. They're jealous of how well we've done with our civic justice and order outside the Assembly of Worlds, and they want their hands on the wealth from our mines."

I had heard much the same in New Edinburgh. Sol's laugh, loud and hearty, was not a response that would be made there.

"Oh, please." Her voice dripped scorn. "Peacemaker command on Earth doesn't care about this planet. You've got a planetary narcissism complex if you think that. I doubt any of them even know Offyonder exists without querying a database. They don't have half the men and women they need for the wars they're already fighting, or trying to prevent, or planets they're running because the places are too fucked up to take care of themselves. The last thing they want is to create another mess they'll have to deal with. Could he be a Peacer deserter? Sure. In which case, he may know strategy and tactics, and he's as likely on your mainland as he is here. I take jobs that will pay."

Willoughby turned away from Sol, color rising in his pasty face. I represented a safer target. "You?" He examined me up and down. "I can't think why they would send a librarian out here."

"I agree that I am a thoroughly useless man," I said. "But I was sent by CenSec HQ. It's worth remembering that fact."

"Yeah." Willoughby pursed his lips. I think he was considering spitting on his office floor. Had we been outside, he would have spit on the ground.

"Did your predecessor assign two CenSec officers to Claire's detail?" I asked.

"I don't know." Willoughby's teeth could have been grinding coffee the way the words came out. "Hernández and Gupta are not here. Bradford may have assigned them to accompany Claire Montaigne, but there is no record of that. I could send a message back to New Edinburgh when the satellite window is open and see if they'll ask him. I would not bet on getting an answer. I'm listing them as AWOL."

If the Directorate was going to use this Bradford in the blame game over Claire's disappearance, I doubted anyone would bother with asking him the question, but long shots do pay off occasionally. So the history books tell us. "I think it would be worthwhile to do that," I told Willoughby. "I will put it in my report."

Willoughby did not say what his facial expression told me he wanted to say. He said nothing, but I was sure he would transmit the question.

"Those two officers, do you know what they did on their time off?" Sol asked. "Did they have women in the town east of here, Edge-of-the-World? A particular bar they frequented?"

"No idea," Willoughby said. "That's what you're supposed to find out, isn't it?"

"Yes. It will be a good start if we can examine their personnel records. And in the meantime, your people are out scouring the hill camps and the fields for Claire?"

"Spare me the bullshit!" Willoughby walked over to his desk, which was bare, so there was nothing for him to pick up and throw. He settled for opening a drawer and slamming it shut. "Yes, I will give you access to their files. Between CenSec and the local police, I don't have enough men and women to scour the dishes in the mess, and I doubt they would be able to do even that properly. If I send them out into the hills, the Spartacists will pick them off, and that will leave the airfield exposed. I won't do that. It's hard enough to get patrols out during the day on the road between here and that stupid Upland town to keep the Spartacists away, and at night I can't maintain even those. And speaking of available resources"—he took the opportunity to direct his glare my way—"we are apparently down to a third assistant librarian."

"Which is why I will be paid," Sol said. "A lot."

On reflection, I had to admit that the approach to assigning blame and punishing failure in the Directorate could use some improvement.

WE WERE TAKEN TO AN EMPTY OFFICE DOWN THE HALL. IT HAD A DESK HOLDING A computer screen with input devices, but no chairs. We stood over the input while I brought up the records for Gupta and Hernández. As personnel records go, these were pretty skimpy. Both men had been stationed at Susan Anthony for a year and a half. Performance ratings were low, without any detail given. Each man had requested transfer back to the mainland on multiple occasions. All requests had been denied. Gupta had been reprimanded for fighting. The only detail of note in the reprimand was that his two front teeth had been chipped. So, in addition to poor performance, he appeared to be a poor fighter.

It took little time to absorb the information in the records. I thumbed the system to Off. "These two were losers," I said. "HQ sent them here to get them out of the way." I rubbed my chin between thumb and forefinger, considering what probably went along with that. "They would probably be corruptible, if you are still thinking of factions."

Sol snorted. "Martin, everyone on this subcontinent is corruptible. It is only a question of price."

I had known she would say that.

From there, we went to see a custodian in the cargo area, with Sol making an offhand comment that she liked talking to custodians. They cleaned up what others discarded, and often items were discarded that should have been treated more carefully. Because people treated them as invisible and immaterial, they also had opportunities to overhear conversations.

Hernández, apparently, liked to gamble. He tended to lose as well. The custodian had retained an IOU Hernández had written out. The amount owed had to be a month's pay in markers. Gupta was a bully and disliked by everyone, according to the custodian. He complained constantly about the lack of a dentist to fix his chipped teeth.

A mechanic who helped maintain the CenSec vehicles told us that both Gupta and Hernández would volunteer for patrol duty on the road east of the airport. This was not a display of bravery, although that duty was considered moderately hazardous. It allowed Gupta to visit the whorehouses in town and Hernández to gamble in the bars.

Sol's conclusion after the conversations was succinct. "We are headed for Edge-of-the-World next."

CHAPTER EIGHT

THE LAND OUTSIDE THE AIRPORT WAS BARREN AND SERE, DULL BROWN AS FAR AS the eye could see. The combination of elevation and dry climate had kept it that way, probably since the time tectonic forces pushed this end of the subcontinent up and drained its Inland Sea. Scrappy clumps of spiky vegetation grew out of cracks between the rocks, and occasionally a tiny animal the size of an Earth mouse could be seen nibbling on them. That was it for the local wildlife. Two CenSec cars, one cruising back toward the airport and one posted at the end of a high ramp offering good views up and down the road, gave evidence of Willoughby's patrols.

It was a two-hour drive through this uninviting territory to reach the aptly named town of Edge-of-the-World. The place was known as the last outpost of civilization on the subcontinent, and there was justice in that label. It was the only civilized town past the coastal mountains, since no one counted the hill camps around the mines as either towns or civilized. It sat lower than the airport, less than a mile high. As we approached the town, the land sprouted fields of waving wild grasses no

denser than the thinning hair on an old man's head, along with clusters of head-high brush adorned with pink-and-white flowers.

Edge-of-the-World was not a place that had grown organically over a period of many years. Humans had not been on Offyonder for all that many years in the first place. The town had been built to serve an obvious need. The mines in the hills to the east and the farms to the north needed the machinery Bannion produced, from drilling equipment to toilets, and all that equipment needed programmers, electrical engineers, and plumbers.

In addition to the grains for the mash, the soil in the bed of the old Inland Sea was suitable for yonderhemp, which supplied the textiles for much of Offyonder's clothing manufacturers. Of course, we grew grains for the mash, but we were also able to grow gene-modded Earth corn and wheat. That meant work for bakers and clothiers because it was much cheaper to do all of this in the Uplands of Serendipity as opposed to shipping the products from the mainland.

On and on it went, down to the barkeepers and the whores. All these people needed to live somewhere, but there weren't so many of them that we needed more than one somewhere. The town sat where it did because the location was a convenient juncture for roads to the mines, the Inland Sea farms, and the route down to Bannion. It was also close enough to the airport without being so close that a civic disturbance could compromise our air traffic. The Directorate always paid attention to civic concerns. That had paid off when the Riots blossomed ten years ago.

Edge-of-the-World stuck up from its surroundings like a pimple on an adolescent's skin. As we went closer, I could see that the buildings were mostly poured concrete—a cheap, easy way to put up structures where wood was unavailable nearby. Some of them were sheathed at the lower half-story with metal sheets riveted into the concrete. The remaining structures were brick. Where gaps existed between the buildings, they were closed by panels of the same metal sheathing, producing the appearance of a solid wall around the town.

The road from the airport ran through the only visible opening left between the buildings. It was guarded by a tall watchtower and blocked by a retractable barrier. The tower and its twin, whose top I could glimpse on the other side of town, gave the police an excellent view over the countryside to watch for the approach of bandits and rebels—or in modern terms, Spartacists. The combination of the solid line of brick and concrete buildings and the watchtowers gave the appearance of an isolated outpost in enemy territory, although it could also have been the image of a prison camp. There may have been truth to both views.

As we drove up to the gate, a crew of workers was busy whitewashing the brick part of the wall on one side of the opening. They had made an oddly shaped white blotch on the red-brown brick but showed no intent to make regular borders or to extend it across the entire building. On the metal-encased concrete wall on the other side of the entrance, the slogan ALL FOR ONE was painted in irregular white letters.

Sol stopped in front of the barrier and I called out to the workers, "What are you doing?"

The man nearest our car responded. "Damned Spartacists painted their 'All for one and one for all,' on the walls. Police told us to get rid of it, but the damned paint soaks into the brick. Too hard to scrub it off, so we're painting over it. Do the other side next." The sun was hot enough that I could see him sweat in his blue coverall.

"Do you mean to tell me that a group of Spartacists walked up to the wall, right under the watchtower, and painted their slogan?" I was not sure which was more astonishing: the Spartacist cheek or the local lack of vigilance.

"Apparently," was the answer.

At that moment, the barrier swung open. No challenge, no check of documents. Nothing.

"Welcome to the far end of civilization," Sol said.

We drove in. Beyond what I can only call an imitation checkpoint, Edge-of-the-World was a miniature Bannion without the smog. The streets were narrow to begin with, some too narrow for cars. The close-packed buildings, with overhanging upper stories casting deep shadows over where people walked, biked, or drove, created a tight and claustrophobic atmosphere. The town had a creek bed through its center, the most open area I saw. It was dry now, but I could imagine it overflowing and flooding the streets when a rainstorm hit, just as the river did to Bannion.

As with the town itself, the inhabitants were also reminiscent of Bannion's people. As Sol inched the car through the streets, the men and women who pulled their bikes to the side or stepped out of the way were mostly shabby, and they turned blank, hard eyes on us as we passed. Poorly educated, if at all, was my immediate librarian's assessment.

The brutish impression they conveyed was not, I should hasten to point out, because they exhausted themselves in physical labor on or in the earth. The bounty of our mines, and to some extent of our mash, allowed us to buy modern earthmoving and excavating equipment from advanced planets in the Reach, even from Earth itself. And with the restoration of civic order after the Riots, the Directorate had been able to produce some fairly sophisticated machinery. The workers I saw in Edge-of-the-World did not need to hack away with pick and shovel or with plow and hoe. However, neither the mine owners nor the farmers could afford to integrate all the machinery across a network and have AI run it. That was beyond us for now. Each machine needed to be run separately and their operation coordinated by humans.

That did not mean the workers needed to understand *how* the machine worked, only what control to tap and when, which meant that it was possible to have a marginally educated workforce that did not do hard physical labor. Our Directorate is always quick to point out that this allowed gainful employment for many people who lacked, or were unsuited for, much education. I have often thought that more effort to educate these people would have led to better lives for them and a greater push to modernize and network our operations, but voicing that would breach GSG and indicate dangerous thoughts. Any slip I make, I blame on a librarian's wish for people to read more books.

In keeping with the nature of its inhabitants, Edge-of-the-World was well stocked with bars. Each block we passed had at least one. In the center of town around a small plaza stood two brothels, each with a bar of its own. The ratio may have been a commentary on the relative popularity of alcohol and sex or, more likely, a reflection of the fact that alcohol was cheaper.

From our conversation with the mechanic at the airfield, we knew Gupta came into town for women. That left us with a coin flip, because both places advertised both men and women for their clients. We chose to start with Peaks and Valleys, probably for the symbolism of its name.

A painted sign by an old-style swinging door left no doubt as to what a peak and a valley represented. The entryway led to a small coatroom and then directly to the bar. The place was half-full, even in the middle of the day, but that wasn't saying much; the area for tables was cramped and the tables were spread out enough for a sex worker to get acquainted with a customer without bumping into someone at the adjoining table. Sol led the way to the bar, a stout structure built from the wood of the handtrees and stained irregularly to a dark brown. Despite its appealing texture, the wood was soft and did not take stain very well, but the amount needed for a bar was readily available by truck from the eastern hills. No one would pay to ship a more exotic hardwood across the sea to build a bar in a whorehouse.

The barkeep was busy drying glasses with a towel that should have been in the rag pile. He had a swarthy complexion on a Caucasian face with a black mustache clipped short. His head came up as we reached the bar, and he gave us a superficial check from under half-lidded eyes.

"If the two of you are looking for a room, you're in the wrong place. Mine are for the girls and boys who work here, not freelance whores."

"Want information, not a room," Sol said.

"You haven't ordered. I need to move the hot mash."

Naturally, we each ordered a hot mash. The drink was cold, in a glass. The heat came from some relative of capsaicin that the grain for this particular mash produced. It obviated any need to think about taste. My eyes watered. I saw no effect on Sol. She asked about information again when she was halfway through her glass.

"Who's asking?"

"Sol from Bannion. I need to know about a C-sucker named Gupta. He used to come here. I've been very patient and polite. So far."

The barkeep's eyelids came up at her name. "Sol. You caught that asshole, Kilmer." Sol nodded. "Normally, I'm careful about anybody who works with the C-suckers or police, but that asshole killed one of my girls. What's your business with Gupta? What do you want to know?"

"Was he a regular here?"

"Yeah. C-sucker he was, and I told you how I feel about C-suckers, but he paid. Never a problem."

"Seen him in the last three or four days?"

"Nope. And that's a long time for him."

Sol considered both the answer and her glass. "Would you know anybody who could tell me more?"

"Maybe." The barkeep's expression said there was a way to find out.

We each ordered another hot mash. Sol actually finished her first one and started on the second.

"I can't tell you this was Gupta, so if it's not, I didn't lead you wrong on purpose." He waited for Sol to nod before he continued. "Heard some talk about something happening to a couple of C-suckers. If you'll wait, and enjoy my drinks, I'll send Jerry from the kitchen to see about … someone who can tell you more. Up to them if they want to do it. You understand?"

"Have Jerry take this." Sol put a full DM coin on the bar. "Final amount depends on what we hear."

The barkeep swept the money off the wooden top and disappeared through a door behind the bar. We sat and waited. While we sat, Sol finished her second drink. She ordered a third when the barkeep returned and finished that.

When she asked for a fourth, I had to say something. "You're drinking too much."

"I can hit a man at fifty yards and I'm doing my job," she said. She did not look at me.

"That wasn't my point," I replied. "That much, it isn't good for you. That's why I said you're drinking too much."

"I'm not drinking enough."

"There's more to the story you started to tell me," I said. "It's on your mind. Is this more about Gilbert Mortimer?"

Sol made a point of taking a drink from the next glass. "I loved him," she said. "That's the story about Gil. As for me, there's always more to my story, but I doubt it's worth telling."

"You never know until you do." I let the sentence hang. If there was something on her mind, that was a good invitation to begin talking. I was ready to listen.

Sol, however, was more disposed to finish her drink than add to her story. When the glass was empty, she stared off across the bar. I thought she would eventually reach the point of talking. Her lips moved, but I heard nothing. She was talking to herself. Before she said any more, the door out to the plaza banged open. A youth with only the beginnings of a beard came through—probably Jerry from the kitchen—accompanied by a woman in blue overalls and a thick woolen shirt, also dyed blue.

Her clothes were dirty, her eyes hard and dark brown, as dark and hard as the rest of her face. I could see the calluses on her large hands from where I sat. "You're Sol, like the boy said?" It was not a trusting voice.

"I am," Sol said.

"Did you really catch the Guttersnipe of Harborside single-handed, the way they tell the story?"

"No," Sol said. "I used both hands. And his brother ratted him out."

Where would humanity be without its rats? I wondered. As if I had spoken the words, the woman turned to me, sized me up. "Who's this? Leftovers from when God made Adam?" Her voice was no softer than her features.

"Martin Allgeier." I did not extend a hand. "Pleased to meet you too."

"Probably not." The woman lost interest in me and turned her attention back to Sol. "Kiara," she said. "Brown," after a pause. "The boy said you were offering for info on two C-suckers."

"I am," Sol said. "Solid Directorate Markers."

"They're dead." Kiara held out her hand.

"Not enough," I said. "Prove it."

Kiara glanced at me, moved her eyes back to Sol immediately.

"I agree with Martin," Sol said. "How do you know they're dead? When did they die, and how did it happen? I want to know who did it."

"You can't blame me for trying to get my money easy," Kiara said. When neither of us commented, she continued. "Was with a road crew out toward Laggard's Gulch. Between the trucks from the mines and the rainstorms, there's always roadwork out there. Saw four independents go down into the gulch."

"Spartacists? How do—?"

Kiara cut me off with a chop of her hand before my next word came out. "You want to get your throat slit, that's fine by me," she hissed, "but mine's not getting cut along with yours. I said an independent group. Pretty ragged. No police, no C-suckers with them."

"When was this?" Sol asked.

"Five days back."

That matched the last day Hernández and Gupta had been seen.

"So, you saw four indies," Sol said. "What were they doing and what does this have to do with our gray-and-blacks?"

Kiara Brown closed the hand she had stretched out and shoved it into a pocket of her overalls. "Come with me," she said. "I'll show you."

Kiara led us to a small all-terrain vehicle and drove us out of Edge-of-the-World. As with our entrance on the other side, the barrier at the exit swung open without question or challenge. In response to my quizzical look, Kiara said, "The guards will usually challenge you if you're coming in after dark."

"How do we know the password?" I thought that was a reasonable question.

"Just yell out 'I'm coming home!' or almost anything else that you think of. Only thing I wouldn't do is shout 'All for one and one for all!'" Her laugh was a harsh commentary on the vigilance of the guards.

The land east of Edge-of-the-World undulated as it trended lower, an abundance of wild grasses dotted with the widely spaced spiky trees that made do with the occasional rainfall. It was also carved by dry washes that would fill with flash floods from the intermittent storms that the hard, stony ground could not handle. Laggard's Gulch was one such feature, named for a bunch of stragglers from a crew headed out to the mines in the days before motorized transport was readily available. A sudden storm had hit, and all that was ever found of them were two unmatched shoes and a handheld light.

At a curve in the road that swung close to and overlooked the gulch, Kiara stopped the vehicle. "There's a gully that runs down into it. Hang on." She switched to off-road.

We jounced and bounced from one pile of rocks to another as we headed down. I rocked to and fro with the car, once banging my head against the side window and thinking wistfully of my padded chair in the library reading room. By the time the ground had leveled out, the entrance to this gully was lost against the sky.

Kiara stopped the vehicle and stepped out. From the rear compartment, she pulled out a shovel.

"It's rained since the day you mentioned," Sol said. "Any marking on the ground will be gone."

"When I saw them, I made sure to watch where they went," Kiara said. "I might not have seen exactly what they were doing, but I'm sure where they were doing it. I'm observant."

We would have to take her word on that.

She picked a spot to the side of the gully where there was dirt as well as rock. After several shovelfuls revealed only darker dirt, she moved a few feet away and started another hole. It took four similar false starts before she let out an "Ah!" maybe a foot into the fifth. She dug more quickly for several minutes. I walked next to her and looked down into the excavation.

"That's a body," I said.

"Fairly recently dead." Sol had come up beside me. "Is there another one?"

Kiara grunted and returned to her spadework. It was not long before we could see two naked bodies in a shallow grave.

"Your two C-suckers," Kiara said.

"Two dead men," Sol said. "One stabbed through an eye, the other garroted, I would say, but they could be anyone who fell afoul of Spartacus. Or maybe cheated at cards. Offyonder doesn't have a gene lab."

"You wanted to know about the C-suckers," Kiara said. "I told you they were dead. You wanted proof. I showed you bodies. What more do you want? I want my pay."

I squatted down and looked more closely. We do not have dead bodies in the library—except in the Gothic fiction section, which is not my favorite—but the sight does not bother me. I have a good eye for detail. Using a nearby shard of rock to avoid touching the corpse with my hand, I peeled back the upper lip of the one with darker skin.

"Gupta had both of his front teeth chipped from a fight. He complained he couldn't have them fixed out here. I don't know how big the chips were, but both front teeth on this one are chipped. This grave is odd, though."

"What do you mean?" Suspicion tinged Kiara's voice.

"My partner is thinking about how shallow it is," Sol said.

I confess to feeling a bit of a thrill when she referred to me that way.

"That's about all it can be around here," Kiara said. "You want it much deeper, you'd need mining equipment."

"If you wanted them hidden forever and you couldn't dig deep, you'd do better going farther away from the road and pitching them into some remote gully. Here, this close to the surface, a rainstorm would eventually wash away the dirt. This close to the road, things uncovered can be seen. It says whoever did the burying didn't care if they were found, as long as it wasn't right away." Sol didn't turn the statement into an accusation, but I heard the skepticism in her voice.

"I never said I could tell you why they put them here, or even why they killed them. I did what I said. Pay me."

"I'll pay you," Sol said. "As soon as we get back to town. Not that I'm thinking you would leave us to enjoy the hike back." She tugged the front of her duster open so that the grip of one of her guns showed. "I am interested in one other question first." She pointed up the gully toward where our point of departure had vanished. "You said you spotted the Spartacists—out here, call them what they have to be—doing something, digging this grave, from where you were working on a road crew. I've got good eyes and I've made a living by being observant. I'm not sure I'm that good."

"What do you mean?" Kiara shifted uneasily where she stood, possibly from Sol's show of armament, possibly from the tone of Sol's question.

"I'm wondering how much you saw and how much you might have heard from someone else."

"I saw what I saw," Kiara said. "Anyway, what difference does it make? You wanted answers. You got them. Why does it matter how?"

"It doesn't. Except that these two were supposedly guarding Claire Montaigne, and we are interested in her. If you know someone who knows more about this, there could be another payday for you."

"Paydays are only good if you live to spend it," Kiara said.

"I wasn't asking you for a name," Sol said. "Only think about it. If someone else wants to come see us, we're staying at the Opulent Miner. If someone does, there would be extra in it for you."

"I heard what you said." That was all Kiara would add. We piled back into her vehicle and drove, without another word, back to town.

CHAPTER NINE

THE ACCOMMODATIONS AT THE OPULENT MINER COULD BE CONSIDERED opulent only if the alternative was camping at the bottom of a mineshaft. I am hardly the sort who lives in luxury, but my small room at the library, which I have by virtue of my position, has real carpeting, a firm bed with clean sheets and blankets, a closet for my small wardrobe, and a modern screen and network connections.

This "room"—and I use the word with some reservation—had a concrete floor without so much as a rug to cover its cracks. It had a single small bed, whose mattress rivaled the floor for firmness—and the floor, at least, would not be as lumpy. It did not have a closet, probably because the people who would take such a room had only the clothes they were wearing. As for electronics, it could have served in the Earthbound days of Arthur and his Knights of the Round Table. That is a small joke. The room did have electric lights.

I surveyed the whole of it with distaste, but the dimensions of the bed were a particular item. I had, in fact, argued that we should take two rooms on general principles. Set against what the Directorate was

going to pay Sol, the small cost of an extra room for Martin Allgeier, while it would never be overlooked by the accountants, would be a matter I could explain.

Sol refused to consider it. "If it is known that we are spending money on two rooms," she said, "the cost of any information we get will at least double." I pointed out that the money was Directorate money, and no one would question what we paid our informants. Sol was adamant. That was not the image she wanted to project.

That left me with the matter of the bed. After the way our nights had been spent at her apartment, what did she expect? What did she want? She had made a point of thanking me for not taking advantage that first night, and I had felt her flinch from an unintentional touch the second night even as she was falling into a drunken stupor. I remembered the way she had told her story, as much of it as she would tell me. I knew the answer to what she did *not* want. I would like to give myself points for not considering what I might want, but the truth is—to the degree that term applies to anything coming from me—those wants were not that important to me, and I feared she would despise me if I acted on them.

"So, we know the Spartacists killed Hernández and Gupta." Sol's voice broke into my contemplation of the sleeping arrangements with a manner that assumed I was thinking through our findings, the same as she. "We can assume they impersonated them, which means they had two of their own join Claire's guards at the airport."

"They could have done that." I am good at a quick mental switch of gears. "The physical IDs CenSec carries aren't like the one I have. They can be faked. I'm sure the technology is available in Bannion, even if not in the Uplands. The New Edinburgh CenSeccers of Claire's guard would have no way to verify them and probably would not think to question them."

"It makes it easy to understand how the ambush was conducted." Sol held up one hand and ticked off points on her fingers. "A Spartacist group could have been notified exactly when the cars left the hospital. The CenSec comms would have had no signal at that point in the road."

"And there were two Spartacists in the cars already, disguised as CenSeccers," I said, to make sure I added a point of my own. "This was bold and very well planned."

"Yeah." Sol hesitated. "Your Directorate makes their recruiting easy, you know. I only first heard of Spartacus a little while after I arrived on Offyonder five years ago. Whatever bands existed here before he started organizing were not much more than bandits and highwaymen. Now, I don't care what CenSec says about them being reduced to half-naked barbarians hiding in caves. They are a functioning rebellion, and the broader your GSG gets and the more people are punished for dangerous thoughts, the more support they have."

"We should not talk about that. Not even here." I knew what she said was true, however, and it was as true on the mainland as on the subcontinent. A librarian reads. The fact that I felt compelled to speak those words validated the thought, even though there was no possibility our room was bugged. The tech to do so wasn't out here. Not a random hotel room. Almost certainly not.

Sol stroked her scar with one finger and smiled. I think she saw the humor in being safer at the far edge of civilization. "We should get some rest tonight. Even if Kiara doesn't give our message to anyone, it will be a busy day tomorrow. I want to talk to people in all the bars and in that other whorehouse."

I did not want to think of how many drinks Sol would have by the time we finished all the talking. Unfortunately, avoiding thinking about the bars and drinking led me back to thoughts of the sleeping arrangements.

"I'll sleep on that couch," she said, as if she had divined my dilemma. The room did have a small couch that she might fit on. "No different than I do at home."

Why did she do that? I wanted to know the answer to that question. It was probably tied in to the rest of her story that I had not heard. I am fairly good at asking questions to find information, but I was not sure how she would react if I pried. I was still debating with myself when there was a knock on the door.

This was not an authoritative "Open the damned door before I kick it down!" kind of knock but a tentative "Should I really be here?" type. We looked at each other.

"That was fast," Sol said.

Too fast, was what I thought.

Sol's hand slid under her duster, emerged with a pistol. I drew mine as well. The distance to the door was short. It would not take any luck for me to hit someone. Sol gestured for me to move to the side. She went for the door, her feet making no sound on the concrete floor.

The knock was repeated, even less forceful than at first.

Sol ripped the door open, dropping into a crouch with her gun leveled at the doorway as she did so.

A young girl stood in the opening. She let out a squeak. Eyes wide as saucers stared at Sol's gun. Her mouth opened wide as well. Her hands went up to cover it.

Sol reached out with her free hand, grabbed the front of the girl's olive overalls, and yanked her into the room. A kick, as Sol pivoted, slammed the door shut.

The girl stumbled across the room before catching herself against the bed. She turned and shrank back against the bed, her eyes fixed on the two weapons now aimed at her. Dark brown hair fell loose in frizzy curls. Her face would have been pale to begin with; fright made it paler. The overalls were pulled tight at her waist by a belt, making her hips prominent. Her chest was nearly flat under the overalls and light shirt. Young indeed. Then recognition came to me.

"Lizzie," Sol said. "What are you doing here?"

I noted that Sol relaxed, but she did not put her gun away.

"I heard—" Lizzie's voice failed after those two barely audible words.

"You heard what?" Sol's voice was flat and hard.

Lizzie licked her lips. Her eyes darted around the room, searching for an exit. "I heard you were paying for information. Information about a beautiful young woman. Blond. Blue eyes."

"You can only have been here a few days," Sol said. "Three, tops. How can you know anything about her?"

Lizzie pushed off from the bed, stood upright, and folded her arms across her chest. "Well, I do." A note of defiance crept into her voice. That made sense. The girl had survived in Bannion as a streetdancer. Now that she realized she was not about to be shot, her innate spunk was resurfacing.

"Why don't you tell us how and what you know about this woman." Sol's gun went back under her duster.

"Are you paying?" Lizzie asked.

"Yes" was Sol's answer. To me she said, "You can put the gun down, Martin."

"Okay." Lizzie took a deep breath. "You said Grandma Toby would get me out of Harborside, out of Bannion. She did. Took me straight to Donovan Black's, like you said, and he packed me into a car with a driver coming here. I had money for one meal. That was it. I figured I could steal what I need, but … Bannion is different. There are a million places to disappear. The streets here … You need protection, and this place is small. People working the streets marked me as new right away."

She shuddered. "They told me what they'd do if I took business from them." Another shudder. "No streetdancers here. The only dancers are in the whorehouses, and they're only dancing to get work. I don't want to sell myself. I mean, I will if I have to, but I don't want to, and I remember you told me not to. My ma did that. I saw how she'd get beat sometimes. I remember her telling me she had to do it so we could eat and then crying 'cause it went to drugs and we still had nothing to eat. Then she got the wheezes and died."

"The wheezes are from the bad air in Bannion," I said. That was probably not helpful.

"Never mind that," Sol said. "I know all about you and your ma. I want to know about this woman."

"You asked how I could know," Lizzie said. "I'm telling you." She met Sol's hard eyes with a stare of her own. "I was here just long enough to be hungry. Just long enough to know there was only one thing I could sell. A man called me over. I was on the street. He could tell I had nowhere to go, no money left. I was telling myself to do what he wanted.

"But he didn't ask for that. Said he could see I was new, that nobody knew me. Said they had a young woman who was very scared, that they wouldn't hurt her, weren't *allowed* to, but she was scared. If I could calm her down and do something with her, they'd pay me. I told him I could dance for her. He said that would be good. I figured I was going to die, but I was going to die anyway. I was hungry. I said okay."

"And he took you to this woman? Describe her," Sol demanded. "What was she like?"

"She's beautiful. Really beautiful. I told you. Blond hair. These pale blue eyes. Her skin is perfect. Even her fingernails are perfect. And she's … I don't know, silly. Not right in the head. She just talks silly all the time. But she was nice. She liked my dance. She hugged me and called me her dizzy-whizzy-Lizzie, if you can believe that. And they did pay me and bring me back here, if you can believe that. The man got me a room at a boardinghouse so he can find me if she wants me to dance again. Told me never to talk about it, but his money won't last forever and I heard you were paying."

"You heard." Sol stopped for a beat after those two words. "How did you hear? Was it a woman named Kiara? Skin dark brown like her hair?"

"No. Nobody like that. It was a server where I bought food tonight. And the clerk at the boardinghouse when I went to my room. Both of them."

"This is too strange," I said to Sol. "A trap, maybe."

"I agree it's strange," Sol said, "but why would anyone set a trap this way? Lizzie, do you realize that woman is Claire Montaigne?"

Lizzie sat down on the bed as though her muscles would no longer hold her. "The Director's niece? But here, with those men … Oh no."

"Oh yes," Sol said. "But she never said who she was?"

"No." It came out in a whisper. "Just talking, all kind of crazy things. And talking to some girl named Abigail who wasn't there. She was quiet when I danced, though, and her eyes, they *watched* me when I danced, not going all over, like other times."

"That must be Claire," I said. "It can't be anyone else. Where is she? I mean, where did they take you?"

"I don't know," Lizzie said. "We went in a car, but I had to wear a blindfold until we were inside the other place and that was just a large room with screens and, I guess, electronics."

"How long were you in the car?" Sol asked. "Can you guess?"

"I think a little more than an hour. I'm good with time. And I did get a peek from under the blindfold when we left because he didn't tie it on right. There was a dome on a building."

"The old weather station," Sol said. "Has to be. It was built when the airport was built, I guess thinking that there would be more settlements. It's odd. They were very clever taking her to be so clumsy now."

"Maybe overconfident," I said.

"Maybe. Let's make sure we don't get too confident ourselves."

I cycled Sol's words through my mind. How Lizzie was able to see the location. The simple fact that they took Lizzie there in the first place. Spartacist cells were said to have informers in many places. A poor neighborhood like Harborside might be rife with them. Could they know Sol was hunting Claire, and was that why Lizzie had been brought to dance? *Overconfidence* was the wrong word. "This is a trap," I said.

"Exactly" was Sol's reply.

Lizzie clutched her hands together and tried to edge away from us but was blocked by the bed again. "I didn't set you up," she said. "I wouldn't. Solly, you know I wouldn't." Fear tinged her voice.

"I didn't say you did. I simply think they decided you were a convenient tool. If not you, they would have used someone else. If we had not found Kiara Brown, we would have found someone else. This town has Spartacist cells and informers." No anger marked Sol's voice. She was matter-of-fact. She would probably have shown more emotion over the weather. "We should leave now. Get there as quickly as we can."

"Wait," I said. "You just agreed with me that this is a trap."

"We need to get Claire." Sol shrugged. "It's not as though we can avoid the trap and go somewhere else. We know a trap is set here; we will watch for it. If we wait and they move her, either we may not find her again or we may not see the next trap. Anyway, middle of the night is always best, and maybe, for all their cleverness, they will not expect us so fast. Lizzie, you will come with us."

"What? No!"

"Yes," Sol said. "I do not want you here to be interrogated about what we said. Also, when we succeed, I do not want them to take revenge on you for the failure of their plan."

"I didn't want any of this," Lizzie said.

"Nobody does. Shit just happens." Sol took Lizzie's hand, gave a tug, and then led her from the room. I followed behind, as I seem wont to do.

CHAPTER TEN

ONCE WE WERE BACK ON THE ROAD IN THE UPLANDS AND OUT OF SIGHT of the eastern watchtower, I asked Sol what she planned to do when we reached the weather station. "I can't imagine that we are going to drive up to the entrance and expect them to drop their weapons and hand Claire over."

"Was that the way they did it in the history books you have in your library?" Sol asked.

"It has happened." I recounted a story from one of the world wars on Earth in which a four-man patrol found an unguarded path into a heavily fortified position, walked in, and by surprise and bluff gained the surrender of an eight-hundred-man garrison.

Sol chuckled. "I suppose anything can happen once. We do have a way to sneak in, but there won't be eight hundred waiting for us. I'm planning to shoot, not count on surrender. Lizzie, you said you saw two men with Claire?"

"Three, Solly. But the third was the driver who took me there and back. What happens to me afterward?"

"We pay you," Sol said. "After we get Claire back to the airport, I'll find a place for you. Somewhere. I won't say 'safe,' because no place is safe, but I'll find a place. Now," she said to me, "that third man may have returned to the station."

"They could have another person, separate from the ones with Claire," I said. "Probably watching the road."

"Good thought. Four, then—and hopefully one will be out covering the road because we will not go up it. The weather station sits on a low hill. Single-lane drive goes up to it from the road, but it goes around the hill and comes up from that side. The result is if you are watching for someone coming to the entrance, you can't see the takeoff from the road. Not a lot of cover on the hill, just low brush, and we have a clear sky with both moons up."

Indeed, Justice, the large moon, was full and the size of a one Directorate Marker coin. Demos was much smaller, but also full, and shone brightly a quarter of the sky away from Justice.

"You are not making this sound good," I said.

"We have an advantage," Sol said. "There is a small gully that runs behind the station. A storage level for supplies was built on the floor below the part of the station where the instruments are, and we can reach that from the gully. I have done … jobs for CenSec in the hills. Most recently a year ago. I've used this station, and I have a key to the storage level."

"How do you know they haven't changed the lock?" I asked.

"I don't," Sol said. "However, nobody else has used it in years. CenSec is not very efficient. This is why life is more interesting outside your library."

———

SOL DROVE PAST THE JUNCTION WITH THE SERVICE ROAD LEADING TO THE WEATHER station. Almost immediately, we crossed a bridge over the gully she had described. She swung the car off the road into a small depression. The weather station was invisible from where we stopped. I liked the way Sol had put this plan together. The beginning looked promising, at least, and she had done it quickly at the end of a long day. I avoided dwelling on the fact that she had also done it after a substantial number of drinks earlier in the day. She appeared immune to hangovers.

We left the car, scrambled into the gully, and started in the direction of the station. Those moons, which I had worried might give us away, provided good lighting for finding a path among the rocks and small boulders. Trying that walk on a dark night with only handheld flashes would have been a good way to turn an ankle.

It was a strenuous hike even with the light. Sol led the way, again without showing any effect of fatigue or the alcohol. Her early training was still there in her musculature and coordination. Lizzie also handled it well. Dancing and hustling on the streets called for both strength and agility. For myself, I gave thanks for the compulsory daily calisthenics required of Directorate professional staff, though I had never appreciated them when they pulled me away from my reading nook. Since I was at the rear of our small column, the occasional puffing and scurry to make up lost ground went undetected and unremarked.

The gully took us to a point directly below the back of the weather station where it sat on its hill above us. The climb up was steep but not too long. I considered grabbing some of the bushes to help pull me up. However, my first tug gave evidence that the root systems were shallow. They would not have held against even a lightweight such as me. Fortunately, the slopes offered plenty of embedded rock and other irregularities, so I was able to negotiate the climb without too much difficulty.

A concrete wall with a door set in the middle of it marked the lower level of the station, exactly as Sol had described. An official installation in New Edinburgh today would have electronic locking, perhaps even facial recognition for an important place. We didn't have that tech on Offyonder when this station was built, and I doubt it would be used in such a remote location even now.

Sol pulled out a set of old metal keys from her duster, selected one.

"How is it that you're carrying around the key to this installation?" I asked. "It's been, you said, a year since you used it."

"I didn't say I haven't used it since," she replied. "I said that was my most recent job in the Uplands for CenSec. It's useful to have a place where no one else goes, and any key I have to a place I'm not supposed to go, I keep with me. Now be quiet. This place is powered off a photovoltaic field. It had power the last time I was here."

Any concern that the lock had been changed vanished in the next seconds as she turned the key and the mechanism clicked. When Sol pushed the door, it swung open without a sound. Darkness lay inside.

Sol stepped through the doorway. She extended one hand behind her and gestured for us to join her. The inside was inky black. There were no windows, so once the door was closed behind us, we were shut away from the light of the moons. Sol clicked on a low-intensity handheld flash. That illuminated little beyond the floor in front of her feet. Stacks of boxes and crates stretched away into the darkness on all sides.

"This way," Sol whispered.

She led us deeper into a labyrinth of piled-up old stores whose purpose and presence had doubtless been forgotten. I could barely see the hand she held up as a stop signal.

"Staircase," came her whisper again.

She lifted the light enough for me to see the stairs rise from the floor beyond a stack of three crates. They ran up to a door ten feet above us. That had to lead into the occupied area of the station.

"Lizzie, you stay right here. We'll come for you. Martin"—she waved me forward—"I know the layout. There's no reason for anyone to watch this door. It opens into a connecting corridor between the living quarters and the area with the instruments. Follow me. We'll take them by surprise."

She put her foot on the first step.

The overhead lights came on. An alarm hooted.

We scrambled backward for the cover of nearby crates. The crackle of automatic weapon fire drowned out the alarm and blew holes in the door at the top of the stairs. Bullets thudded into crates and sent a stream of liquid pouring out of a punctured drum.

"Okay, not the best plan I've ever had," Sol said from where she crouched behind the crate in front of the one sheltering me.

"Ha ha," I said. I admired someone who could make a joke, however poor, after being shot at.

Sol's handgun was trained on the door at the top of the stairs. So was mine. We waited for several eternities, because time stretches out and slows when your adrenaline pumps in a crisis. I doubt it was more than two minutes, which was long enough with nothing more happening.

"You don't blast a magazine through a door and never bother to check what might be there," Sol muttered. "Cover the rear door, Martin. Maybe someone is coming around the back."

I found a spot that allowed me a shot at anyone coming through the rear door while still being able to turn and see Sol and the staircase. Lizzie cowered under the overhang of a large box between our positions, all but invisible. A distant roar came from outside the building. It could have been an internal combustion engine. No sounds came from the vicinity of either door.

"They can't occupy this place forever," Sol said. "Not without people running supplies to them. However, we can't wait forever either. Let's try this."

The staircase had a handrail on each side supported by a row of metal spindles. Sol edged over to it, careful to stay away from a direct line to the door. She holstered her pistol under the duster and grabbed hold of the spindles. With a grunt, she pulled herself up along the outside of the staircase. Hand by hand, she worked her way up along the spindles until she was even with the door. One of the shots had smashed through the latching mechanism so that it was now a fraction of an inch ajar.

With her legs dangling free, she was able to use her arms to pull up and then flex her body so that she wedged one foot into the angle where a spindle was bolted to the staircase. Holding herself rigid with only one hand and that wedged foot, she drew the pistol with her other hand. She extended the muzzle of the pistol under the grip of the doorknob and pulled back. The door swung open. No shots came. No shouts. No sound of feet.

"What the hell?" Then she said, "Come on, Martin."

With my weapon aimed at the open doorway, Sol again holstered her pistol. She got a two-handed grip and swung herself up and over the railing to land on the top platform. Still no response to her activity. Gun out ahead of her, she crouched low and went through the open door. After another eternity, during which I heard nothing, she reappeared in the opening and waved for me to come up. I did, telling Lizzie to come as well and to stay behind me.

We followed the corridor and emerged in a utilitarian room with windows that gave a view out toward the road. A few chairs near a console with screens suggested that this had been the control room when the station was in operation. All the screens were dark.

"No sign of them," Sol said. Her words did not mean she was relaxed. Her weapon was out and she scanned back and forth to the doorways on either side of the room.

"This makes no sense," I said. "You're saying they detected us below, fired a random blast through the door to that storage area, and then bugged out? Did they think we brought an army?"

"No answers," Sol said. "I've checked the rooms on either side. One is a bunkroom. The other holds equipment."

"So, they ran and took the Prin … Claire," I said. "If we have to hike back to the car, we'll never be able to track them."

A banging noise interrupted my gloomy thoughts. The sound was coming from the door to the right, where Sol had said the bunkroom was located. Cautiously, we advanced to that door.

"The bunkroom was empty before, but I didn't go beyond it," Sol said. "I wanted you upstairs before I got too far away from the stairway door."

That was logical. Whether it was a mistake would depend on what happened next. With me covering her, Sol burst through the doorway, dived, rolled, and came up next to a double-decker bunk. The speed and athleticism of her entry were wasted. The room was empty. Nothing happened.

Well, the room wasn't entirely empty. It held two of the double-decker bunks. One bed was still neatly made. The other three had sheets and blankets pulled down in disarray. A pillow was on the floor. I try to make a point of noticing details like this. Had the alarm we triggered surprised them in their sleep? A sudden alert like that in the middle of the night could have panicked them, made them think they were facing a more dangerous force than a bounty hunter, a streetdancer, and a librarian. But hadn't anyone been keeping watch?

The pounding came again. It was followed by what could have been vocal sounds that did not take the shape of words. All of it came from an alcove off the far corner of the bunkroom.

Sol and I reached it in three strides. In the back was a partially closed door leading to the center of the station. More banging came from beyond it.

Sol turned her palms up to the ceiling in a gesture of puzzlement. She followed that with hand signals that told me to cover the door. She brought her knee up to her chest and slammed the bottom of her foot into the door. It flew open. Sol was through in an instant. I was close enough behind her to be hit by the rebounding door. That knocked me sideways, and I'm not sure how much use I would have been if our sudden entrance had started a fight. There was no fight, however.

We had found Claire Montaigne.

CHAPTER ELEVEN

W E WERE IN A SMALL KITCHEN DESIGNED TO SERVE THE CREW WHEN THIS station was manned. Claire's hands had been bound together with rope. Another rope was looped around the first bond and tied to a wall mount that also held up a rack of pots and pans. A wide swatch of cross-ribbed elastoplastic tape ran from one cheek to the other and served as an effective gag. Her feet were free.

When she saw us, she started jumping up and down while yanking futilely at the rope tying her to the wall. All along, she was making incoherent sounds through the tape.

"Hold still. Hold still." Sol put her weapon away and tried to undo the binding, an almost impossible task with Claire bouncing around. "Wait a second, goddammit!"

On the counter near Claire, Sol spotted a plastic block with a knife handle protruding from it. She grabbed the handle and withdrew a chef's knife that looked razor sharp. It was all I could do to hold Claire still enough for Sol to slice through the rope without taking off a piece of Claire. It was ironic, I thought, that the knife was close enough for

Claire to have used it to saw through the rope herself, if she'd had the presence of mind to manage it.

When the rope parted, Claire jumped back, away from the blade and out of my grasp. She fell against Lizzie, whom we had forgotten about but who had stayed behind us as we advanced through the station.

From the little I knew of Lizzie, I would never have expected her to soothe anyone, but that's what she managed with Claire. She stroked Claire's arms, hugged her, and patted her, as though Lizzie were the parent and Claire a frightened child. It worked. Claire calmed down.

In person, Claire looked nothing like the favored niece of the Director that Dr. Lomell had described. Her hair was now a wild mess of blond straw that stuck out and hung down in various places. She wore the sort of standard blue coverall a male worker might use, except it was at least one size too large, and she had overalls on top of that. Heavy boots appropriate to a mine worker were on her feet. From the scuff marks all along the wall, it was probably a good thing the boots were stout.

Lizzie took a corner of the elastoplastic tape in her fingers and tried to gently tug it loose. That did not work. The tape did not come off. Every tug led to a head shake, and a jump, and an incoherent shout.

"That's not going to work." Sol pushed Lizzie to one side. She gripped the barely loose corner of tape and said, "Sorry about this," in a voice that did not sound sorry at all.

With a mighty jerk, Sol ripped off the tape. Claire was so surprised she did not let out a sound. At first. Her mouth made a silent O in the middle of a red rectangle that stretched across her lips and cheeks. Her eyes went wide enough to swallow the rest of her face.

Then she screamed.

"Oh, how horrid! You are horrid, horrible, horridable! As bad as those evil, devil men!" Claire clapped her hands to her cheeks, then shrieked again as her fingers hit the skin that had been abused. "Oh, that hurts! I cannot bear it! But I could not bear to be bare, either here or there."

She pointed to the door leading to the bunkroom. "But we are rescued! Abigail, Abigail, we are rescued! Uncle Joshua has come to rescue us! That's wonderful, isn't it, Abigail?" Claire was looking over her right shoulder as she said that, again out through the doorway and not at any of us.

Then her eyes found Lizzie. "And he brought my Lizzie. Lizzie-whizzy, whizzy-Lizzie!" Claire grabbed the girl by her upper arms and spun her around with a strength I would not have suspected, so that Lizzie's feet came off the floor as she was twirled in a complete circle. Lizzie's face registered shock and she fought to maintain her footing when Claire planted her back on the floor.

It was late at night and I was tired, but ten seconds of Claire would have been exhausting even if I were well rested.

"Who is Uncle Joshua?" Sol asked.

"My uncle Joshua, of course," Claire said. "Where is he? Where is he? I must thank him properly for rescuing me."

"That would be Joshua Montaigne," I told Sol, "youngest brother of the Director and head of CenSec and ArmedSec." Claire nodded vigorously. "Joshua Montaigne is not here," I told her. "He has heavy responsibilities. He has sent us." In a manner of speaking, that was true, as any CenSec action ultimately derived from him. "I am Martin Allgeier, third assistant librarian of our Central Library in New Edinburgh, and this is Sol." I could not see going through Solange's full name. More candidly, I didn't want to get it wrong in front of her.

An already strange adventure became stranger.

"That is impossible." Claire drew herself up and smoothed down the sides of her baggy coverall and overalls as though they were one of the finely fitted gowns she wore in New Edinburgh to public events. Her voice was imperious, but her eyes, to the extent they focused at all, were fixed on empty air to her right. "This is not possible, is it? I am *the* Princess Claire. I cannot be rescued by a third assistant librarian." There was no mistaking the sarcasm when she gave my title. "I must be rescued by my uncle Joshua. Uncle Joshua must come for me. He swore he would if there was any trouble. Abigail says so too. That is how this must perspire."

"Perspire?"

Claire turned to Sol at the question. "Yes. Things perspire, don't you know? They happen. They go on. The way this is perspiring now is not right. Lizzie, they are not listening to Abigail. Tell them what to do."

"What?" Lizzie's voice was a squeak. "What should I tell them?"

"That Uncle Joshua has to come and rescue me. The Princess Claire cannot be rescued by them."

I found it a bit curious that she wanted Joshua Montaigne and not the Director, who doted on her, but I supposed that even someone in a state of mind like Claire's would realize the Director could not simply leave his post. "There is a plane waiting at the airport," I said. "We will take you there and it will fly you back to New Edinburgh. Joshua Montaigne will meet you at the airport there. I will call my hand … my contact to be sure he knows you are coming."

"That is not acceptable." She jerked her head up to toss her hair around. "Uncle Joshua needs to rescue the Princess Claire himself. He must be here. Uncle Joshua does not need a call. He will remember. Because I am a member of his club. You are not, so he will dismember you and you will remember. Abigail says so, and Abigail is always right."

"Who is Abigail?" Sol asked. "Was she a friend you had as a child, someone who died?"

"Don't be stupid," Claire said. "If Abigail were dead, how could I be talking to her? She is right here with me, like always." Again she turned to her right, eyes wide and unfocused.

"Look, *the* Princess Claire. Whatever you want to say about your uncle Joshua, he is not in this room. Right? You can ask Abigail and she'll tell you." An edge was forming in Sol's voice. "If you want your uncle Joshua to come save you, we have to get you out of here or he won't be able to get you. This place is dangerous, and it is probably more dangerous with every second we waste. Come with us to Edge-of-the-World and we'll work it out with Joshua. Okay?"

Claire smiled under vacant eyes. "That's the first sensitive thing you've said all night. Abigail says that Uncle Joshua is not here and we need to do something else. Abigail agrees we should go to Edge-of-the-World."

I can be forgiven for thinking, for a brief moment, that if Claire could somehow be conveyed directly to Spartacus himself, without the tape over her mouth, the insurrection might be brought to its knees without any other effort by CenSec.

CHAPTER TWELVE

I BRACED MYSELF FOR ALL SORTS OF TROUBLE MANEUVERING CLAIRE TO THE CAR, BUT in the event I was pleasantly surprised. Once we started moving, she followed directions without questions or crazy talk. Except for one remark to Abigail that we were leaving, her invisible companion stayed out of the picture. Even more surprising, she proved agile in descending from the storage room down to the gully even though the moons were lower in the sky and not nearly so bright as when we arrived.

The car was where we had left it. There was no sign anyone had disturbed it. We put Claire in the back with Lizzie. Sol drove while I rode with my pistol out, scanning from one side to the other until my neck ached. It seemed impossible that the Spartacists had panicked and run away, but no one approached the car or tried to stop us anywhere on the road back to Edge-of-the-World. I told myself that irregulars, not even trained soldiers, who have deserted their post in fear are more likely to vanish entirely than rally and reengage or report to their comrades. That kind of luck was possible.

The only disturbance during the drive came from Claire. After that stretch of cooperation in leaving the weather station, she decided to resume her conversation with Abigail, mostly asking Abigail's opinion of the road and of Sol's driving. I could see Sol's clenched teeth from where I sat, but she stayed focused on the road and the dark land around it.

We were challenged by the watchtower at the end of the drive. It was a welcome end to the stress of the drive, but it brought its own concerns.

A lone guard with a rifle stepped into the road to halt us. Judging by his posture and his voice, the presence of other guards in the watchtower did not provide him much reassurance as he walked over to Sol's side of the car.

Sol gave him her name and told him we were staying at the Opulent Miner.

The guard shined a handlight into the car. My weapon was out, clearly visible. He made no comment. I will confess to a frisson of tension when he shined the light on the two women. Would Claire keep her mouth shut? We had never considered her spontaneous and crazy talk when we had discussed getting past the guards.

"Who's this in back?" the guard asked.

"Got a contract to bring back two whores that ran off to a hill camp," Sol said.

"Whores, huh? Word in town is that you're hunting some rebel for a bounty."

"Yeah, Spartacus himself." Sol laughed. "Rounding up whores is easy money. I'll take it when I can get it. Now, can we pass? These girls need to work, and I need to sleep."

I prayed that Claire would keep her mouth shut—or if she did not, that whatever she said would be so crazy the guard would laugh it off. Not a sound came from the rear seat.

The silence lasted only until we reached our room at the Opulent Miner.

"The Princess Claire does not share a room with this many people. Such a room would mean doom, especially if it went boom. There is barely room for Abigail. I need a separate room. Or I could take one with my whizzy-Lizzie."

"No," Sol said. "I cannot wake the proprietor to get another room at this hour, even if he has one. And even if I could, I am not letting you out of my sight."

"That's mean." Claire folded her arms over her chest. "You haven't called Uncle Joshua for him to come rescue me. I talked to Abigail on the drive. We need to stay here until he comes."

Sol turned away from Claire, her head clutched in both hands. "Part of me wants to go straight for the airfield now, not chance even one night in this town," she said to me. "But that road is not patrolled at night and I can't believe the Spartacists aren't looking for us by now. We can't risk it in the dark. It will be dangerous enough by daylight, even if I can get an escort from the CenSec post here. And the truth is, we need a few hours of sleep. Especially if we need to fight."

"I agree with you." I meant it too. I didn't say it simply to let her feel that she was in charge. "Figure three hours for sleep, then go. Does that sound reasonable?"

"Yes." Sol turned back to Claire but did not have a chance to speak.

"Ooh," said Claire as she stuck an index finger in Sol's direction. "Look at her head. How did you do that to your head?"

Sol ran her fingers over the white scar that ran across the shaved side of her head. "I screwed up," she said. "It was many years ago."

"Why do you shave that one side?" Claire asked. "Won't the hair grow there? That's too bad because you have nice hair. You could braid your hair if you grew it. Or I could braid your hair on a dare. And mine to compare." She started to twist strands of her blond hair into a crooked braid.

"I keep it that way so I can see it when I look in a mirror," Sol said. "It's a reminder."

"Ooh, that's a story!" Claire clapped her hands together. "Story time. Story time!"

"No," said Sol.

"Then I'm not going to sleep, and I won't go to the airport," Claire said.

"Solly, if you tell it, just short and quick, Claire will sleep in the bed with me," Lizzie said. "Right, Claire? I'll even make room for Abigail."

Claire nodded enthusiastically, her eyes now looking at something none of us could see, far beyond the walls of the room.

"Shit," Sol said. The room was quiet for a minute. Claire perched on the bed with Lizzie next to her. Then Sol began to speak.

"It was on Ascension. That's another one of those semicivilized, garbage-dump worlds out in the Reach where people went to build a utopia and made themselves a hell instead. I was nineteen. I'd been hunting with Gil for three years. Long enough to know better, be smarter.

"Our target was a high-value one. Half of Earth had been after him for one thing or another, but he'd skipped on that by joining the Peacers and going into the Reach. When he deserted the Peacers, all those charges came back in force. We had a local working with us. Don't remember his name. Not important anymore."

Sol took a deep breath and blew it out in a big gust. She continued speaking, but in the direction of the window, not to us.

"We'd run him down in this slum of mud streets and hovels of drywall and cardboard the locals called buildings. He was trapped. Said he'd surrender. Gil moved in to make the capture, and the target took a shot. But this local stood up, too, and the bullet hit him instead. It would have killed Gil if that guy hadn't stood up. When the target fired, he exposed himself. Just a little. Just enough. One shot. I killed him. First time I'd ever killed." Sol seemed to have forgotten anyone was in the room with her. She put a hand on the wall, leaned on it, and spoke to the dark street beyond the window.

"It was a dead-or-alive contract, so killing him was no problem. We'd still get paid. But when we were back at our room, Gil was ready to bounce from one wall to another and then off the ceiling. He was drinking, of course. He'd taken some stuff. I don't know what. We both drank and used whatever we got our hands on. But he was pretty wild. I should have understood. Should have realized that Gil knew if that guy hadn't stood up, the bullet would have gone through him. I should have known.

"Well, when we closed a contract, Gil always needed to, as he said, fuck off the tension. And that's what he wanted that night. I didn't want to, though. I was thinking about killing and it was my first time for that and … I didn't want to. 'Goddammit, Solange,' Gil said, 'just take your clothes off and get on the bed. I need to fuck. I need to fuck you.' I knew that. That's what he always needed. I knew what he needed. But I couldn't do it that night. I didn't want to. I told him no."

The narration stopped for maybe a minute. Sol fingered her scar.

"Gil finished what was left in the bottle, took a pill he found in one of his pockets. Screamed at me. 'Solange, I'll take your damned pants down myself and bend you over the bed and do it that way!' I said no, I didn't want to. He grabbed the waistband of my pants. I knocked his hand away. He smashed the bottle against the side of my head."

We all waited for Sol.

"I woke up two days later. He had, somehow, gotten me to the one hospital in that excuse for a city and they closed up the wound, gave me anti-concussion meds. Linear skull fractures heal themselves, with time. Gil had sat by my bed the whole time, waiting for me to wake up. He was so sorry. Said he would never lose control like that again. Said it wouldn't have happened except he had thought he was going to be shot and then I'd been so stubborn at the wrong time and we needed to be careful about that and he would be and was sure I would too. And he was right, you know. I knew what he needed, and it must have been scary to know you had almost been killed and he could never say he was scared, and I knew that. It was all because I picked the wrong time to be stubborn and I should have known better. It was all my fault."

Sol's head bowed, her hand on the scar.

"It was not your fault. He was an asshole." The words rang out while I was still digesting the story that had poured from Sol. They came from Claire, sharp and penetrating. Her eyes focused on Sol like a pair of lasers.

"Claire?" I took a step in her direction. Sol snapped her head around to stare at Claire as well.

"Abigail said Solly didn't do anything wrong." Claire's voice went back to its usual singsong. Once again, her eyes were empty windows in a vacant building.

I had no time to wonder about that flash of a different Claire. "Sol, what Claire said is right. There is no way that was your fault. The fault was his. All of it."

Sol shook her head. Sobbed once. "No. If I hadn't done what I did, said what I said, it never would have happened. I loved him. I needed to be more careful."

Lizzie left Claire and put a hand on Sol's arm. "Solly?"

Sol shook it off and turned away from her.

I decided that I would take Gil Mortimer to the deepest circle of hell—which is where I will be consigned—and watch him burn for eternity. Other forms of torment passed through my mind as well, and I will admit to indulging in them. Some people deserve to die horribly.

Sol made her way to the couch. It was not long enough even for someone of her modest height. She lay down with her head on one cushion and her feet over the other armrest.

"Solly, you should take the bed," Lizzie said. "The Princess Claire and I will be okay sleeping on the floor."

"No, this is fine." Sol's voice was weary. "I shouldn't have said any of that. Should have just told a lie, like always."

"Why didn't you?" I asked.

"I don't know. Tired. Maybe tired of lying. Started and I didn't stop." Sol rolled over so her face was to the back of the couch.

I waited for a little while until Sol's eyes were closed and her breathing regular. A chair with a poorly cushioned seat and a plastic back stood in the corner of the room across from the couch, so I sat in that. Lizzie and Claire were asleep on the bed next to each other. As I watched Claire, I thought again about her outburst. That had been like a reappearance of the young Claire.

Had the shock of losing first her mother and then, soon after, having her father, Geoffrey, murdered by the insurrectionists made her into what she was today? Or had there been something more?

Some part of the Riots that directly touched her? I might wonder why Sol's story had brought back a flash of that old Claire—the child people had once called Golden Girl—but there was nothing I could do with that wondering.

I checked the time. The satellite window was open. I slipped out into the hall to make the connection to my handler. That was not a call I would miss, and I was not going to make the call in that room.

CHAPTER THIRTEEN

WOKE WITH THE SORT OF PAIN IN MY NECK THAT WOULD MAKE HAVING MY HEAD chopped off a good solution. I needed to stop sleeping in chairs. I would have done better to curl up on the concrete floor. Judging from the wan light through the window, and confirmed by a check of my comm, it was early morning.

I made a futile attempt to massage my neck, then decided to be thankful my sleep had been limited to only a few hours. We could not afford more. We needed to move.

Lizzie and Claire were still asleep on the bed. Sol was awake, standing in the small gap between the foot of the bed and the wall. She was staring through the window opposite the bed.

I stood up and joined her. "Did you get any sleep?" I asked. "You must have. You needed it."

"An hour or two. It will have to be enough."

"If it was because of what you said, don't worry about it. You were right, and he's still wrong and ought to be dead wrong." I will confess to feeling protective for no reason I could discern.

"Not so simple." Sol tried to stifle a yawn. "Simpler if I hadn't said it. Shit slips out at the worst times."

Ha. I like bathroom humor. "Something else is bothering you now," I said. Sol's tense half crouch by the window conveyed her feeling without the need for words.

"Yeah." She traced her scar with two fingers. "This has been too easy. Just too damned easy. From the moment we arrived in Edge-of-the-World, it's been like dumping a jigsaw puzzle out of its box and having the pieces all drop into place. Our room overlooks the street entrance to this hotel. I've been watching, and I don't see any sign of someone watching us. I've been at this trade long enough now. This is not how it goes."

"I understand what you mean. That's not the way it happens in mystery and detective thrillers either."

Sol turned from the window and regarded me. I waited for a smile but did not see one. "That what you read in your library when you're not cataloging your history section?"

"Sometimes."

Sol let out something between a snort and a chuckle. "Okay. Did you make whatever contact you needed, and is Joshua Montaigne going to pick her up at the airfield?"

"Yes to the first and I doubt it to the second," I said. "It probably doesn't matter, because once we are at the airport, Claire is going on the plane one way or another. What happens after that isn't your concern. You're paid off once she is on the plane. You only need to get her from here to the runway."

"Right." Sol straightened. "It's late enough for truck traffic to start and the patrols to be out. The sooner we get going, the better. Let's get them up."

When I stepped over to the bed, Claire's eyes were open, staring up at the ceiling. Had she heard our conversation? Would it matter if she had?

"Let's go," I said. I gave Lizzie's shoulder a shake to get her started.

"I'm hungry." Claire sat up and swung her legs over one side of the bed. "My stomach is growling." She mimicked a storybook tiger with clawed hands and bared teeth. "You need to feed me. Indeed you need. Feed is the deed. If you do the deed, you could reseed. If you reseed, you get corn. I want a fried corn on the cob."

I could believe she was hungry. I had no idea when she had eaten last. It had been a long time for us as well, but jobs came before food. Lizzie said nothing. From the little she had said before, I was sure there had been plenty of times she had gone hungry. "We have some food in our packs," I said.

"The Princess Claire expects breakfast." Claire stood and smoothed down the front of her overalls. "It should be on clean white dishes. With a cup of real hi-caf tea. Which comes after S, which stands for sassafras, although I don't know what that is. Abigail is hungry too. Abigail says she doesn't want to go to the airport until we eat."

Play the fantasy, I thought. That is what you are supposed to do in this type of situation. "Princess Claire, there will be a breakfast set for you at the airport. With the hi-caf tea we grow on the Hastings Peninsula south of New Edinburgh. We will put out a setting for Abigail."

"Breakfast with Uncle Joshua at the airport?"

"Of course."

"I don't believe you!" She thrust one fist up with the middle finger raised. "If Uncle Joshua were going to be there, you would have said that first. Abigail says she does not want to go to the airport. We should eat here first."

What part of this job was too easy?

"Your uncle Joshua will meet you when you get off the plane. I am sure of that. And you will have a very nice breakfast with Captain Willoughby at the airport. And we need to go now so we're not late for breakfast."

"I want Lizzie-whizzy for breakfast." She grabbed Lizzie's hands. "Not roasted, though. Not even toasted. I want my whizzy-Lizzie. I want breakfast now."

"We need to go. Now! We are going to the airport. Now!" I put a real snap in my voice. I can do that, although I have rarely had the need. Patrons of history and historical fiction are neither rowdy nor boisterous in rooms marked QUIET.

The street had a reasonable amount of traffic when we left the hotel, enough that we were not conspicuous, while not crowded enough for someone to come close without our noticing. Sol's long duster did differ from the attire of other pedestrians and bikers, who all wore some variant of the coveralls or baggy shirts and pants, but it was not outlandish enough to draw looks.

A brief early morning shower had left the center of the streets wet. Under the overhanging second stories it was dry, which meant the garbage in the gutters had not gotten wet. That would keep the smell down for the morning.

Living areas were stacked on top of businesses as a second story. They projected over the streets, because the streets needed to be wide enough for cars, and people wanted more living space than the ground floors permitted. As the town had grown over time, third stories were added, which further deepened the shadows on the streets. Building up was preferable to spreading out, because the presence of people and business brought bandits the way garbage brings rats. Those sporadic bandits had become rebel gangs, and now the Spartacists. I have wondered why our civic order has been so precarious despite the effort expended to maintain it. The library holds many volumes relevant to that question, nearly all of which have been flagged as off-limits for reasons of GSG or civic justice. Nevertheless, a librarian can access anything, and without leaving a trail.

My thoughts were directed along the lines of civic order—or its lack—because our vehicle was not where we had left it.

Sol stared at the empty space. The space was not under an overhang, and the bricks that had been under the car were dry. "I wouldn't call this town law-abiding," Sol said, "but stealing a car is unusual. There are too few places to put it or sell it that it won't be found, not unless you take it out to the hill camps or the farms. I'm guessing it was taken right around the time I was saying this job was too easy."

"You don't believe in jinxes, do you?"

"No, I'm just finding it funny." Sol's face said she did not find any part of it funny. "The contract will pay Toby for the vehicle."

"Of course," I said quickly.

"And whatever I need to pay for another one, unless I steal one." Sol sighed. "Let's go back over to the whorehouse and see what we can do about transport to the airfield."

Sol had not taken more than ten or twelve steps away from the vacant bricks when she came close to me and said in a harsh whisper, "We have a tail. Behind on the right. Boots suitable for rough country. Worn coverall in faded blue. Knit hat. Spotted him earlier and wasn't sure. Now I am."

I did not spin around to look. Even I know that much. I did turn toward Sol as though I wanted to say something only to her, and in doing so, I was able to look back without making it obvious. The man was there, as she had described.

Our car had been stolen and we were being followed. Part of me regretted not having made a dash for the airport last night, but these same occurrences meant that being alone, in the dark, on that stretch of road would have been likely to end in disaster. I told myself this was a poor time for an internal debate. What I needed to consider was whether we would be attacked in the middle of the street. The grip of my gun under my coat was welcome reassurance.

"Claire, Lizzie, come walk ahead of us," Sol said.

Lizzie slipped an arm around the crook of Claire's elbow. Just as they came even with us, Claire sang out, "Abigail's got a tail! Abigail's got a tail! Wag your tail, Abigail. Dogs wag tails, not Abigail. It would make a good tale, if Abigail had a tail. Are you going to tell us another tale, Solly, one that will make us wail without fail so I would cry in my lunch pail? I'm still hungry. Get me some of what he is selling."

What had captured Claire's attention was a street vendor selling beef skewers from a cart. The man smiled and held up a skewer. I thought of food poisoning.

The outburst brought us attention of the negative kind. People drew away from us, leaving a zone of open ground all around us. Eyes were averted, fixed anywhere except on our group. In New Edinburgh, this would be a healthy desire to avoid doing anything a CenSec informer might consider disrespectful to a person with obvious mental issues. I was surprised to see that attitude in Edge-of-the-World, since the CenSec presence here was limited and I doubted they had a large informer network. But perhaps the behavior was so ingrained on Offyonder that it continued the way Pavlov's dogs salivated. This was another aspect of our prized civic justice and order that had stimulated much thought and late-night reading on my part. I had not seen it in Bannion. I had no time to dwell on it now.

"We are all hungry. We will get you something to eat, Claire, when we have a car." My tone may have been brusque; I was hungry too. I did not receive any protestation about how Princess Claire should be treated. She came along with us.

"I don't see that man anymore," Sol muttered. "Not since Claire's little performance."

"He can't have lost us," I said.

"No," Sol said. "He has probably passed us to someone I haven't identified. How many of them can they have here? They keep their cells small for their security."

"We can turn left at this intersection," I said, "then right at the next, and then another right will bring us out near the brothel. See if anyone stays with us."

"You do read too many of your books. But, yes, the street grid is basically rectangular."

We had not reached the next corner before Claire let out another yell. "We need to go in here!"

"Here" was Thornton's Dry Goods and Electronics, a nondescript storefront whose door was almost hidden in the shadow of the second-floor overhang.

"No, Claire, we need to keep moving." Sol's voice was as harsh as mine had been.

"No! I need to pee!" Claire screamed. She stood rooted in front of Thornton's with one leg crossed over the other.

"Not now!" Sol snapped. "I don't know this place. It's not safe. We need to reach—"

Claire hopped up and down a couple of times and broke into what Sol was trying to say. "Ohh no! Ohh no! Help me! I wet myself!"

It took only a quick glance to see the spreading dark stain at Claire's crotch. This was a situation I was not well equipped to handle.

"Please," Claire said. "It's dripping in my boot."

"Martin, you might as well take her in there." Sol waved at the entrance to Thornton's. "See if they have something she can change into. Take Lizzie with you. I'll watch out here, and let's hope that's all I do."

I could not think of a reasonable alternative, so I pushed the door open and motioned for the two of them to follow me. I gave a silent thanks that Claire did that much without any further comment.

The inside of Thornton's was small, cramped, and packed with goods for sale. On a positive note, it was well organized. Clothes were to the left, everything from work bibs to coveralls to baggy casual pants and shirts. All of it was fabric of yonderhemp or wool, none of the expensive printed filament or off-world cotton that a high-end store in New Edinburgh would carry (and that I could not afford).

To our right were stands holding knives and machine tools. A locked case containing electronics—everything from comms to simple trackers—stood next to the pay station near the entry. I was surprised to see comm units as good as you could buy in New Edinburgh, with backcountry battery packs good for two weeks between charging, all of Offyonder manufacture.

A thin woman in blue coveralls, with the lines on her face and the gray in her hair to speak to twice my years, watched us closely from the pay station. Her eyes narrowed whenever Lizzie or Claire drifted close to a display table.

"We've had a bit of an accident," I said. "Do you have clothes for her?" I pointed to Claire. "A coverall or top and bottom." I fished out my electronic voucher and held it for her to examine.

The sight of the card relaxed the wrinkles on her face. The pitying look that followed when she looked Claire over saved us any further discussion of what was needed.

She introduced herself as Molly Thornton. "I've got a coverall that should be the right size, or close to it," she said. "It will be less expensive than separates if you'll take the yonderhemp. No need really for overalls on top of the coverall."

"I need undies," Claire said. "And one of my socks is wet."

"I don't carry underwear," the woman said. "For that, you would go to Bogart's, that's closest, but they'll charge you an arm and both legs."

Claire's face went so downcast that the corners of her mouth were ready to drip on the floor.

"No choice on that," I said. "You'll have to do without for now."

I paid for the coverall. When the woman brought it over, it proved to be a cheap, coarse weave of the yonderhemp. It would probably be rough and scratchy to wear but should be endurable for the trip to the airport. A never-lose-it tag in the electronics case caught my eye while we were making the transaction. I purchased that as well.

"Where can I change?" Claire asked. "I can't change on the range." She swept her arms around the store. "I need a place that's in range. While she makes change."

The woman looked away from Claire. "There's a dressing room downstairs you can use." She pointed to a door at the back of the shop. "It has a mirror, though I don't imagine that's the most important thing right now."

"No, it's not," I said. "Come on, Claire." I put one hand on the small of her back and used the other to gesture toward the door.

Claire jumped as though I had applied an electronic shock. "No! I'm not doing it with you there. You can't … I won't …" She began bouncing up and down on the balls of her feet.

"All right. All right." I took my hand away from her and held both of them up in the air. "How about if Lizzie goes down with you?"

Claire nodded.

"Come on, Claire. You'll get out of the wet things and it will be fine." Lizzie took both of Claire's hands and Claire calmed down immediately. I was finding myself grateful we had Lizzie with us, although that led to thoughts of what would happen to her after this was done, and that was best not thought about.

"One moment," I said. "I'm only touching your hair." I stepped behind Claire and used the band of the never-lose-it to pull her hair into a loose ponytail. A tap on my comm paired the two devices.

"What's that?" Claire asked.

"So we'll always know where Abigail is," I said.

"Oh, a tracker for Abigail. Isn't that wonderful, Abigail? Although I always know where Abigail is. But thank you."

Claire seemed delighted enough and occupied enough by the never-lose-it that was now in her hair that she lost all her trepidation about changing clothes. She went with Lizzie without another word.

Another customer came into the store while I watched the two of them disappear through the back door. He paid no attention to me and went to the display of knives. The proprietor went to talk him up for a sale. Sol stuck her head in through the door and I explained the situation. She had spotted another person she believed was watching us and told me she would take care of that but not to take too long in the store. When Sol left, I watched the new customer test the weight and balance of a six-inch bowie knife while complaining that the price was too high for the grade of steel. Time passed. The dickering over the price of the bowie continued. The never-lose-it had not changed location. How long does it take a young woman to change out of urine-soaked clothing?

An alarm bell went off in my head.

"You!" I snapped at the proprietor. "Come with me. We're going back there." I stuck my head out the front doorway and did not see Sol. "Sol!"

There was no answer. This was too like many of the novels I had read. When I turned back from the door, the man who had been looking at the knives had stepped close to me. He had that bowie gripped in his fist, the blade close to his chest and half-hidden by his open jacket. All at the same time he saw my eyes fasten on the blade, he snarled and whipped forward a backhand stab at my chest. By the grace of any deity you wish to name and a giant dose of luck, I was alert. I had no time to draw my gun. But ever since the Riots, the Directorate has trained all its personnel in weapons defense.

I had no time to think, only to react. My left arm came up in a block. Our forearms cracked together in a parody of a plus sign. His hands were thicker and stronger than mine, but the pain of that impact loosened his grip. My hands were quick. I put him in a wrist lock, twisted and snapped. He gasped. The knife hilt slid into my hand. I stabbed into his belly, yanked the blade up toward his ribs and then across his abdomen. He screamed and toppled forward with loops of bowel hanging out as he went down.

The proprietor froze. I let the bloody knife drop to the floor and drew my gun with one hand while I pulled my comm out with the other. I tapped Sol's code and yelled, "Urgent!" I put the comm away and did a fast one-handed frisk of the man. No other weapon. No ID either.

Sol burst through the door a moment later, gun in hand. The proprietor raised her hands and put them on top of her head. Sol frisked her quickly and relieved her of a small pistol that had been hidden in a fanny pack at the back of her coverall's waistband.

"I always carry that," the woman said. "Nothing to do with you. I mean, how would I know you would come here? I'm often alone."

I shrugged. "I don't care whether you're telling the truth or not. You are going to lead us through the door to where they went, and if there is any trouble, the first bullet will go through you. When you come back upstairs, assuming you do, if this is alive"—I kicked the moaning man on the floor—"call your police to come get him. You will explain it this way." I stepped close to her and whispered in her ears some words my handler had given me for touchy situations such as this. When I finished, the woman's face was several shades lighter than her hair.

Sol could not hear those words, nor was she supposed to. She used the time to lock the door to the street and switch the store's sign to CLOSED.

"Move." I used the barrel of my gun to start the woman toward the back door. Past the door was a poorly lit landing and a narrow staircase leading down. We had to go single file down the stairs. I kept one hand on the collar of the woman's coverall, and the pistol, as a reminder, touching the top of her head. At the bottom was a corridor running both left and right. In front of us was a door with DRESSING ROOM stenciled on it.

Sol stepped forward and banged on the door with the butt of her pistol. There was no response. She tried the doorknob. It was unlocked. A push swung the door open. The dressing room was empty, save for a wet coverall and overalls draped over a stool. No, there was one other item present. Looped over a corner of the mirror on the wall was the never-lose-it.

ACT II

TYRANNY, LIKE HELL, IS NOT EASILY CONQUERED; YET WE HAVE THIS CONSOLATION WITH US, THAT THE HARDER THE CONFLICT, THE MORE GLORIOUS THE TRIUMPH. WHAT WE OBTAIN TOO CHEAP, WE ESTEEM TOO LIGHTLY: IT IS DEARNESS ONLY THAT GIVES EVERY THING ITS VALUE.

THOMAS PAINE, *THE CRISIS*

CHAPTER FOURTEEN

Sol and I went up and down that corridor below Thornton's shop, forcing Thornton to come with us. Multiple doors were set into the walls, some marked with the name of a shop, others simply as storage, a few without any marking. Most were locked. The unlocked ones were empty, other than a single one containing junk. In one direction, the corridor dead-ended. The other ended in a T-junction with a crossing corridor.

"These are mostly storage rooms for the shops above," Thornton said after I prodded her with the end of my pistol. "The underground corridors were built with the town because the winters are harsh here, and most have these storage rooms even if it is only houses above. There is no space aboveground for storage, and building another story for that is too expensive."

"Convenient for storage," I said, "but underground corridors could also be convenient for Spartacists." If they had been following us aboveground, could they have had people below as well? "Did you signal them that she was going downstairs? Where could they take

them from that dressing room? Where would they have to come up?"

She squinted at me. "I have no idea what you are talking about. How would I even know that you were going to come into my shop and that she would need to go downstairs?"

What the woman said was pretty reasonable. If Claire hadn't gone in her pants on that particular street, we would not ever have entered Thornton's. Yet something was wrong about this woman. I'd seen how people reacted when the Spartacists were mentioned, especially if they could be personally involved. They flinched, at least a little. She had not.

"You're lying! I know it!" The way I got the words out, I am sure they sounded a bit unhinged. Well, that could be a good thing. "You remember what I told you upstairs. I could put a bullet in you where you'll die slowly and leave you in your own dressing room. By the time they find you, all they'll do is bury you along with the rest of your family."

I am not given to threatening language and I don't have a menacing appearance. In this situation, however, I had a gun in my hand and was waving it a little, and my words came out, I am sure, rather like a crazy man's. After all, the situation was dire. Alive, Claire would have value to the Spartacists; Lizzie would not.

I told myself that I had become fond of the waif only because of the way she had helped Claire, but the obvious fact that Sol cared about the girl affected my feelings as well. Maybe that was most of it. Whatever the basis, I obviously looked like a maniac who would happily commit murder.

Whatever defiance Thornton had gave way. She was an old, scared woman. "Listen, listen, this is what I know, really all I know. That man who came in, the one who attacked you, I didn't know he was a … you know. Most of us know about them, whether we say so or not, but that doesn't mean we know who they are. I didn't know he was going to try to knife you. But even if I did, I'm not stupid enough to give it away. I didn't know anyone would take the girls. I didn't know! They could take them out through any of the shops. They all have stairs down like mine. And the corridors connect along the streets. They could come out anywhere along there or stay in one of the places that are really working with … them. That's all I can tell you!"

I suspected that truly was the limit of what she could tell us. We had turned into her shop almost at random. I simply had a desire to make someone pay for our problem. I was saved from that by Sol.

"If you wanted to get a message to the Spartacists, could you do it?" Sol managed to sound as if she were asking a server if the restaurant could make eggs for breakfast. "It would be worth your while."

The woman licked her lips. She looked from Sol to me and back again. Fear battled avarice on her face. Avarice won. "How much?"

Sol named a price.

"And my family is safe? His … friends will stay away?"

"You are safe from us." I will swear that Sol winked at me. "We will pay for the return of the girls. Both of them. The payment will be worth it. Have someone leave a message for us with the desk at the Opulent Miner. You can tell them that I'm Sol. If either of the girls is harmed, I have a reputation for finding people."

After receiving a friendly pat on the shoulder from Sol and with a terrified backward glance over that shoulder at the two of us, the woman retreated up the stairs to her shop, where she would need to deal with that man, or his body.

We put our weapons away and went up every set of stairs to the ground floor of every establishment they led to. Most of the doors at the top were locked against anyone coming from below. We banged on them until someone opened them. The reactions ranged from apathy to annoyance. The answers to our questions were always variations on the same theme. No, no group that had included a girl and a young woman had come up from the lower level, gone through the shop and out to the street.

One man took it further and questioned whether we had been born stupid or become brain damaged later. Sol's lips pressed together could have been misinterpreted as a smile, but her hand going under the duster carried a different message. The man drew the same conclusion and backed out the front door of his own shop in such a hurry that he tripped and fell on his ass in the crowded street. Sol stood over him, and I wondered if she would do something drastic—like shoot him in plain view of everyone—simply out of frustration.

It is possible that the man owed his life to a vendor on the other side of the brick road who waved to us. This was the same vendor selling the beef skewers Claire had wanted. His cart was positioned in the shadow of the building overhang. The contrast of the sun's glare on the middle of the road with the darkness at the side was enough to make him nearly invisible from our side of the road. He gave us a second wave.

"Come on," Sol said.

We worked our way through the stream of people in the street and dodged one bicyclist who seemed intent on running us down. The vendor, when we reached him, was a burly man whose loose pullover and baggy pants were liberally stained with grease. His face could have used a shave and his body could have used a bath.

"Saw the way you came out of that store," he said. "Made me think you didn't get the right answer to a question you asked. Made me think I might have some information you would want."

"Implying you saw something recently," Sol asked.

"My meat is good," he said. "Never spoiled. Your choice of toppings. You might buy one each. A good tip is always appreciated."

"How do we know that what you're going to tell us is worth anything?" I asked.

"You don't," he said. "But you will get a good beef skewer even if it's not."

Sol handed over an outrageous number of DMs that the Directorate would have to cover.

"Very generous of you," he said. "A young woman, a blonde, came out of Herlick's Smokeables with two men." He pointed to the shop at the end of the block. "I would say she looked like the woman I saw with the two of you before you went into Thornton's. She wanted one of my skewers, I am quite sure. I thought it was interesting that she came out with the two men. I thought it was more interesting the way you two just came out."

"It is interesting," Sol said. "Did she look like she was being forced? Did she look afraid?"

"I didn't see a weapon, if that's what you mean. Hard to tell what a person's feeling when you're looking into shadows, you know. But that blond hair. Can't miss that."

"Where did they go?" I may have been abrupt, but I did not have the patience for question-and-answer games.

"Are you sure one skewer is going to be enough for your appetites?"

Sol bought another one and suggested she might buy a fourth if she heard something that stimulated her appetite.

"A car pulled up to that corner and all three of them got in. That car is from the D'Ascenzo farm. I know that because Ralphie D'Ascenzo got roaring drunk three weeks ago at M'Bele's Bar and scraped the whole side of his car along the brick wall. No way of missing that."

Sol bought the other skewer. "You said a blond woman. What about a girl with them? Early teens. Thin girl. Dark hair."

"You mean the other one who was with you when you came." The vendor shook his head. "Not with them. Haven't seen her." He looked at our hands filled with his beef skewers. "I'd say what you've got ought to fill you. Wouldn't be right to sell you another one."

Sol started away from the man and his cart, her face grim. I had to hustle to catch up with her as she headed back across the street to the row of shops we had been in.

"Sol, where are you going?"

"Lizzie wasn't with Claire when the men put her in that car. I need to check that lower level again."

"Sol, I'm sorry about Lizzie." I was panting as I followed her while she stormed through the shop we had just come out of. "I'm sorry about Lizzie, but we need to get Claire."

"I'm going to be sure there isn't a body down there." Sol took the stairs down two at a time. Trying to keep up with her made me fear I would trip and go headlong down them, and then I would be the body at the lower level.

"We can't go after Claire without a car," Sol said. "We can afford the five minutes to check the storage areas on that connecting corridor."

It took more like fifteen, which was fifteen too many in my estimation, and it was not only the connecting corridor but then the next one that connected to. It was wasted time. We found nothing, although perhaps not finding a body meant the time was not wasted. Again, no one in any of the shops could recall seeing a girl who matched Lizzie's description. Naturally.

When Sol finally gave up, we emerged from the underground and stood in the street around the corner from Thornton's. From the scene on the street, nothing out of the ordinary had happened. Presumably, Molly Thornton had found somewhere to stash the man who had tried to kill me. Either that or the police response was even slower than I would expect for the fringe of civilization. Sol was breathing heavily, as though she had sprinted a mile.

I decided I should sound empathetic. "Sol, I know you're attached to that girl, but there's nothing more you can do. We have to get Claire back and we have a lead as to where she's been taken. We need to see this D'Ascenzo place."

"I am not *attached* to her," Sol said. "I'm not attached to anyone. I told you before: she reminds me of someone, and that's it. Beyond that, she's nothing more than another Bannion street kid."

She reminds you of you. The thought burst into my mind, but I managed to keep it there. What I said was "In Bannion, you risked your life to save her. You knew you were walking into a gunfight back then."

Sol's lips twisted into more of a grimace than a smile. "Risking my life is not putting anything of much value at risk."

It is to me. Again I avoided voicing my thought. We were together solely for the purpose of this mission. Such sentiments were not helpful in doing our jobs. In fact, I should not be having such thoughts at all.

"Anything that risks you risks our job of recovering Claire. I'll thank you to consider your value from that perspective, if not from any other. Now, what do we do about obtaining another car?"

CHAPTER FIFTEEN

A LONG WALK WITH NO FURTHER CONVERSATION SAW US BACK AT PEAKS AND Valleys. We took a table; Sol downed a serving of the hot mash and struck up a conversation with the bartender about a car. This resulted in a series of men and women coming to our table for brief chats with Sol. All of them seemed to know of her or represented people who knew of her. More of the Directorate's money changed hands. I could see that I would need to call on all my knowledge of fiction to properly craft a report of my expenses.

At length, the discussions came to an end with a final payment—on the high side, I would have to say. Sol sat back in her chair and ordered another mash. From across the table she looked me over in silence, as though this were the first time we had met. I had the uncomfortable sensation that her eyes were seeing under my skin and inside my head.

"Tell me something, Martin," she said at last. "You told me that you are a third assistant librarian. Correct?"

"No. I am *the* third assistant librarian." I almost laughed when it struck me how much that sounded like Claire proclaiming that she

was the Princess Claire. This was not a moment for laughter, however.

"Let's forget the article," Sol said. The air over the table had a charge, as though an electric storm were coming. It was a small table. "Today, with no warning, a man attacked you with a knife. You left him gutted on the floor. I heard the way you threatened the woman from Thornton's. This does not strike me as what *a* third assistant librarian would do, someone who was assigned this job because they are a nobody whom no one will notice. Please explain this to me, and not with that line about how all Directorate personnel are given self-defense training."

I tried to restrain my blush and failed. "I suppose I do need to tell you the truth," I said. "I have wanted to be a CenSec officer for a long time. Since the Riots, when I was finishing my studies and saw CenSec stand up and save the civic justice and order of our Directorate."

"I wasn't on Offyonder then. That was ten years ago, correct?" She looked to me for confirmation. "I have heard plenty of stories from many people, and they describe it differently. Barricades stormed. A crowd massacred in a stadium. Some grisly executions that haven't been used since the medieval period on Earth, drawing and quartering being one. I went to school long enough in London to have learned about that."

I reflected that the unofficial, word-of-mouth database on the subcontinent rivaled our official one on the mainland and might be, in some respects, more complete. "There were excesses at the end that should not have been allowed." I could admit that much. "You have to understand, it was almost civil war. What the rioters demanded as 'free speech' would have allowed people and groups to be targeted, would have allowed hate, would have sent us back to the uncivil, unequal society we left. They murdered Geoffrey Montaigne, Claire's father. We had to do what was necessary. You need to set those excesses at the end against the earlier atrocities by the rebels and the threat to our civic order and justice."

"I see," Sol said as if she did. "And now you have free speech as long as it is consistent with GSG. Never mind. Let's set aside who did what to whom. That doesn't matter very much to me. You wanted to join CenSec. Did you? Is the librarian bit a cover?"

"No. I tried three times. I failed every time. Each time, they told me my scores did not meet standards. I think"—and I lowered my voice at this point—"it's because CenSec officers are supposed to look the part. There is a height guideline, a chest guideline, a guideline for almost every measurable. They are guidelines, officially, so I was allowed to try, but as you know, guidelines are mandatory. A CenSec man is supposed to look like a *man*. I'm ..."

"A man," Sol finished when I hesitated. "Just a small man." Her smile softened her face, even if it did not change the words.

"I have this assignment because they wanted a nobody, someone who looked the part. I took it because it is a last chance for me."

"It's ridiculous to fail someone because they don't look the part." Sol's index finger tapped against her glass. "It hardly seems fair."

"It's not fair," I said. "Many things are not fair."

Sol smiled once more. "That comes close to a GSG breach," she said. "Risky for a CenSec candidate."

There are dangerous thoughts that go with the words that would be called dangerous and a breach of GSG, but those were best left unspoken.

"I don't suppose it matters," Sol said when I did not reply. "You obviously learned something in your training, even if that didn't matter to your evaluators. A librarian with some level of CenSec training will do better in certain situations. Which you demonstrated. Which is probably why CenSec picked you for this and not some other nobody. I'll only caution you not to be disappointed in the end, when they no longer need your help."

"I understand what you're saying. But if I didn't take this chance, there would never be another one. I'm sure of that." I put all my earnestness into that statement.

Sol drank her mash and ordered another. That kept her from commenting on the likely ephemeral chance I had at that career for the time it took a young woman to come over to our table. From the amount of cleavage and leg her outfit revealed, she had to be one of the whores.

I was not offended that she focused on Sol. "I was told to tell you that there is a package for you at the Opulent Miner. They said you would be wise to pick it up immediately."

She fled before I could look from her to Sol and back.

"Odd way to deliver a car," I said.

"I doubt it's the car," Sol said. "I think we should go back there now. I would suggest that you have your nonlibrary skills ready for use."

———————

SINCE WE DID NOT YET HAVE THE CAR SOL HAD NEGOTIATED FOR, WE HAD THE SAME long walk back to the hotel. We were greeted in the lobby by an agitated clerk. *Agitated* may be an understatement. The clerk looked like he had stood by the door, sweating and waiting for us, oblivious to the rest of the world.

"I was afraid you had left." The clerk mopped his forehead with a cloth that had seen much recent use. "Of course, you had left—that is, you've checked out of your room, so it isn't your room anymore—but I didn't know what else to do and the owner will expect you to pay."

"Take a breath," Sol ordered. "Hold it. Now release it slowly." The clerk did not look any better after doing that. "Now, slowly, tell us what is going on."

"A man came by. He insisted that I let him into your room. Please understand that I had to let him in and that, for now, it is still your room. He said there is a message for you, and he left her in your room." I have never believed a man could dissolve in his own sweat, but there is a first time for everything.

"'Her'?" My question was abrupt. The Specials, the officers who reported directly to the Montaigne brothers, were reputed to occasionally leave "messages" for people in the form of bodies of family members. The ones working for Joshua Montaigne being the ones most talked about. However, if it was only one man—and the clerk would have said if it had been a group—it would be both difficult and public to put a body in our room. So, the "her" was alive. I doubted any of Joshua's Specials was in Edge-of-the-World. There were never very many of them. "Her who?"

"I don't want to talk about it," the clerk said. "Just go upstairs and then please take her and get out of here. I don't even care if you pay."

"Easier to go up and find out what this is about than try to pry anything useful out of him," Sol said.

The hallway in front of our door was quiet. Sol gave me a silent signal to stand to one side. She took the other side of the door and drew a gun from under her duster. I did the same. No sounds came from the room. With a sudden move, Sol jumped in front of the door, brought her leg up, and kicked the door in. It wasn't a very strong door. The framing around it splintered as the door flew open. Sol was through it before it had time to bang off the inside wall and rebound. I was right behind her.

Other than the furniture, all that was inside was a small body curled into a ball on the couch. Lizzie. Her head came up, which told me she was alive, and the fear on her face vanished when she recognized Sol.

"Solly! Oh, Solly!" She launched herself from the couch, a missile direct to Sol. She clung to Sol and sobbed into her chest.

"Lizzie, what happened? Tell us what happened." Sol allowed a brief hug, then pushed her back to arm's length.

"Solly, Claire saved me. Claire saved my life!"

"Claire saved you?" I was mystified. Claire, who had peed her pants in the middle of the street, had saved Lizzie?

Lizzie nodded furiously. Her chest heaved with sobs.

"Take a breath, Lizzie," Sol ordered. After the girl had gulped some air down, Sol said, "What happened when you went downstairs? What happened from that point?"

It took a moment for Lizzie to start, but once she did, the words came tumbling out without a pause. "Claire went into that changing room. Said there was only room for her and Abigail. I mean, fine with me, I wasn't going to change her. I'd wait outside the door. A man came down that hall. Pulled a gun. Said one sound, any sound, he shoots me right then. Turns me. Shoves my face into the wall. Someone put a bag over my head. Had to be someone else 'cause that first man, it was his voice, said, 'We should slit her throat and get it done. She saw my face.'

And I felt a blade. I felt a blade!" Lizzie put a hand up against the right side of her neck. "That's when I heard Claire say, 'No!' and she said it twice and then she said, 'Abigail says no also,' and they didn't cut me, and that first man was cursing and cursing, but someone else took me, let me feel a gun against my ribs, took me upstairs, took the bag off my head, told me I either acted fine or I died, took me out through some other store, just me. I don't know what happened to Claire. He put me in the back of a van, wouldn't even let me go piss." She sucked in a quick breath. "Not sure how long. I'm good with time, but it seemed like forever. Then he brought me here."

"Lizzie, you saw those men. Would you recognize them if you saw them again?" Sol asked.

"Yes! I mean, no. I don't know." Lizzie balled her hands in front of her. "First one was a white man. Brown hair. Somebody busted his nose really bad once; it's really crooked." She drew an angle in the air. "The other was Black. Maybe short hair. That's all I remember."

"That's not much," I said. Even with a broken nose on one. "But what about Claire? You didn't see her at all when this happened?"

"No." Lizzie shot me a glare for not valuing her description from the relative protection afforded by her proximity to Sol. "I'll tell you something, though. You know how she sounded when Sol told that story? How she sounded different, Solly, when she said it wasn't your fault?" We both nodded. "That was her voice when she said no, that they shouldn't kill me. It was that different voice."

Sol turned a quizzical face to me.

"I don't know." I ran my fingers through my hair. It would have been nice if I could have pulled a brilliant insight out of my mind by pulling my hair, but I don't think my mind has brilliant insights. "Before her mother died and before her father was murdered in the Riots, Claire was normal. Supposed to be really smart, although I'll agree before you say it that the Directorate would have claimed that no matter what she was. Maybe the person she was is still inside and comes out in certain situations."

"I think you're a librarian, not a doctor, and clearly you don't read the medical books," Sol said. "What interests me more is that they didn't kill Lizzie, and from what the guy selling the skewers said, Claire went with them. Could she somehow be cooperating, or they want her to cooperate and that's why they didn't hurt Lizzie? I can't see Claire managing that. She barely cooperated with us."

"People can act that way," I said. "It's called identifying with the aggressor. They used to call it Stockholm syndrome. It's in the history books."

"Stockholm is a city on Earth. I don't know about a syndrome." The puzzlement showed in Sol's voice. "I don't think we have time to find a psychiatrist. I doubt there even is one in the Uplands."

"We don't have time," I said. "The vendor said that car came from a particular farm. D'Ascenzo was the name. I want to talk to them."

"The farmers of the Inland Sea are big supporters of the Directorate," Sol said. "I can't see them helping the Spartacists, although I suppose some of them could be playing both sides."

"Maybe everyone is playing both sides," I said, looking at Lizzie.

"I'm not! I swear it!" Fear came back into her face. "I don't know what I'm into, Solly, I don't. I wish I was just dancing for my coins, and even worrying about if I'd have anything to eat tonight would be fine. But Claire saved me, and I want to help her. Look." She dug into one of her pockets. "When that Black man put me in the truck, he picked me up to make me get in. I felt something in his pocket. I am very good at this." She glared at me again.

When she opened her hand, a heavy signet ring rested in her palm. Sol picked it up with two fingers and held it so I could see it as well. Engraved in a fancy monogram was the lettering *TD'A*.

"I don't know about the *T*, but the *D'A* could stand for D'Ascenzo," Sol said.

"People wear jewelry like this in New Edinburgh," I said. "Would they do it here?"

"Unusual." Sol rubbed at her scar. "Someone who wants to show off, make out as though they are important even if your GSG doesn't allow them to say upper class."

"Stolen," I concluded. "The car probably as well. Before the Riots and before Spartacus, it was bands of thieves running around the Uplands. Old habits die hard. So, the D'Ascenzos are loyal to the Directorate, and what we are trying to find are a bunch of old-time bandits working for the Spartacists."

"Maybe." Sol stared at the ring. "This could be valuable. I think we should still see the D'Ascenzos. Maybe they will be grateful to have this back." She put an arm across Lizzie's shoulders. "Maybe you're important to Claire. You're coming with us."

CHAPTER SIXTEEN

THE CAR WAS DELIVERED A LITTLE AFTER SUNDOWN. FOR THE AMOUNT OF money spent, I was not impressed with the vehicle. Not a fender or a door was free of dents and dings. One headlight was cracked and the other did not light at all, but a string of glow-bulbs had been strapped across the hood and gave off enough illumination that we would be able to see ahead in the dark. The interior was, if anything, worse. All the seating surfaces had been scratched and torn. From the smell, the car had been used to haul materials around a farm, including some that had come out of animals. To top the list of deficiencies, it was an IC engine that growled and sputtered ominously when Sol hit the ignition. We would not be making a silent approach anywhere we went.

"It has an engine that runs and wheels to roll on," Sol said when I waved a hand in front of my nose.

"An IC engine," I said. "We have all the resources here for batteries, and whatever electronics we need to import are light. The starships bring them in quantity."

"IC is cheaper and more reliable in the Uplands," Sol said. "It's the same reason I wanted an IC for coming out here."

"I've smelled worse," Lizzie said. A rear door gave a loud squeak and stuck when she tried to open it. After three tugs, the opening was barely wide enough for her to slip in.

Sol offered no complaints as she played with the balky levers to adjust the driver's seat. That left me with no alternative but to get in and ignore the interior. I poked with one finger at the emblem peeling from the dashboard. "Equity Auto Works. Made here on Offyonder. It should be a point of pride to own a vehicle built here."

"This is a farm vehicle," Sol said. "Getting their work done is what is important to them. Points of pride are important only to the Directorate."

"Keep going like that, and you'll breach GSG and be accused of having dangerous thoughts, Solange Marie-Valerie Louise de something." I tacked on the other names as a way of making light of the first part of what I said.

"You know it's true, Martin," Sol said. "The Directorate defines what is considered compliant with GSG, and across the ocean you have to be careful of what you say. Isn't that something they taught you when you took your training programs? Or is that why you failed?"

"That's not why I failed. And anyone working for the Directorate has to know GSG thoroughly and be sure their thoughts are consistent. Even as the third assistant librarian." Of course, given my position, I had access to the library and all the words and thoughts in it. I knew the differences.

"To say 'dangerous words' or 'dangerous thoughts' is a curse on the streets." Lizzie's voice came from behind us. "People say 'words' or 'thoughts,' but you're talking as though some words are actually dangerous."

"They can be. To your health." Sol's laugh lacked any humor. "The Directorate sets the GSG, which is supposed to be how you can talk without hurting or offending anyone. If you don't follow it, that means you might not be thinking properly either. Dangerous words, dangerous thoughts. Of course, today the Directorate is mostly worried about speech that would harm *it*. Am I making you uncomfortable, Martin?"

"Yes." It was all true, though. I knew it. It had been true before the Riots and had been one of the reasons the Riots had occurred. I had simply been young enough to accept what we were taught as the natural order of things. Having free access to a library can make you see what you were taught in a different light. The library itself was not pruned, because whenever a starship came in-system and downloaded to our library database, whatever had been deleted would return. It was more efficient to ban what needed to be banned and track anyone who accessed it. Librarians had ways of having access. I said only, "It is necessary to preserve our civic order and justice. That is valuable."

"There is precious little civic order in Bannion," Sol said. "You've seen that. Maybe that is why no one there cares much about GSG, not even CenSec. You don't need to worry about it, Lizzie, not as long as you live here."

"I just want to live, Solly. That's all I want."

"I'll do my best," Sol said.

"So will I," I added. I have a dark heart, but, surprisingly, I meant it.

THE D'ASCENZO FARM WAS IN WHAT HAD BEEN, MILLIONS OF YEARS AGO, THE Inland Sea. The barren and rocky uplands sloped downward into a huge basin. The air turned moist, the soil fertile. The farms of the Inland Sea grew both Offyonder and Earth produce in quantity. They were a triumph of the hybrid ecology humans had planted on Offyonder.

Reaching this farm was a nearly four-hour drive from Edge-of-the-World, much of it on a road that might as well not have been a road. The car rocked and bounced from bumps to holes, bottoming out from time to time. Sol pushed it as fast as she dared.

"There are advantages to coming in the dark," Sol said. "If there is any chance the D'Ascenzos are playing a double game, I would like to keep the element of surprise."

The first surprise was ours, however, when we came around a low ridge. Lights blazed out ahead of us. The farm was all lit up.

"This is a farm, a farm where people do a lot of the work. I would expect them to be in bed," Sol said. She brought the car to a stop, stared through the cracked windshield, and drummed her fingers on the steering.

"No way this car is going to get close without alerting everyone," I said. "Maybe we just drive up and see what kind of reception we get." I made a point of checking that I had a full magazine in my pistol.

Sol took us forward slowly, if not silently. The farm was brightly lit but I saw no sign of anyone up and around. The outbuildings were quiet. Not even animal sounds. A building behind the farmhouse could have been a dormitory for farmworkers. There was no movement there. Crops stood tall in the fields beyond the buildings, illuminated by the moons. I could see yonderhemp growing in the fields to one side and Earth corn, probably gene-modded, to the other. They waved in the gusts of wind.

Sol stopped the car at a distance from the farmhouse. We got out and a squeak from a rear door told me that Lizzie had as well. We advanced on foot from there, trying to keep to the shadows as much as possible. Our approach had hardly been silent, but we saw no sign that we had been detected. Nowhere in the open area in front of the house did I see a car with a scraped side. The front door was open, with light spilling out.

"This is all wrong," Sol whispered as the three of us crouched behind a small toolshed.

I flattened myself on the ground and peeked around the corner of the shed. From there to the open door was maybe ten yards of open ground. No cover.

"Do you think you can reach the side of the house on our left?" I asked. "Maybe get a look through the window there?"

"I can try." With a weapon in each hand, Sol took off in a sprint, fast and silent. She drew neither a challenge nor gunfire from the house. Once there, she pressed herself against the rough brick side and peered through the window.

Abruptly, Sol straightened and waved to us. Then she walked to the front door.

Inside, we found the D'Ascenzos: a man and a woman, probably in their mid-forties; two younger men in their twenties; and a girl, probably in her late teens. They had been stood up against the wall across from the front door and executed. Multiple bullet wounds marked their chests and abdomens. Their bodies were grossly swollen and discolored. One finger of the older man had been cut off. A large dog had been shot as well. The wall behind them was pockmarked with bullet holes and splattered with now-dried blood. More blood had pooled and clotted on the floor.

"Sprayed with an automatic rifle," Sol said. "The Spartacists do not, supposedly, have access to those weapons. Another bit of wrong information. Dead about three days, I would guess."

"This wasn't done simply to steal a car and a ring," I said. "You said these farm families are loyal to the Directorate and support CenSec. This is a message."

"In conjunction with taking Claire, yes. This is a very strong message," Sol said. "Something is about to start, although how the Spartacists think they can use Claire is anybody's guess right now."

"I feel sick," Lizzie said.

The comment startled me. I had managed to forget we had her with us. "If you need to be sick, just step aside and do it. This makes me sick too."

"Martin, if you can avoid being sick, come with me," Sol said. "We need to see if these are the only ones."

Of the three of us, Sol was the only one to sound unaffected. She went through a door leading to the back of the house. I swallowed once and followed her. Lizzie did as well, her fear of staying with the bodies stronger than her fear of what might be beyond. The next room was a parlor of sorts, with armchairs and a coffee table. While we were gazing at the artifacts of the same civilized life we would see in a New Edinburgh dwelling, so out of place in a farmhouse beyond Edge-of-the-World, a sound came from farther back in the house.

We rushed forward, weapons ready, no longer concerned about silence. The sound changed to crying. A small back room was the laundry, full of modern cleaning fixtures. Piles of laundry were heaped on the floor. A small head topped with curly black hair stuck up out of one of them. The crying and tears escalated as we came closer.

"Oh, you poor thing!" Lizzie's own fear and sickness dropped away. She pulled a child, a girl of about four, from the clothes and sheets that had hidden her.

The little girl bawled without stop as Lizzie hugged her. The girl's dress was caked with dried vomit, her panties fouled. Lizzie paid no attention to that. She stroked the child's head and tried to calm her.

———————

There was little else for us to do at the farm. A quick search turned up four more dead, two men and two women, in the dormitory behind the main house. The farm animals had been killed as well, a thorough-going slaughter that had missed only this one small child. Lizzie found clothes amid the piled laundry that fit the girl and, if not clean, were better than the filthy ones she was wearing. We all tried to soothe the girl, Lizzie doing the best job of it.

We could not contact CenSec from the farm. The farm did have an antenna, but Edge-of-the-World was too far, and the satellite window was not open. Our comms would not connect. We put the child in the car and drove back to Edge-of-the-World.

We found the same lackadaisical approach to guarding the entrance we had seen before. That would need to change. I was gratified to see the panic in the female guard's face when we informed her of what we had found, and I could hear it in her voice as she used her comm to call the CenSec captain in charge of the town. I was certain there would be changes.

Captain Inoue was a short man—that is to say, no taller than me—and of equally spare frame. He was not happy to see us in his office on the ground floor of the police station, a small two-story structure of brick and stone three short blocks from the entrance to the town. He seated himself behind a small metal desk holding nothing other than a decorative plaque with the logo GSG GIVES RESPECT. CENSEC PROTECTS RESPECT. He rubbed at the wisp of a beard on his chin. "The D'Ascenzos were strong backers of the Directorate. I'm sure they were deliberately targeted. I am equally sure the story is already tearing through the hill camps and the mines. Automatic weapons, you said. Are you sure?"

"Yes," Sol said. "There is no question about it."

"I do not have any modern ones available here. I will need … That is not for you to discuss." He pried himself out of the chair behind his desk and paced back and forth in front of us. Four strides was all it took to cross that small space. "Could you get anything from that child?"

"She can't be more than four," Sol said. "She is scared out of her mind, and she hasn't eaten for maybe three days. She can't even tell us her own name. No matter what we ask, all she says is, 'Marco says kill them.' She must have heard one of the Spartacists say that before they shot the family."

"How did they miss her?" Inoue asked. "Do you really think she had the presence of mind to hide under a pile of laundry?"

"Or someone couldn't do it when it came to murdering a four-year-old," Sol said. "That can happen, you know."

Inoue let out a growl and ground his teeth. That gave me a chance to break in with a question. "The name Marco. Does that mean any-thing to you?"

He turned toward me. I could tell he was more impressed with Sol. "It might. We've picked up rumors that Spartacus has a new field commander with some number of men under him. Marco is the name we've heard." He ran his fingers through black hair that fell straight to his collar, then gave his hair a tug. I was surprised none of it came out.

"Just what we need. Some new hotshot rebel who wants to prove to Spartacus and everyone else what a terror he can be."

"Or worse," I said. "The Director's niece has been taken; her guards killed. There have been no demands. This massacre happens. Spartacus may be starting an operation and this Marco is only a part of it."

"Thank you for telling me what I already know." Inoue balled both hands into fists. "Yes, this will be part of something Spartacus is up to. Damned Peacer is what he is, and this is why we should never have our people going into the Peacers. All they will do is disrupt civic order wherever they go, and then they will bring that disruption back here." He stopped for a breath. "So, we have one who ran away to here and is doing the only thing he knows how to do. Damn. One of my officers will find a family to take care of that child. I will send a police group out to the farm, and we'll see if they can find anything. I am telling you that if you have any information on the Director's niece, you give it to me. CenSec should be in charge of finding her. Not the two of you." A distinct inflection marked his last two sentences.

"I am sure you understand that I need to fulfill my contract." Sol picked up at the end of Inoue's words without missing a beat. "Naturally, I would show my appreciation for the critical role you would play in providing assistance and your availability."

Inoue's stance visibly relaxed. I would swear that his face showed both satisfaction and a glint in his eye. Sol had read him perfectly.

Normally, the presence of the gray-and-black CenSec uniform would instill confidence that any problem would be handled efficiently and competently. Looking at Captain Inoue, I did not feel that emotion. If I felt anything, it was a troubling sensation in my stomach that CenSec had its hand out and that such behavior was expected. I reflected that there was a reason a significant level of authority had decided that Sol and I should be after Claire, rather than any local CenSec. Perhaps my handler would pass that to Captain Inoue.

CHAPTER SEVENTEEN

B Y THE TIME WE WERE DONE WITH CAPTAIN INOUE AND ABLE TO LEAVE FOR THE hotel, it was fully light. The streets were filled with the same sort of early morning traffic we had seen before. I made a point of asking Sol to go past the street where we had seen the vendor and also past Thornton's store. The vendor, with his supply of meat skewers, was in the same place and was making the same pitch to passersby. The only difference was a different pattern of grease stains on his clothing. He gave no sign that he recognized us. Thornton's had a CLOSED sign on its door. If I were the wagering sort, I would bet Molly Thornton was permanently gone.

The owner of the Opulent Miner was at the desk that morning, and I would add him to the lengthy list of people not pleased to see us. The displeasure changed to obsequious joy with the payment of a 50 percent bonus for our room. We could have it as long as we liked. Its door showed an obvious, hasty repair job from yesterday.

The window shade in the room was far from opaque, but it could have been made from cheesecloth for all that I cared. The fatigue

from the last day lay on me with the weight of a concrete foundation. I intended to sleep. Sol palmed a few pills from one of her many pockets when she thought I was not looking. Two of them went to Lizzie in a handover that would have been concealed had I not seen her pull them out in the first place.

Lizzie might well need some pharmacological help to block out the horror of what we had seen at the farm. As for Sol, I was forming the belief that whenever she was not actually doing something, she chose to blot out her thoughts and maybe her memories with whatever was handy. I thought I should ask her about that and perhaps offer to listen, but as long as the ghosts in her mind did not affect our job, they were not truly my business. I am not the type to pry into personal matters unless they are also business. I would not need chemicals in order to sleep.

Sol flopped onto the not-long-enough couch while Lizzie had the bed to herself. Based on my memory of the chair, I decided I was still young enough to sleep on the floor. That concrete floor was more comfortable than the chair, and I was asleep as soon as my eyes closed. No dreams troubled me.

I woke without any sensation of having slept; however, the light coming in through the window was fading. We had slept the day away. My first emotion was anger. We had squandered valuable time that should have been spent searching for Claire. I forced that feeling away. In the absence of any leads, the rest was more important than an aimless drive around the Uplands. This was not one of the histories in my library, in which the most unlikely and impossible events actually took place.

From my position on the floor, I could see Sol still asleep. I came to my feet with a set of aches that told me my body was, in fact, past the age when the floor made an acceptable bed. I arched my back in the forlorn hope that the vertebrae would pop back into proper alignment. A glance at the bed showed Lizzie still sound asleep as well. A time check showed the satellites would allow me to check in. The day might have been wasted, but there was a great deal of information

I needed to pass to New Edinburgh. I slipped out into the corridor to make my call.

It proved to be a disturbing conversation. It was clear that the news of the D'Ascenzo murders and the revelation that the Spartacists were toting automatic weapons was unwelcome. The reaction made me suspect that Inoue had failed to make a report, although it was possible that he had and the information was being closely held. Neither possibility was promising from the perspective of a good response by the Directorate. My handler also had information for me that was very problematic.

As soon as I ended the call, I was back in the room to speak to Sol. I was glad she was now awake.

"Someone, a Spartacist obviously, has sent the Directorate a message about Claire. An odd one." I recited the verse exactly as my handler had given it to me:

Now Spartacus has made the call,
It's time for Joshua to fall.
Or not all of his Specials and all of his men,
Will put the Princess Claire together again.

Sol massaged her temples with her palms and sat forward on the couch. "Aside from the bad verse, that sounds like a demand for Joshua Montaigne to leave the Directorate, voluntarily or otherwise. And if that doesn't happen, Claire will suffer."

"I agree," I said. "The verse is probably a way of showing to the Director that they really have Claire."

"Yes. Anyone who has spent time with her will pick up on the rhyming." Sol sat up straight. I saw bloodshot eyes. "I can't imagine the demand will be met."

"No chance at all," I said. "No matter how fond the Director is of Claire, Joshua leads CenSec and ArmedSec. The Director has no one capable enough to replace him, even if Joshua would agree." I took a deep breath. "When Geoffrey Montaigne used to joke about the three brothers being the Three Musketeers, he would call Joshua the Dark Musketeer, and it was not because of black hair and nearly black eyes compared to the other Montaignes' blond hair and blue eyes. It was his moods and his tempers. The hair and eye color had people talking about parentage. Suddenly that kind of talk became a violation of GSG. People disappeared. Bodies appeared. Joshua will not appreciate this verse."

"Do you think Claire knows how much danger she is in?"

"Probably not." I rubbed my own eyes. "From the description of the way she went with those men, she probably thinks it's a game she's playing with Abigail. We need to move fast."

Before I could make a follow-up remark about moving fast with no information, the sound of knuckles on the door broke into our conversation. I spun around and had my gun in my hand as I opened the door. The shopkeeper Molly Thornton was on the other side. The muzzle of even a small-caliber pistol can look as wide as the mouth of a cannon when you are on the wrong side of it. Every bit of color vanished from a face pallid to begin with. That made me smile. It would probably lead Sol to comment later about my failed CenSec training showing through.

"Well, Mx Thornton," I said, "it is a pleasure to see you again, even if you are not so pleased to see me. Do come in."

Lizzie sat up in bed, totally disheveled, but her glare for Molly Thornton was murderous. Thornton shuffled past me, her hands held rigidly in front of her chest as if I might take any movement as sufficient reason to blow her head off. She stopped in front of Sol, trying her best to ignore me.

"You said there was money in this," she said to Sol.

"There is."

"Good." The tip of her tongue ran across her lips. "I hope it's good, anyway. Listen. That young woman who was with you was seen in a car that came from the D'Ascenzo farm."

"We already know that," I said. "If you want to earn, tell us something we don't know."

"I have more." She clutched her hands to her chest, refusing to look at me. "It wasn't any of D'Ascenzo's family or workers driving it. The driver was a Spartacist man. Not only that, someone who has been seen with Commander Marco. You think about what you want to do with that. Everybody has heard Marco is a killer."

"Good to know," Sol said. "It would be worth more to know where they went."

Thornton was trying to keep her hands from shaking and having only partial success. Still, her cupidity won out over her fear—as always.

"I can't tell you where they ended up, because I don't know. What was said to me was that the car went on the road to Lithia Unit One. There's a hill camp along the road before the mines. You can ask there. Now you pay me—for me, and for the one I got this from."

Sol paid liberally. I suspected that the split between Molly Thornton and her source would depend on how scared of that person she was, but I did not really care. We had a tangible lead to Claire. That was all that mattered.

A GLANCE AT THE WINDOW AFTER THORNTON WAS OUT THE DOOR SHOWED THAT THE time with her had consumed most of the remaining daylight. While I wanted to be on the road immediately to make use of the information we had obtained, I had to admit that would have been a mistake. Taking the road in the dark through the Uplands was risky, and arriving at the hill camp and mine in the middle of the night offered no advantage to balance the risk. We found food for the evening and resigned ourselves to another night in that room.

At break of day the next morning, we took only enough time to fuel the car and ourselves before we were back on the road, with Sol driving and Lizzie in the back. I was, I will admit, skeptical about having Lizzie with us. While I had no doubt a street kid could fight, and probably do so quite viciously, she had no training with any weapon, which made her a disadvantage in any fight we would be in. The likelihood was too high that she would either be in our way or be hurt.

She insisted, however, that she was more scared of what would happen to her if we left her behind, and she claimed that she would be able to keep Claire calm whenever we found her. Sol sided with Lizzie. I acquiesced. I had hired Sol, after all, for her experience in these kinds of matters. Murders, kidnappings, and battles to the death were common enough occurrences in the books of the library, but they did not happen to the librarian.

"What do you know about Lithia Unit One?" Sol asked after we left Edge-of-the-World behind us.

"Of course, I know about the mine," I said. "This is where the first big spodumene find was made. When they started mining to extract the lithium, they found the diamonds, basically by accident. That was the beginning of the boom for us. I mean, I can't quote you how much we ship to other planets in the Reach, but these mines are why we have regular starship calls at Offyonder and why New Edinburgh has the same level of sophistication as a city on Earth. Close to it, at least. We could join the Assembly of Worlds if we wanted to."

"More to the point," Sol said, "the starships that haul your doped diamonds across the Reach also bring people here, people who hear that Offyonder is rich and uncrowded and think they can get rich quick."

"Usually from planets where they thought it would be easy to set up a successful colony and it wasn't." Those types showed up with every ship that came in-system. "They have been a challenge for our civic order and justice."

"Well, one of them did get rich quick. Me!" Sol laughed without mirth. "For the rest, your Directorate ships them across the sea to Bannion. Some of them end up in the hill camps around the mines, where they join dissidents who survived the suppression of the Riots and were transported here. None of them can return to the mainland. It's easier to take a starship seven hundred light-years across the Reach to Earth than to travel across the sea from Bannion to New Edinburgh."

"There is work for them here. Many of them."

"Yes, because until and unless you put a nuke plant over here, there is not enough power to handle all the grunt work associated with the mining operations and the farms, never mind the power Bannion needs. Photovoltaics are useless in the soup. There is a certain irony in having an interstellar economy built on the backs of people working with pickaxe and shovel. Between the trouble caused by gangs, police, and CenSec in Bannion and dissidents and off-worlders in the hill camps, I never lack for work."

I lacked a good rejoinder. The way our economy worked was no secret. That was the price that needed to be paid for civic order and justice. It made sense. Except to the people paying the price. Which was why we first had bandits in the hills, then gangs of rebels—and now an organized underground, thanks to the arrival of this Spartacus. I never indulged in the conspiracy theories that claimed he was an agent of the Peacers, sent to destabilize the Directorate so the Peacers would have an excuse to take over the mines and *assure* the shipments, but I could see how some people believe the stories. The fact that he was probably one of those people—ex-Peacer or not— who arrived on a ship and brought with him a talent for disruption did not help.

We drove back into the grasslands of the former Inland Sea. The road was broad and smooth here, pounded down by the haulers that brought the minerals from the open pit mines located farther into the hills down to the transports at the Bannion docks. Wild grasses akin to the ones we cultivated for our mash grew thick and high to the sides of the road. Blue bolts, foot-high green stalks with bright blue flowers up and down the stems, grew among the grasses, and turned a distant view of the grassland blue. An ill-defined cloud hovered over the sweep of green and blue, its shape constantly changing.

"Buzzies," Sol said in response to my question. "The blue bolts attract swarms of them. They go to flowering plants from Earth, too, so they're effective pollinators for us, even if they're a major annoyance to be around."

Buzzies. From too small to see without a magnifier to an inch in length, they filled an ecological niche of insects on Offyonder. The blue bolts did not grow nearly as densely anywhere on the mainland, so I had never seen a buzzie swarm like this. I could hear the buzz even in the car. I thought about Sol's remark about how they pollinated Earth plants as well as Offyonder ones. Another triumph for our hybrid ecology.

Eventually, the road climbed off the ancient seabed into the foothills on the eastern side. Soon enough we were into the outskirts of the hill camp.

First it was one ramshackle hut that appeared near the side of the road, seemingly planted amid the grasses and the blue bolts. Then there was another and another, followed by a cluster of them and still more, singly or in bunches. They were built of planks from the handtrees bound together with ropes of yonderhemp. The yonderhemp stretches over time—which is why it does not make very good rope, even though it is convenient—and the planks did not appear to have been fitted together well in the first place, so the walls of the huts sagged, with gaps all across. Eyes stared out through some of those gaps as the car rolled past. The roofs were made of large mats of the yonderhemp and handtree leaves, fastened loosely to the ropes holding the planks together. None of these places looked like they would stand up to a strong breeze. The only sign of paint on any of them was a sloppy *S* in white that appeared on nearly all of them. The most prominent wildlife were rats, in evidence wherever there were huts. Naked or nearly naked children ran among some of the clusters of huts, mixed in with dogs, cats, and the three-tailed kits.

"*S* is for Spartacus," I said. "They're all over. Except there." I pointed to two rectangular structures cantilevered against the side of a steep hill. Those were covered in gray paint.

"Dormitories for paid employees of the mine," Sol said. "They paint over the *S* whenever somebody puts one up." She stopped the car in a place where the *S* was visible no matter where I looked. "When I first came out here about five years ago, there were gangs people called rebels, but you didn't see any *S* signs. That was about the time Spartacus, whoever he is, consolidated the gangs and became the leader. Even up to a year ago or so, you only saw a few *S* signs here and there. Now they're all over. Tells you how it's going."

"We're seeing the *S* on the mainland too," I said. "Even in New Edinburgh. CenSec is working to root them out."

"Sure. That's why the signs are increasing in number."

I looked at the structures that barely held together, at an open cookfire by a clump of huts with barefoot people grouped around the flames, at laundry hanging from lines attached to shacks so flimsy the laundry might pull them down. Intellectually, I had always known conditions in the hill camps were not good, were backward. Seeing it had an impact that reports in a database did not. "It's hard to believe we're on Offyonder. It's as though we left civilization behind."

"There are planets in the Reach where this would beat the best the people have. The cats here remind me of a time Gil and I ran down this woman on a planet called New Dawn. Shacks like that"—Sol pointed out her side window at a row of them, with laundry hanging from the lines that hadn't dropped to the ground and windows of oiled paper rather than glass—"were the best you saw, and the only thing keeping the people alive was a detachment of Peacers running an aid station and a soup kitchen. The cats could eat the native wildlife and had gone feral. They were all over. All the Peacers wanted to do was leave that cesspit of a planet, and all we could do was sit with them until one of their relief ships showed up. Gil did some fast talking to get us out in that ship with our capture."

"That was the man who hit you with the bottle." Those were the first words from Lizzie in hours. "Was this after he hit you?"

"Oh yes. Long after." Sol sounded surprised at the question.

"Why did you stay with him?" Lizzie asked. "Why stay with him after he hurt you?"

"I loved him. And he was sorry about what happened. That and other things. He was always sorry, and I loved him." Sol said it as though that was always the answer to any question about Gil Mortimer's behavior.

After Lizzie and I both stared at her for a moment, Sol added, "You have to realize that he was the famous bounty hunter with a reputation that stretched from Earth across the star systems of the Reach. Without him, I was nothing."

"You are far from nothing. That's why the Directorate had me hire you." I believed I could say that much without allowing any of my feelings to interfere with our job.

Lizzie's emphatic concurrence took away any attention Sol might have paid to the inflection in my voice, while I considered inventive approaches I could pursue should Gil Mortimer ever fall into my hands.

"First stop is the mine manager." That was Sol's way of ending the conversation.

CHAPTER EIGHTEEN

THE MINE MANAGER, AVISH DOS, WAS NOT IN HIS OFFICE WHEN WE ARRIVED to see him. When I told the CenSeccer stationed at the door that we were representatives of the Directorate to see Mx Dos, I received an immediate "Right away, right away." It was, in fact, right away, since the office was a small square room attached to one side of a prefab bungalow that served as Dos's residence.

Dos came out of the bungalow at a quick step. He was a thin man two inches taller than me, with jet-black hair combed straight back to the nape of his neck. A brown face with the smoothness of youth was creased with lines of worry. He ushered me and Sol into his office— we had decided our roles would look better if Lizzie stayed in the car, lying as flat as possible between the rear and front seats.

His office was sparsely furnished. He had a utilitarian desk of metal and plastic holding a computer screen, input devices, and a framed picture of a young woman. Four metal chairs lacking cushions were the only places for visitors to sit. Dos waved us to two of the chairs, but went no further than putting a hand on the back of his cushioned

recliner behind the desk.

"You are here to talk about … of course, the diamond quota. It would be best to show you the mine as we discuss that." With that comment, he pushed his chair under the desk and led us back out the door we had just entered.

We were *not* in his office to talk about a diamond quota. Sol caught my eyes as Dos went through the door. It took no words to see we were both thinking the same thing. *Dos is nervous about something, but let him fill in the blanks.*

A path led from his office door in the direction of the wild hills to the rear of the building. With us and the CenSeccer trailing him, he took the path at a brisk pace. It made a jog to the right and ended at an overlook with a railing. The view was of the open pit mine, a great gouge in the earth. Dos came to a stop at the railing. The CenSeccer halted a discreet distance behind us on the path.

"I'm new here," Dos said. "Just started my term two weeks ago, the usual rotation for someone at my level. I remember my predecessor said to always assume the office is bugged. He said I might never know who was bugging it, but no matter what I did, there would be a bug. Now, if you are here from the Directorate, it must be about the killings."

"The D'Ascenzo family, you mean," Sol said. "I have a contract."

Sol's manner said she had every right to be there and ask him questions, but I pulled out my Directorate identification card and held it up as backup.

"Yes, yes, of course. That is a very fast response. Appropriate." He intertwined his fingers in front of his chest as a means of keeping his hands still. "We've never had an incident … Well, I mean there have been incidents, naturally, but never anything like that. Relationships with our farming families have been good. That is where our food comes from!"

"You are sure this was a Spartacist operation?" Sol asked.

"What else could it be? We pick up rumors, the workers talk, saying that Spartacus has appointed this man Marco to lead a unit around here. A wild man, if half of what I hear is true. He must have done this, although I can't see what they gain from it."

"I am also looking for a young woman from the Directorate. Midtwenties. Blond hair. Kidnapped, we believe, by this same unit. Any word here about this?"

"A kidnapping also?" Dos shook his head. "Not here." He scuffed his soft leather boots against the ground. "You should understand, we and the Spartacists … Well, we coexist. Uneasy, but we coexist. For all Spartacus and his people run around, they're little more than thieves at the margin, stealing enough to stay alive and barely that. They know better than to kill the hen that lays the eggs.

"I and the other mine managers, we lack enough gray-and-blacks to really chase them down and eliminate them, and I'm not sure the workers would support us if we tried. So, Spartacus, he steals some here and some there but doesn't really threaten us. We catch a few here and a few there, but never really threaten them. And life goes on."

"Until now," I said.

"Yes. Until now." The wind was not that cold, but he shivered. "Are you after this Marco? Is that your contract?"

"If necessary," Sol said. "I also need to recover the girl. We will want to speak to some of your workers. We will also be around the hill camp by the road."

"Of course. Of course." Dos shivered again. "I would be careful asking about this Marco. From what I hear, he makes Spartacus look tame by comparison."

"We'll be careful," I said.

———

"A FOOL OR A COWARD. POSSIBLY BOTH." THAT WAS MY SUMMATION AS WE WALKED back to the car.

"Or possibly nothing more than a junior bureaucrat who needs to serve his term in this bleak post in order to have any chance at advancement and is hoping against hope that the place won't blow up before he is able to leave." Sol did not open her door immediately. Across the car's roof, I could see a faraway look on her face. "You saw the picture on his desk. His girl, I'm sure. He can't bring her here; he can't go back until his rotation is over. He will do anything to keep the peace, even the illusion of peace, until he is able to go home."

"If I didn't know you better, Sol, I'd call that romantic."

"Hah." That motivated her to yank the door open.

I wished I could have phrased my remark so that it sounded like a compliment. That was what I had wanted to do, but I lack expertise in that area.

"Avish Dos is not important," Sol said when we were both inside and Lizzie was sitting up as well. "We saw him only so that he knows we are here and will not have the gray-and-blacks interfere with us when we talk to people who have information. We should go see a contact of mine who has performed well before."

"Agreed," I said. "Your ability to work in these communities was, as I told you, a key reason the Directorate hired you." That was the truth and had to be said, but I did not like the way her jaw tightened and her eyes narrowed when I said it. I much preferred that faraway gaze when the lines on her face were softer. Of course, my personal preference in this did not matter.

———

It was a short drive to a building made up of two of the same type of bungalows that had served as Dos's residence. COMMISSARY was the hand-painted sign hung over a pair of old-fashioned metal doors. Sol parked the car on the hard-packed dirt right in front of the entrance.

"Almost everybody in a hill camp uses the commissary, or whatever name they give it, from time to time. Whenever I'm in a place like this"—Sol looked down the slope of the hill to where huts were visible among the handtree trunks, brush, and ubiquitous blue bolts—"I cultivate whoever is running it. Best source you can have where you don't have bars or whorehouses."

Sol led the way in. This time, we took Lizzie with us.

Inside, a stocky woman with gray hair and a sharp nose on a pale white face fixed us with eyes that could have been gunsights. Her attitude conveyed equal parts interest in what we would purchase and alertness against what we would try to steal. At the sight of Sol, her lips compressed into a thin line.

"Olga." The name was directed at a young woman with dirty pants frayed up to her mid-calves who was picking over a basket of dried fruit of some sort. "Out." The older woman jerked her head to the door.

Olga gave a tiny jump and scuttled out the door without a word.

"Sol," said the woman once the other was gone. "Great to see you again. I hope."

"I hope so too," Sol said. "Irina Semenova, this is Martin Allgeier and Lizzie."

Irina gave me a perfunctory greeting and examined Lizzie. "Is this one free-to-hire or for sale?"

That brought a gasp from Lizzie.

"Neither," said Sol. "She has work to do for us, and Lizzie will never be for sale."

"Fair enough," Irina said. "Who are you hunting, and what will the information pay?" She shifted her position to stand next to the pay station, where she reached out and flicked a switch. Music blared out in the shop. I recognized it as a band that had been popular in New Edinburgh when I was a child. No bug manufactured on Offyonder would be able to filter out that noise.

"I'm looking to retrieve a girl—a young woman—age about twenty-six." Sol went on to give a physical description of Claire. "Something is not right with her." Sol tapped her head where the scar ran. "If you hear her talk, you'd think she's a young child or maybe plain crazy. What I know says the Spartacists took her. Could have come here a day or two ago. I need to bring her back."

Irina took a package from a basket and picked at the tape holding the paper cover closed. Her hands were twice the thickness of mine. "Is there a name that goes with this girl?"

"Unless you've already heard it, I can't say it," Sol replied.

"Interesting." Irina continued to pick at the tape. "Nobody has mentioned a girl like that. And you said in the last couple of days?" Sol nodded. Irina shook her head in response. "Nah. Good-looking girls, they don't stay good-looking too long up here. It would be remarked on. And talking crazy, like you say. People would talk about that for sure. You're certain it was the Spartacists, and you're sure they came here?"

"It was Spartacists," I said. "That much is definite."

"And I was told they came here," Sol added. "One of the men who took her, he was a white man with a nose that looked like it was bent with a wrench," Sol drew a slanted line across the middle of her own face. "He was driving a car that came off one of the big farms. The D'Ascenzo farm. Does that stir a memory?"

"Oho." Irina stuffed her hands into the pockets of her coverall. Her eyes narrowed over a mouth and chin set like a block of stone. "Dan Knutson would fit that description. He was through here and he talked about that car. About that car and about what else he did."

I may be forgiven for the swift chill that passed through me along with her words. "Does he run with this Commander Marco we've heard about?"

"Aiyuh."

Irina's cold blue eyes dared me to say what came next. So, I did. "We were at the D'Ascenzo farm. We know what Marco and his gang did."

"Not all of it, you don't." Irina's eyes flicked over to Sol, who nodded. "Ralph D'Ascenzo, his brother, and two of their workers came up here a couple of weeks back. They grabbed a girl, a young one. They forced her into the woods and took turns raping her. Damn mess she was when they were done.

"Word came down that Spartacus sanctioned them himself. That was what we heard. Marco, he jumped at the chance. That's what we heard. You won't find anyone here who'll say a word against Marco. Understand me?"

"The D'Ascenzos aren't any part of my business. All I need is to get this girl back, and if I can do it without bothering Marco, I will." Suddenly Sol's brow furrowed and it was her eyes that narrowed. "Marco didn't shoot the girl, did he? She wasn't part of what the D'Ascenzos did."

"Didn't hear anything about that girl, like I said before, and any executions Marco did weren't done here. Although …" She allowed the word to trail off into silence while maintaining a placid face.

"Although what?" I knew what came next would cost extra. The Directorate could afford the payment more than I could afford the annoyance of haggling over it.

"Knutson and some of the others who run with Marco now use an old shack out in the trees and bush when they're around here. People heard shots out there last night."

"Last night?" I asked. "Has anybody been out there today to see what happened?"

Sol allowed herself a tiny smile. It broke the hard set of her features and was welcome, but I didn't understand the reason for it.

Irina nodded in Sol's direction. "Sol knows the answer," she said. "None of us will go out there to investigate. Spartacus, if it's not something he ordered, he'll send someone when he hears about it—but that's not business any of us will touch."

I was going to tell Irina that if those shots involved Claire, I would see to it that the business involved her and everyone else in this benighted encampment, but Sol drew her hand across her throat. That movement stopped the words in my throat.

"Give us directions to this shack," Sol said, "and let me settle our bill."

CHAPTER NINETEEN

RINA'S DIRECTIONS SENT US TO A BEND IN THE ROAD PAST THE HILL CAMP IN THE direction of the mine pit. It was about a half mile from the commissary, so we had not passed it before. Tire tracks led away from the road into the trees. Sol turned off the road to follow the tracks.

We had not gone very far when a combination of more closely set trees and lower growth blocked any further advance with the car. The dirt in this spot was packed down, rutted, with tire marks evident. Others had stopped their vehicles here. A footpath led from this impromptu parking area into the greenery.

"The ground is fairly hard," Sol said, "but there are a couple of boot prints in the dirt off to the side here."

She bent over one of the prints to examine it more carefully. "It's a man's boot. A pretty large man. And it was made since the last time it rained here, but that's about all it gives us."

We followed the trail through the surrounding brush into the woods. An occasional additional boot print indicated the presence of a second man in what we decided was the same time frame.

"Nothing that I would say is consistent with a woman of Claire's size," Sol said.

"But if she walked only on the hardpack, we wouldn't know," I said.

"Correct," Sol said. "All the stories about a captive deliberately veering off to the side to leave a distinctive footprint are nice stories, but if it didn't happen, there's only so much we can get from studying this."

The trail ended at a crude metal shack set not in a clearing but in the available space among the trees. Its metal walls and roof were thin and the whole structure was flimsy enough that it rattled even in the light breeze that blew through the forest. It had only one door and that was open. Intermittently, the wind would slam it against either the exterior wall or back into its frame, in each case with a bang that resounded over the shaking of the sides. Windows in the walls were narrow panes of dirty glass.

"Lovely little vacation getaway," Sol said. "I would call that a bullet hole." She indicated a round puncture about gut-high in the wall adjoining the doorframe. From the outward splay of the metal, the shot had come from inside.

We were not met with a challenge, but Sol called out a greeting in case someone was there and hadn't seen us. No answer came.

"Empty?" I asked.

"One way to find out," Sol said.

She walked to the door in the open, hands up and empty. For what it was worth, I covered her from my position in the trees, with Lizzie next to me. No movement, no sound. Sol reached the door and pulled it wide open. She reached under her duster, took out a handlight, and shined it into the dim interior.

"Come look at this," she called out.

I tried to make my run from trees to door a dignified one. Lizzie followed at my back.

The interior lacked almost all furnishing. This shack was more a waystation or temporary shelter, not a habitation. Wrappers, loose rags, and scraps of food were strewn around the floor. Also on the floor were four soiled mattresses. Two of the mattresses bore holes surrounded by dark stains.

"Shot in their sleep?" I asked.

Sol crouched by one of the mattresses and poked at the stain. "Could be blood," she said. "Dried now. Nothing to test it with, but what else could it be?" I thought the question was rhetorical.

Sol stood up again and surveyed the room. "This is odd. I'll grant that it looks like someone murdered two people in their beds. But where did the bodies go?"

"Whoever did it removed them," I said. "That would have to be. Unless Irina was lying and the people from the hill camp came and took them away."

"It's still odd," Sol said. "If someone dragged them out, you would expect a path through the crap on the floor. Okay, maybe if there's more than one who came up here, they could pick up the bodies and carry them out, but there's no blood anywhere else. No blood dripped on the floor."

"If they came long enough after the shooting, it would all have been clotted," I said. "No dripping."

"Could be." Sol swept her light around the room. "You could throw this shit around afterward to make it look like no one was pulled out of here, but the mattresses and the bloodstains are still here, so it's not as though you can't tell what happened. And someone still had to take the bodies somewhere."

We left the shack and searched around outside but found no evidence of graves.

"Whoever was shot here isn't buried here," Sol said. She arched her back to stretch it and groaned.

"How far could you pull them into the woods to bury them so that the graves wouldn't be seen?" I asked.

"Quite a distance, if you have help." Sol put her hands on her hips and scanned the area. "There's plenty of undergrowth, though, and a lot of it is that spiky bush. We haven't seen any sign bodies were pulled through it. Not recently. Yes, you could cover your tracks, but it wouldn't be easy. If you were going to that much trouble, you could go back to where the cars park." She snapped her fingers. "The mine! An open-pit mine is a good place for two bodies."

"Are you thinking they killed Claire?" Lizzie asked. "I heard what you said at the hotel."

"I don't know." Sol looked at me. "That rhyme you told me about, that was new? The Directorate just got it?"

"As far as I know," I said.

"Then this doesn't fit," Sol said. "Even if there was an immediate refusal, killing Claire would give away any chance to use her to gain some leverage, and they went to a lot of trouble to capture her. And that shack has *two* mattresses with blood and bullet holes. Internal disagreement? From what I hear in Bannion, Spartacus has control of his people and has been in control for nearly five years, but no one knows for sure—just as no one knows for sure who he is. Martin, did your Directorate contact give you any information on that?"

"No. I mean, CenSec knows a lot more than they told me. I'm sure of that. When you get past the … we should be frank … official line about 'bands of near-naked thieves,' everybody talks about the Spartacists like they're an army. Although maybe this new one, Marco, is splitting away and will challenge Spartacus."

"Find the bodies, maybe we'll get some answers," Sol said.

"I have to find Claire, alive or dead," I said. "If she is one of those bodies, I have to know."

"I'm paid either way," Sol said.

"Yes," I replied. "That was the agreement."

"I don't want Claire to be dead," Lizzie said. "She wouldn't hurt anyone."

CHAPTER TWENTY

IT WAS A SHORT ADDITIONAL DRIVE FROM WHERE WE WERE TO THE MINE COMPLEX. The open road ended at a guard post even less sophisticated than the one at Edge-of-the-World. Here was only an open-sided shack with a crossing gate that barred our passage. Two bored guards watched us from under their roof. They wore the olive coveralls that Lithia Unit 1 used and a brassard bearing the lettering POLICE. When it was clear they did not plan to move, Sol and I left the car to walk over to them. The dull roar of mining machinery rose up from the ground beyond the gate and enveloped us. A cluster of poured concrete buildings with sheet-metal roofs stood on the ground behind the guard post. Past them was the open lip of the mine where it was cut into the hill in front of us. Rows of photovoltaic panels coated the hillside above the mine.

The guards could not be persuaded to raise the gate and let us into the complex, but a bribe from Sol was adequate to open and lubricate a conversation. Yes, of course, vehicles came from the hill camp on a regular basis. How did we think the workers came and went for their shifts? The guards were adamant, however, that no car meeting the

description we gave of the D'Ascenzos' vehicle had come when either of them were on duty. Could it have come when they were not on duty? How would they know if they were not on duty? They had a good laugh when I asked to see the video clips of all arriving vehicles. Did their post look like it had any electronics, never mind cameras and videos? Maybe in New Edinburgh we had that tech, but not out here, behind the beyond. An additional bribe persuaded them to show us the logbook of arrivals and departures. That was uninformative. It was a written book, ink on paper. Eventually we gave up, returned to the car, and headed back to the hill camp.

"That was useless," I said. "Bribe those guards enough, and it probably does not need to be very much, and they will forget to write down an entry. The event never happened. Either that or threaten them enough."

"One bribe can always be topped with another," Sol said. "Even threats have a price. We saw enough of that area from where we were standing, though, that I don't think it matters."

"Why not?"

"Because that mine is nothing more than a big hole in the ground. The guard post is to keep track of people going in and out, but the rest of it isn't even fenced off. They don't care if somebody sneaks into that pit, and if you are where you shouldn't be and you fall in, that's your problem. It makes me think that Dos might be right when he says the Spartacists coexist with them. The Spartacists don't want to shut down the mining. If the flow of minerals into the Reach were cut off, most of the starship traffic would stop coming here. Once stopped, it might be hard to restart. Planets become *forgotten* out in the Reach. They are never updated in the databases if ships don't come through. I'm from Earth, and I've chased people who went to ground on planets like that for exactly that reason. I understand. Offyonder is a long way from Earth. Supposedly, the Spartacists want Offyonder to join the Assembly of Worlds. They won't jeopardize that by shutting down the mines."

I took a few moments to digest what Sol had said. Assuming that this Spartacus was cold and calculating—and it seemed likely that he was—her argument made sense. I arrived at that conclusion through my own cold analysis, having nothing to do with any bias in favor of Sol.

"That makes it a great place to dump any number of bodies," I said with a sour taste in my mouth. "Nobody is really watching the pit. Drop the bodies in the path of an automated crusher and there's nothing but a thin smear of organics on the minerals. What do you want to try now?"

"Back to the hill camp," Sol said. "Somebody had to have been in that shack to clean up. We don't need the actual bodies as long as we know who they are. Correct?"

"If we say one of them was Claire, we need proof. Really solid proof."

"Understood," Sol said. "We also need a place to stay."

<hr>

Irina Semenova grew an expression of disbelief when we told her what we had seen at the shack. She held a hand to her mouth and gestured for us to go outside. She joined us and walked ahead of us to a clump of low handtrees twenty yards from the commissary.

"Even with the music on inside, I am more comfortable out here." The rigid brace of her shoulders said she was anything but comfortable. "I am not doubting what you say. Sol, I would not doubt you, and anyway, what value would there be in lying to me?"

It seemed that Irina was trying to come up with a reason, but when she could not, she resumed speaking. "I cannot believe anyone from the camp would have done that. The cleanup, never mind the shooting. It is dangerous to be involved in anything the Spartacists do. Life is dangerous enough. However, I told you people heard the shots. Let's see if anyone saw something as well."

With us trailing her, Irina led the way to one of the cookfires we had seen that formed the center of a small group of huts. There she found three children and summoned them to her.

The oldest was a girl of about Lizzie's age. She had dirt on her face. Her exposed skin, including her face, was dotted with tiny red insect bites, and her feet were bare on the stony ground. Her clothes had more holes than solid cloth. Had Lizzie run all the way to the hill camps, this could be her. From the way Lizzie's eyes fixed on this girl, I knew the same thought was in her mind.

Irina gave terse instructions. The girl in turn tapped the two younger children, made a set of hand gestures, and the three of them sprinted off.

"If there is anything to learn," Irina said, "it will be from the camp followers out here. The shift workers at the mine"—she jerked her head in the direction of the uphill dormitories—"will not have been out there. So, now we wait, but we will wait at the commissary where we do not need to swat at these." She waved her hand through the air at the cloud of barely visible buzzies. "They don't get anything from biting us, but we get a local allergic reaction."

I reflected that this was a downside to our hybrid ecology.

We did not wait long. A man or a woman would appear in the commissary. They would be as shabby and dirty as the children we had seen. They would not buy anything, only say to Irina that they had something they were hoping to sell. We would head over to that stand of handtrees and they would speak. Sol always provided a reward in solid DMs. I do not think an e-voucher would have done any of them any good.

The first few told us they had been in the area of the shack but had seen nothing. Then a man named Jacques said that he had seen lights moving across the trees and heard two voices talking back and forth, although he had not been able to make out what they were saying. With the next few people who came to see us, more people had been detected moving and talking among the trees by the shack. With each further telling, the number of people around the shack increased until, if you gave the tales any credence, you would have concluded a battalion had made camp out there.

"I am sorry for the waste of your money," Irina said with a shrug as she finally closed up the commissary. Her tone said she was not sorry at all that Sol had been giving out money to members of the community. Even though these were Directorate funds, and I was responsible for their expenditure, I could not find it in me to take issue with her. "Word gets around very fast out here, and people will embroider the story more and more in the hope that you will pay more and more. By tomorrow, if you give any indication you will listen, you will probably get a tale that Spartacus himself, ten feet tall with lightning flashing from his eyes, cleared that shack. Of course," she chuckled, "none of them will tell you what Spartacus looks like, because none have seen him, nor know anyone who has."

"Do you think there is a Spartacus at all?" I asked. "Or is he a myth, all made up, nothing more than a fiction to scare some and rally others?"

From the flash of fright on Irina's face, I had caught her off guard. "He is real, or I believe so. But he is a wise man and guards himself well, and speaking too much of this man is a good way to shorten your life."

"Martin was not asking if you had ever seen Spartacus," Sol said. "From the little I know, he has a very small command cell and is careful to work at a distance and through others. This is why the rumor that he is a renegade Peacer makes some sense. And I would not say the money was wasted. From those tall tales, I think it is safe to say that no one actually noticed anything in the area around that shack, and that in itself is interesting because we know someone was there."

"Thank you," said Irina. "You are good to work with, as always. My place is not much, but it is clean and dry, tight enough to keep out the buzzies."

"Yes, those buzzies," I said. "You would think, since the people here know the blue bolts attract them, they would have the initiative to clear those plants away from their shacks. As it is, they live right in the middle of them."

A long look from Irina told me that had been a mistake on my part. "What you probably don't realize," she said slowly, "is that, even though the plant is indigestible by humans, the flowers can be used, along with a ground fungus that grows among the trees, to make a soup. It's not great food, but you can survive on it. Catch a rat and add some meat. Those children I sent off, that's what they eat."

I felt heat rise in my cheeks. I do not like being a fool. "I'm sorry" were all the words I could find.

Irina shrugged. "That's life, such as it is here. We will have stew for dinner and the meat in it will not be rat. You are welcome to stay with me tonight."

I thought as we walked away from the commissary of all that Sol and Irina had said. My mind pulled up the histories I had read about how a strict cell system was used by underground commanders and what this implied for the type of man Spartacus was. I liked the way Sol's mind worked. She was definitely the right person for this job. Mentally, I congratulated my handler, who had told me to hire her. I did wish that circumstances would allow her to smile a little more often.

I did not sleep well that night after we ate. It had nothing to do with the food, Spartacus, or thoughts of Sol. Humans had bent the laws of physics to their will in order to fly to the stars so their descendants could subsist on soup of flower petals, fungi, and pieces of rat. Something was very wrong with this picture.

CHAPTER TWENTY-ONE

IN THE MORNING, WE ALL AWOKE AT ABOUT THE SAME TIME—NOT SURPRISING, since Irina's hut was a small single room. Irina reached over the side of her bed to switch on the space heater. While that banished the nighttime chill, I sat up on the planking of the floor where I had slept. If this mission continued as it was going, I would end up inured to sleeping on the ground. Either that, or I would be an early candidate for a nursing facility.

Irina turned on a hot plate and put the pot with the remaining stew from last night on it. She did not light her stove. I watched the care she took with every item that drew power. It was shameful. Our people had come to Offyonder in starships across multiple wormhole transits and many light-years. In New Edinburgh, we prided ourselves on having all the electronics of any planet in the Reach, with the peace from a civic order few could match. Yet here, where people had power at all, they watched every erg they drained from their batteries. It was not my job to fix what was wrong in our Directorate, but something was wrong, and someone needed to fix it.

"We should talk about what we can try today," Sol said. "There are a few farms within a day's drive. I don't have contacts among the farmers the way I do in the hills, but they may be willing to talk to us. After what happened to the D'Ascenzos, and it will not matter why it happened, they will be alert to anyone in the vicinity of their steads."

"Makes sense," I said. "What about fuel?"

"I can sell you the mix that car runs on." Irina said. "Most farms will sell to you also. People do take care of each other where we are spread so thin."

"Most of the time," Sol said.

We were handing the empty soup bowls back to Irina when we were interrupted by buzzing from Sol's comm. She pulled it out of her duster and looked at its face. A frown formed immediately. She held the comm for me to see.

ID NOT REGISTERED.

"I've never seen that." I hadn't. Some CenSec officers had comms that came up as "ID withheld," as did the comm I was carrying, but that was a different type of result. "I don't know how a comm can be on our network if the ID isn't registered at all."

The comm kept buzzing.

"It doesn't matter, I suppose," Sol said. She tapped the comm. "Hello."

"Solly-wolly! Wolly-Solly! Why haven't you come to get me?" There was no mistaking Claire's voice on the comm.

"We need to go outside." Sol's words were as much for Irina as they were for us and Claire.

Once we were away from Irina's hut, Sol asked, "Claire, are you okay? Who is with you and where are you?"

"Of course, I'm okay, Solly-wolly. But no one is with me, except Abigail, naturally. I'm alone and I'm scared. Why haven't you come to get me?"

"We'll come for you," Sol said. "Where are you?"

"Well, how should I know? That's why I'm lost, and you need to come get me."

Sol tilted her head back and looked at the sky. We don't believe in imaginary deities on Offyonder, but I recognize a plea for help from one when I see it. She refocused on the comm. "What's around you, Claire? What do you see?"

"I'm right next to a big metal pole that sticks up in the air. It's got little metal sticks coming out of it, and those have like long metal needles coming out of them. It looks like a stupid metal tree."

"Transmission tower," Sol said to me. "There's a chain of them to keep communications open among all the mines in the hills. Some farms can connect to them as well." She spoke back to the comm. "Claire, there should be a sign at the bottom of the pole. Letters and numbers. Can you read them to me?"

Claire did.

"Got it." Then, sotto voce to me, Sol said, "There aren't that many roads out here, and I'm sure the commissary will sell us a printed map." She raised her voice into the comm again. "I know where you are, Claire. We're coming to get you. It will take a while, probably a few hours. Don't go anywhere."

"Well, why would I go somewhere if you're coming here? It's not like I'm going out for dinner. Although I'm hungry. You could bring food. To here." The call cut off.

"How did she get a comm?" I asked.

"If I wanted a comm, I'd steal it." Lizzie had come out with us. From her worldview, that was a logical comment.

"From whom?" was my question. "We're not on the streets of Bannion. If she was being held at that shack and somehow escaped what happened, possibly the comm could have come from one of the people who was shot. But then how did she get from here to there? This is *Claire*."

Sol shook her head. "It's just as possible that she was never here, that the shack is about something else, and she was being held near that tower. But again, how does she have a comm and how did she escape?"

"Could this be a trap?" I asked. "Think of the threat Spartacus made."

"Can't rule it out," Sol said, "but you know Claire. Do you think you could get her to cooperate in setting a trap? This all feels a little odd." She blew out a long breath. "There's one way to find out for sure if it's a trap, isn't there?"

Some questions are rhetorical.

WE TOOK A TURN OFF THE ROAD TO THE MINE TO A ROUTE THAT LED US DOWN OUT OF the hills. The descent toward the ancient seabed brought us back out of the handtree forest. Wild grasses covered the ground here in a dense mass, a land of waving stems and seedpods broken into a checkerboard of blue bolt lakes. Here and there, the occasional spike bush stuck up above the rest. The road was bare, packed earth, easy to see as it ran through the grass. Turnoffs were few, which made it simple to follow the exorbitantly priced map we had obtained from the commissary. The result was a boring three-and-a-half-hour drive, but boring is a good type of drive to have when you are worried about being attacked.

The transmission tower stuck up over the open terrain very much as Claire had described it. When we were close enough to see the base of the tower, we could see a car off the side of the road near it. A blond woman wearing overalls on top of a coverall was jumping up and down next to the tower.

"Ooh, you're here, you're here!" Claire screamed as we pulled up. "Did you bring anything to drink? I finished all the water they left in the car. And I'm so hungry! And you brought my Lizzie-dizzy, dizzy-Lizzie." When Lizzie got out of the car, Claire grabbed her and hugged her while continuing to jump and twist. Whether Lizzie was delighted or dismayed was hard to tell.

Sol had a bottle of water with electrolytes ready. She pulled the nipple top open, then had to dance around the spinning combination of Claire and Lizzie to hand it to Claire. Once Claire had it in her hands, she stopped twirling, tipped her head back, and chugged the entire contents of the bottle.

"What happened to your arms?" Sol asked.

With her arms raised to drink from the bottle, the sleeves of Claire's coverall fell back, revealing angry red marks around her wrists.

"They tied me up. But they were stupid. And if I don't see the marks, they don't hurt, but now you made me see them, so that's not good. But they were stupid. Their rope had no hope, but I didn't mope because I could cope and they were dopes. Stupid people get what they deserve. I knew you would come get me, which you did."

"Claire, did they hurt you anywhere else? Let me check you quickly."

As Sol moved in to check, Claire let out a shriek. She pulled Lizzie between her and Sol.

"Claire, you should let Solly check you," Lizzie said. "She knows what she's doing. It will be okay."

"No, no, no! No way okay, not in any way." Claire danced backward.

"Let it be," I said. "She can't be hurt that bad, not dancing like that, and once we bring her back, CenSec can check her. More importantly, Claire, try to focus, please: What about the men who took you? How did you get away, and where are they?"

"They were stupid," Claire said. Her voice firmed a bit, and her eyes did focus on me. Possibly I just wanted to believe that. "Two of them took me to this metal building in the trees. It smelled bad. It was dirty. They tied my hands in front." She put her wrists together in front of her stomach, so the rope burns on one touched the burns on the other. "It was night. They said I should sleep. One of them went to sleep. The other one sat up on his mattress to watch me. But he went to sleep too. Stupid. My fingers are good with knots. Why not? They say a boat goes fast in knots, but you can't tie a boat in knots. You can't tie me in knots, because my fingers are good with knots, so their knots were not working."

"Claire, slowly, Claire." Her words flew past my ears so fast I worried I would miss what she said. "Claire, are you telling us that you undid the rope?" I did not want to use the word *knot* again. "And then you ran away while they were sleeping? You took their car while they were sleeping?"

"No, no, no." Claire looked to her right. Then she gave me and Sol a sly side-eye. "Abigail told me what to do. Abigail is smart about these things. Abigail said, 'Take his gun and shoot them both.' I listened to Abigail. I took his gun and shot them both."

I stared at the cherubic smile that spread across her unlined face, her blue eyes that focused far in the distance, if anywhere. I had come to think of Claire as a young child, perhaps a demented child. Now she was telling us that her invisible and imaginary friend had told her to shoot two men in their sleep and she had gone ahead and murdered them. "Did you really shoot both men while they were sleeping because Abigail told you to?"

"Yes. I said so. The second one woke up when the gun went bang but I shot him anyway. I can show you the place."

"We've already been there. We've seen it. Did you leave the bodies on the beds?"

That seemed to startle her for a moment. Then her eyes lost focus again. "Bodies, bodies everywhere. Abigail said to leave the bodies. Busybodies will find them. Are you a busybody?"

I dropped that line of questioning. Claire could not have moved the two bodies by herself. The more critical question was whether she still had the gun. I asked her.

"Abigail says I should keep the gun. Don't touch me. Lizzie knows to keep her fingers out of places."

"I'm not! I won't!" Lizzie had her hands up and backed away from Claire.

I said that I wouldn't touch her either. I put both my hands up, empty palms toward her. I would not lay my hands on Claire Montaigne, gun or no gun. Soon this would not be my problem. "Claire, was one of the men named Marco? Did you hear the name Marco?"

"Marco? Marco Polo! Marco Polo went to China. Did you know China is on Earth? They have a great wall there. If you have chalk, I can draw you a picture of the wall here." She brushed sand off the concrete base of the antenna with her boot.

"No chalk, Claire," Sol said. "You took the car and drove here?"

"Yes. I can drive. Although I don't drive so good. I got stuck here because it stopped working. And nobody came."

We walked over and examined the car. It was the same car the two men had used to abduct Claire from Edge-of-the-World, the one from the D'Ascenzo farm.

"Out of fuel," Sol said. "So, if you took the car and drove here after you shot them, you've been here, what, going on three days?"

Again Claire startled briefly and focused on us for an instant. "Days and days when you're in a daze," she said. "I had to pee in the dirt."

In the meantime, Sol looked through the rest of the car, including the trunk. Scraps of food and empty water bottles were scattered over the front seats. "Fuel containers in the trunk. This could be refueled. More water and food packs also."

I looked her over from a distance. Claire was in good shape for having been alone for two to three days, although having some food and drink in the car helped. But why had she come to this transmission tower? It was not on the way back to Edge-of-the-World, nor anywhere close to it. Had she had a different destination in mind? Being careful with the way I phrased the question, I asked her where she had been going.

"Away" was the answer.

I reflected that this was the only time Claire had given a one-word answer. "Just away?" I asked. "Wasn't there some place you wanted to go?"

"I wanted to go away because I made them pay and I didn't want to stay, and I came here and you didn't until today."

I translated that to mean that Claire had driven off down the road she'd found in the magical belief that it would take her to … the airport, Joshua, home? Whatever had been in her mind at the time, even if she could recall it, probably did not matter. Claire was lucky the car had run out of fuel near the transmission tower, where we could find her easily. She had never thought to look in the trunk for more food and fuel. Similarly, the comm must have come from one of the men she shot, which meant she had the presence of mind to take it but then did not think to use it right away. But that raised yet another question: If this was a somehow-unregistered Spartacist comm, how did she have Sol's code? She could not have tapped into our information system. Not from here and not with that comm even if it could have connected. I asked that question.

"Where is the number from? It's in the comm, so it's not random, which means I don't need ransom. Does this mean Uncle Joshua is coming?"

Once again, the multiple sidetracks of Claire's mind converged on a single fixation.

I held my hand out toward Sol as though I had that comm in it. "Does it make sense that your number would be in a Spartacist comm?"

She shrugged. "It's possible. Certainly, my number is known to CenSec and I have worked in the Uplands. Could a client have been a Spartacist?" She shrugged again. "I don't test my clients on affiliation or GSG."

Sol did appear to have a level of notoriety on Serendipity that extended to the Uplands, the hill camps, and, I daresay, people who would know Spartacists, even if those details never made it into the thin dossier we had on the mainland. Claire's good fortune could have extended to picking up a comm that had the number she would need. She was also lucky because the direction she was going, if she had not run out of fuel, would ultimately have taken her to another hill camp, where there would be more Spartacists, or at least their supporters.

My mind conjured yet another crazy possibility. Could the Spartacists have put a wire and transmitter on Claire? I dismissed that thought as soon as I had it. People did not put a wire on someone they were holding captive and were not planning on releasing. Not to mention the fact that searching the body of Claire Montaigne for a wire that did not exist would lead to significant consequences for me later. Associating with Claire was making my mind take wild flights. I did not mention any of this to Sol. It would have made me look bad.

"Let's get out of here and back to the airport," I said. "None of this will matter once we get there."

"Is my uncle Joshua coming to rescue me?"

"We've been out here finding you," I said. "We won't know about Uncle Joshua until we reach the airport."

That shut her up and I didn't even need to lie. That was good because I had other issues to think about. Claire had blown a hole—two holes, actually—in whatever scheme Spartacus had concocted to force Joshua Montaigne out of power. This might leave Spartacus embarrassed in front of his own people. If Spartacus was strong enough to hold on to his leadership position despite this, we likely had a furious Spartacus after us. Not a good situation.

CHAPTER TWENTY-TWO

THE D'ASCENZO VEHICLE WAS IN FAR BETTER CONDITION THAN THE JUNK HEAP we were motoring around in, but Sol did not want to take it. I agreed. If the story of the end of the D'Ascenzos had made it out to the hill camp, for sure every farmer in the Inland Sea had heard it. Being seen in that car would raise suspicions, and there were undoubtedly some who would shoot without bothering to ask questions.

Those considerations were even more important because we would not reach Edge-of-the-World before dark. In fact, we would be left with a substantial drive after sundown. The sky had clouded over, which would further dim the moons, now long past full. The road had neither pavement nor lighting. We also had to think about the risk that the Spartacists would be out searching for Claire. That could argue for pressing on to reach Edge-of-the-World as fast as possible, but the argument that it was riskier being on the road in the dark was as strong. As crazy as the idea of Claire being wired was, I was uneasy about camping in the car overnight in the middle of nowhere. We

agreed, after a short discussion—without any mention of a wire—that we should try to find shelter for the night.

But where? It would be unwise to head back to the hill camp.

"I have some connections with the people there, as you've seen," Sol said. "However, the way it is now, with these two murders, someone will sell us out. Bet on it." She paused for a moment. "The farms are widely separated, and the farming families are suspicious of strangers. Still, asking for a night's shelter is probably our best chance."

Who was I to argue? The map we had obtained from Irina showed roads but no farms. It did show us a route that would take us back to the West, toward the Uplands. The road network was sparse enough that we were unlikely to miss a turn.

We saw no other cars and no sign of habitation for the first two hours after we left the tower. The landscape shrank to our immediate surroundings: waving grasses on all sides, already grown high enough to block our view of the blue bolts or anything distant. These were not Earth species either. This was all Offyonder biota. Earth had yet to establish a beachhead in this area. The car windows blocked out most of the drone of the buzzies, although the intermittent splats on the windshield announced their continued presence.

It took us until the shadows were long before we passed the fences and tended fields that marked a farm. A sprinkler shot water high in the air, identifying a field of Earth crops, which usually needed more water. A little farther down the road we came to a turnoff. That way led to buildings. That was also the moment the sun kissed the horizon in the far west. I breathed a sigh of relief.

Sol blasted the horn three times as we drove down the narrow lane to the farm buildings. We did not want to surprise people already on edge.

Four vehicles were parked in a clear space before the front door of a large farmhouse. At the front end of one of the cars stood a man pointing a rifle at us. I stared at the rifle as we came to a stop. It was a modern automatic rifle, the same as ArmedSec had. It would not have been out of place in a Peacer unit. Not only did the Spartacists have, apparently, top-grade weapons, but these tools of war had also made their way to an isolated farm on the isolated subcontinent of Serendipity. The implications for civic order were not good.

Sol stopped the car ten yards from the nearest of the parked ones. Slowly, showing empty hands in the air, she exited. I copied her and was glad to see Lizzie and Claire do the same.

"You're not Matthews nor any of his," the man with the rifle said.

"No." I liked how Sol not only looked but also sounded completely calm at gunpoint. "My name is Sol. Martin"—a tip of her head indicated me—"and I were hired by her father"—she made a slight turn toward Claire—"to retrieve her from the Spartacists. We were able to free another girl as well. We do not want to be on this road after dark. All we ask is a place to sleep for the night."

"You're armed?"

"Of course." Sol made it sound like the most natural thing in the world.

I took stock of the man while he considered Sol's statement. He was taller than me, which I understand is not saying much, with dark brown hair that fell across the forehead of a white face. A thick drooping mustache mostly covered his mouth, and eyebrows almost as shaggy as the mustache shadowed his eyes. He did not wear a coverall. Instead, a coarsely woven shirt decorated by dyed horizontal stripes of purple was tucked into blue pants of a tighter weave.

"If you said you weren't armed, I'd shoot you for liars, and you'd be too stupid to live if you were telling the truth. Retrieved these girls, did you?" His eyes went to Claire and Lizzie, both of whom thankfully stayed quiet. It was the girls who apparently tipped his mind in our favor. "This may be a good thing. I'll invite you to join me and my family and … others. We will be having some discussion over dinner. I'm Rory Hilliker."

We had not yet reached Hilliker's front door when the crunch of tires on the unpaved drive announced the arrival of another car. The driver, who bounded out with an apology for his lateness, was a Black man with an unkempt mass of black hair and a tall, thin frame. He reached behind him into the passenger compartment and pulled out a rifle that matched Hilliker's. Quick introductions established that this was the Matthews Hilliker had expected. He and the four of us trooped into the farmhouse behind Rory Hilliker.

The front room of the farmhouse had been set up for what would pass as a feast in this backward part of Offyonder. A large table was piled with typical offerings. There was a bowl filled with hard-boiled eggs, platters with various parts of chicken in three different sauces, cereal from Earth-derived oats sprinkled with sugar, loaves of warm bread, plates of Earth vegetables, rashers of bacon, and a baked ham. More significant was a platter holding slices of what had to be beefsteak. Farmers were careful about using their cows for meat.

Gathered at the table was the Hilliker family: his wife, three grown children, and three younger ones. Two more adults were probably spouses of the older Hilliker children. They were all dressed in the same type of clothing as Rory. An older man, whose thinning hair was several shades of gray lighter than the barrel of the rifle he gripped, was dressed in a standard coverall. At a snap from Rory's fingers, his grown children hustled out of the room toward the back of the house. They returned with a small table that they abutted to the larger one. The combined table was still two chairs short of having seating for all of us, which resulted in the two smallest children being banished to eat on the floor in a corner. Their protests died fast at a growl from Rory. When the rest of us were seated, Matthews to Rory's left, the older man to his right, and the four of us grouped around that smaller table, Rory introduced the older man as Jefferson Calhoun. Then he repeated for Calhoun's benefit the story Sol had told outside.

"This may be both fortuitous and fortunate." Calhoun had picked up on my New Edinburgh origins and had chosen words to convey the impression of education. "The way these fiends behave, you were lucky to get away unscathed."

Claire chose that moment to break her silence. "Abigail said to take the man's gun and shoot both men. It's important to do what Abigail says, so I took his gun and shot both men. Bang. Bang. Two dead men."

Calhoun stared at Claire. Furrows formed on his forehead as he frowned. "You killed the men holding you?"

"Yes, I," said Claire. "The Princess Claire. I went bang, bang. Shot the gang. Lullaby and good night to their scheme. To scheme, to dream, to sleep, perchance to dream, although they won't dream anymore, but I will have good dreams tonight."

Now Hilliker and Matthews were staring at Claire along with Calhoun. So was Hilliker's family. Claire started humming to herself.

"Her name is Claire," I said quickly. "She was named after our Director's niece. I'm sure you understand that some families in New Edinburgh do that. The thing is"—I tapped the table with my forefinger to help draw their attention—"the stress of her captivity has affected her … greatly. She thinks she is Claire Montaigne. It is best not to try to disabuse her, at least until we get her home."

I hoped Claire was not going to argue with me. Thankfully, she closed her eyes and continued to hum.

"And who is Abigail?" Hilliker asked.

"An imaginary friend," I said. "I told you, the stress of her captivity—"

Claire's eyes went wide and she cut me off. "Abigail is not imaginary." She gave us all a sunny smile. "She's right here with me." Claire looked off to her right, to where Abigail always was for her. Since she was at the corner of the table, only empty space between the table and the fireplace was in that direction.

"I see," Hilliker said. "I think." After a brief silence, he continued. "We should eat and then we need to talk about the business at hand. We have plenty of food for all, and the participation of our unexpected guests is welcome. In fact, not only welcome but possibly important too."

With that, plates were filled, emptied, and refilled. Hilliker and his wife seemed set on adhering to our Offyonder custom, dating to the earliest days of settlement, that guests be fed to the point of either bursting or vomiting, an expression of pride in our ability to feed ourselves on a new planet. Hilliker's wife rose to fill every guest's glass— and these were glassware—with mash, then got up again to refill them. A large dog I had not noticed when we entered left its blanket by the fireplace and became quite active under the table.

Most of the attention was on the food and drink, but I noticed everyone studiously avoiding even a glance in Claire's direction. It was fortunate that the only consequence of her outburst was for her to be ignored.

The business of the evening began as the food and drink disappeared. The older man rose and cleared his throat, nodding at their host. "Rory, thank you for hosting me and Matthews tonight and for being able to host these unexpected guests as well." Rory beamed at Calhoun's acknowledgment of his prosperity. "We need to talk about an Inland Sea self-defense organization. I have received communications from the mainland on this, which is why we are here tonight. I know we are busy with our farms. I know the work they require. I am a farmer as well, one of you.

"However, we cannot allow that outrage at the D'Ascenzo farm to pass without notice. If we remain as we are, isolated and vulnerable, we will be picked off one by one. I have no idea who could be next. Rory, it could be you."

"We have had this discussion before, Jefferson," Rory said. "We cannot get enough robotics from New Edinburgh to completely automate our farms. We must be here to work them, and we need the help of our families. And how would you defend our farms anyway? There are not enough of us to form an army. Even if we could, that army could only be in one place at one time."

Hilliker's wife, older children, their spouses, and Matthews all began to talk at once. Calhoun cut them off with a sharp, "Please!" He waited until the talk subsided. "I do not want to rehash old arguments. It must be different now. This is precisely what I have heard from my contact on the mainland. He is … well placed. Sometimes to defend, you need to attack."

With those words, he had their attention. "We need to go on the offensive. We need to form a unit and attack these hill camps one by one. We are getting the weapons now, as you see, through my contact." He patted his rifle. "We attack the hill camps. The people there are no better than savages anyway. They are not real people. We can drive them out. Scatter them. Kill any who resist. Burn everything down.

The Spartacists need those camps the way a bottom fish needs the slime it eats. Destroy the camps, and the Spartacists will be finished."

I thought of a girl like Lizzie, one with rags for clothes and bites across her skin; I thought of people who lived on thin soup of rat who would spin any tale for a coin. These people could barely support themselves; they were not the foundation of an army. This would be terror for the sake of terror. I kept my thoughts to myself, of course.

"If we interfere with the mining operations, we'll have CenSec down on us, if not ArmedSec," Rory protested.

"First of all, CenSec doesn't have enough force to do anything out here. Why do you think they don't do anything about the Spartacists in the hills? The Directorate isn't going to send ArmedSec over here; they need them on the mainland. Anyway, CenSec is not going to bother us. Without the food we produce, Bannion can't exist, and without Bannion, they can't ship out the mining products. And we're not going to bother the mines or the workers." Calhoun stretched himself upward. "It's only these subhuman camp followers who live around them. Drive them into the wild and kill them. That's how we beat Spartacus."

"What if the Spartacists defend the camps?" Matthews asked. "Will we have enough men and women to beat them?"

"If we all fight together, we will. Don't forget, they're not an army either. Nothing more than bands of thieves before they came up with a name." Calhoun smiled. "Most important, they cannot match these weapons, not even this crazy Commander Marco."

"It's not this Marco that worries me," Rory said. "It's Spartacus. I heard that Ryan, you know from north of here, sent a spy into the hill camp around Lithia Unit Two. He said Spartacus was there himself with some of his fighters. He's a huge brute, six-five at least. Black hair and a long black beard. He's got them all terrorized. Some man argued with him over food; he split the man's chest and ripped out his heart."

Calhoun laughed at that, but his laugh was a nervous one. "That spy of his would do better earning his coin as a tale-spinner in the Bannion markets. Either that or Ryan needs to quit drinking. First of all, we know Spartacus has brown hair and is clean-shaven. Very particular about his appearance. Those reports are reliable. And even if he's got the scum in the hill camps in fear of him, that doesn't mean they can fight, and they still don't have the weapons, even if they could. We can do this."

"Are you sure about the weapons?" That was one of Hilliker's sons. "We know Spartacus used to be a Peacer, whatever name he used then, and when I was at a bar in Edge-of-the-World, I heard one of the gray-and-blacks talking with local police. They were saying Spartacus still has friends in the Peacers, and his groups on the mainland are getting weapons from the Peacers when the starships come in. They said smugglers are bringing them in through Bannion now, so the Spartacists in the hills could have them."

"Do you hear what you're saying?" Calhoun tried to sound forceful but could not pull it off. "The Peacers are fighting and patrolling on more planets in the Reach than I can count. Do you think they have time for one former officer on what is to them just one more planet? Please."

That did not end the conversation about Spartacus, his personal characteristics, or his connections. If anything, it acted as an invitation for everyone at the table to chip in whatever they had heard about the man, however remote the teller's connection to the source.

Among the most memorable: that Spartacus was even bigger, a giant approaching ten feet tall, a Black man with skin darker than the coal that fouled Bannion's air and a shaved head he polished with wax, so it gleamed in the sunlight. Another description had him equally large, but a redhead whose beard and shaggy hair all but hid a pale face festooned with scars. Or that he had a vicious squint in his left eye, and that eye would blink uncontrollably when he was about to order the deaths of captives. That on one occasion his fighters had taken control of the most remote of the hill camps so that he and this brutal Commander Marco could have a competition to see who could rape the most women in one night.

I began to doubt that any of these stories had any connection to a person who had actually seen Spartacus. Rather, the accounts were being made up on the spot to top the one that had just been told by someone else. It was not very different from the way the stories told by the camp followers in the hill camp—people these farmers thought of as subhuman—kept escalating when we asked about that shack. Doubtless these tales would be repeated on other occasions with other groups of people, becoming yet another entry in the legend of the barbarity and depravity of this rebel.

From the smug expression on Calhoun's face as these chronicles wore on, he was pleased with this use of time. The more Spartacus was made out to be an inhuman ghoul, the more agitated Matthews and the Hillikers became. They were scaring themselves silly. At last, Calhoun put his hand up.

"Please," he said. "I think enough has been said. We should remember that there are children here." He pointed to the corner, where eager young faces leaned forward to catch every word, obviously wishing their bedtime stories could be this dramatic. "Whatever beast Spartacus really is, and whatever human slime he has with him, we need to recognize some hard truths."

Calhoun waited until the chatter had died down and all eyes were on him. "There have been bandits in the hills from the day the mine camps were established. For many years now, the miners and New Edinburgh have called them rebels against our cherished civic justice and order." His harsh laugh at those words would not have been heard in New Edinburgh. "The civic justice and order across the ocean here we have made ourselves. As long as the crime stayed in the hill camps and mines, we could go about our business and raise our families. However, it is five years now since this Spartacus took over these bands. In that time, the danger to us has grown. They have attacked the shipments we send to Bannion. That is our lifeblood, the source of our fortune. Now they have murdered the entire D'Ascenzo family. These animals will not stop unless we stop them. Who will join with me? Who will join so that we can lay waste to those hill camps and starve Spartacus of his support?"

Hands went up around the table, a hand from every adult. Calhoun turned to us. What about you, Sol and Martin? The young woman, Claire, is old enough and, I guess, has already drawn blood—"

He got no further because Claire broke in. "Yes, I have drawn blood with a crayon. And the thorn of a rose draws blood without a crayon, but it's madness to hate roses because you were stuck by one thorn, but we don't have roses here, so that would be a thorn in your side, which I don't think you can abide, especially if you don't know which side. Is that the problem? That we have to choose a side?"

A long pause followed before Calhoun said, "I would agree she would be of no use in a planned attack. But what of you two?"

"I do whatever I have contracted to do," Sol said. "For now, I am under contract. Once that is paid off, my business will be whatever the next contract is."

She received a nod from Calhoun, as if he understood the sanctity of a contract and was already calculating what to offer. His eyes went to me.

"I am obligated to see Claire returned to her family. I must also make provision for the other unfortunate with us, whose family may have given up on her. In any case, I am not a fighter by trade, only by necessity. I am a functionary of the Directorate." From my reading of history, the grasp of strategy and tactics I was hearing suggested that if Spartacus had half the intelligence ascribed to him, these people would head straight to disaster. I would much rather be on the other side of the planet when it happened.

I also considered that the invocation of civic justice and order was lip service and nothing more. The hell they promised to create in the hill camps was even worse than what they accused Spartacus of doing. Did our civic justice and order have any standard-bearers in this benighted wasteland?

Deep lines etched a scowl into Calhoun's face. The evasion I had given him did not sit well.

"Abigail says the camps will not expect you," Claire said in a sudden burst of words. "Attack with your band, take them in hand, and shoot them all. Abigail says to shoot them. Shoot anyone in a suit because that will suit them. Doesn't that suit you?" She smiled and clapped her hands in front of her face.

"I believe you have your hands full for the moment." Calhoun's words were slow and evenly spaced.

"Yes," I said. "My hands are quite full."

CHAPTER TWENTY-THREE

The Hillikers offered Matthews and Calhoun places in the house for the night. Neither of them was interested in making a long drive in the dark and quickly agreed. We were offered space in the barn. Instead, Sol and I elected to have the four of us sleep in our car. The story I gave Rory was that I felt my allergies coming on and the night air in a barn, redolent with animal odors, might worsen them. I also commented that the car seats, thinly padded as they were, had more padding than a bale of hemp. Rory accepted my explanation with an air that said it was what he expected from a New Edinburgh functionary.

Once in the car, I twisted and poked at the seat. A bale of hemp might, in fact, be softer.

"I did not want to make accusations," Sol said as she watched me knead the seat, "and I am glad you didn't either, but my business has taught me to be suspicious of everybody all the time. It would be too convenient for them if our car did not start tomorrow."

"I share your suspicions." I always liked the way Sol thought. "I do

not think they are ready to rush off to an attack, but I would not want to be their guests until they do, with them expecting us to join them in their barbarism."

Sol gave me a tired grin, but I was glad to see it. "It's good we think alike on this," she said, "although I can't imagine you have problems like this at your library."

"Never. Civilization out here seems to be only on the surface."

She reclined her seat as much as she could without crowding Claire behind her in the back seat and rested her head on its back. "We'll take watch and watch, and we won't make the mistake Claire's captors did."

"Agreed." I drew my gun, not to aim it anywhere, only to have it ready on my lap. "I'll take first."

After that, the only sound for a while was Claire humming to herself in the back seat. I couldn't catch the words, but the tune sounded happy.

"Solly? Solly, are you still up?" That was Lizzie talking over Claire's tune.

"Yeah."

I was surprised Sol hadn't fallen asleep immediately, or didn't ignore the question so she could go to sleep.

"Solly, I know—I mean I've heard, you know people talk—you've been paid to kill people. That's true, isn't it?"

Sol shifted in her seat so she was leaning on one shoulder, but she did not sit up and turn around. That left her facing me. "Sometimes the bounty on a person says dead or alive. Sometimes dead is the way it goes. One reason or another."

"Then you have. You have killed for pay."

Sol returned to lying on her back, face to the windshield. "Lizzie, you can't tell me you're realizing this for the first time."

"No, no. That's not what I meant." Lizzie paused. "Please don't get angry. What I'm asking is if you would take money to do what that Calhoun was saying. Go into the hill camps and kill the people there. Like that girl we saw, the one with the torn-up clothes."

"Listen to me, Lizzie." Sol's voice was no longer sleepy. "If I was out to collect the bounty on a man or woman and someone got in the way, like that girl, say, the answer is yeah, I might kill that person if I had to.

Depending on what they were doing, I might not even be sorry. My job and my skin come first."

I thought that was the end, but it wasn't.

Even though Lizzie said nothing else, Sol spoke again. "Would I take money to do Calhoun's job? Go there and kill people—not because they had done something, not because they were in the way, or someone's shield, just kill them to get rid of them even if the Spartacists aren't there? No, I don't think I'd take that contract."

Once again, the only sound from the back was Claire humming her happy tune.

Sol sat up and pushed her fingers through her hair. "Martin, I think I'll take first watch, if you don't mind."

AFTER SOL WOKE ME FOR MY WATCH, I SAT STILL IN MY SEAT FOR A FEW MINUTES. SOL went to sleep almost immediately. The night sky gave us almost no light. I could not see her features, not really, but I did not need to. I had memorized every one of them. The passenger compartment was narrow; our seats were close enough that our shoulders were nearly touching. I would not reach out across the remaining inches. Of course not. I thought about it, though, built touch into my mental constructs of the two of us on a trip together. Not a job. A trip to the mountains of South Hastings or the beach near Port Gandhi, where couples go when they are courting. Those daydreams were safe because they would never happen.

I got out of the car to spend my watch standing guard outside. That was much better. Only me, the night, and thoughts I could substitute for reality.

I WOKE SOL AS SOON AS THE SUN WAS UP ENOUGH TO LIGHT THE CLOUDY SKY. Whether because of our vigilance or because no nefarious deeds were planned, the night had passed without incident. Other than the chickens, the farm was quiet. A small figure passed between buildings and went into a barn.

"The children are up at their chores, but the adults may sleep later than usual after all the eating and drinking," Sol said. "I would prefer not to impose on Rory's hospitality any further and be away before they are up and about."

"What is the fuel situation?" I asked. "I would feel better if we were away from them, but if we do that, we cannot ask them for fuel."

Sol started the car and studied the readouts on the dash and the map. "It will be close, but I think we can make it to Edge-of-the-World. We will have to stop there to refuel. I'm certain we can't make it all the way to the airport."

"Let's do that." Edge-of-the-World wasn't much, but it was a beacon of civic justice and order in this uncivilized wilderness.

Sol pushed the car as fast as she dared on the uneven road. I switched between checking where we were headed and where we had come from with such frequency that I thought my neck would need adjustment—if I ever returned to New Edinburgh. All the checking was for naught, and I told myself to be glad that was the case. The Hillikers did not try to bring us back and we did not drive into a Spartacist ambush. I did give a sigh of relief as the road inclined steeply and we drove out of the grassland of the Inland Sea. The barren moors of the Uplands outside Edge-of-the-World might be bleak territory, but they offered fewer hiding places for those who would do us harm.

The eastern watchtower of the town was a welcome sight from the moment we first saw its top. Poor reflection of our civilization on Offyonder as the place was, it was still an important marker. We had left the backcountry behind us.

In contrast to our previous experiences, the barrier was not only down, but the road was also barred by two armed, alert, and nervous local police. They wanted a password, which we did not have. Sol argued back and forth with them that we did not need a password and that Captain Inoue of CenSec knew us and that she had something for him. They wanted to take us to the CenSec office, but Sol did not want to go there and that was a problem for them anyway because they had no one to relieve them at the barrier. Captain Inoue was not immediately available to come to the barrier. In the end, Sol gave them her name, told them all we wanted was to refuel, said we'd be having something to eat and drink at Peaks and Valleys and that Inoue could find us there to pick up what Sol had for him.

"The way I left it at the end, when we spoke with him before, he is going to expect a payment," Sol said after we cleared the checkpoint. "Even if I hadn't said anything, he would expect something, call it providing 'safe passage' if nothing else. It's probably better for us if he doesn't think we are trying to skip out without any payoff for him."

The seating area in front of the bar was not crowded at this hour, but it was not empty either. A mix of clients occupied some of the tables: those who, having slaked one appetite in the previous hours were now dealing with another, and workers hungry from their honest labor overnight. I made certain to order Claire exactly what Abigail wanted. I figured I would be done worrying about Claire's imaginary friend soon enough that it was worth the indulgence now to avoid hearing complaints during the drive.

The food had not yet arrived when Sol said, "Gray-and-blacks."

In fact, three CenSeccers, led by Captain Inoue, came through the front door. They came straight to our table and spread out from one another as they did. I did not like the little swagger in Inoue's gait.

"It is good to see you again," said Inoue. "I see your efforts have been crowned with success."

Sol's face was a mask, absolutely still except for eyes that narrowed slightly. I knew her well enough by this time. Behind that mask, she was making calculations and not liking what she saw. Was she weighing in the fact that there were three CenSeccers? She must be.

"I appreciate your congratulations," I said, "but I am surprised you felt the need to bring reinforcements in order to give them."

Claire chose that moment to jump out of her seat. "I want a sticky bun from the kitchen!" She sprinted past the bar and through the door that led to the kitchen.

Inoue made no move, gave no order to stop her. "The mind of a child, and not a bright one at that." His face wore a smirk. "Cameron, go collect her so that we can take her to the station."

"We are on our way to the airport with her," I said. "I am expected to turn her over there to CenSeccers who will fly her back to New Edinburgh."

"No." Inoue's gun was out. Sol was where it was aimed. "We will take charge of her and contact CenSec at the airport."

"My contract says I bring her to the airport and receive payment. If you are taking charge here, I expect my payment now." Sol was looking not at the barrel of Inoue's gun but at his eyes.

"We will collect at the airport the payment you were expecting, not whatever pittance you thought you would leave here," Inoue said. "You should take your continued life as adequate payment for yourself. Put your hands flat on the tabletop, fingers spread apart. We know enough about you that if you even twitch, I'll shoot."

Slowly, very slowly, Sol did as she was told. She was still calculating. That concerned me. A CenSec officer could hit a target from a distance of three feet. The other CenSeccer had not drawn his weapon, though, and the one called Cameron had not yet returned from the kitchen.

Was this merely avarice on the part of these CenSeccers, to take the opportunity to claim whatever Sol had been promised and maybe an additional reward for themselves, or were they sufficiently venal to take Claire and sell her to the highest bidder if they could get more that way? I decided I should bring the weight of my official position to bear on the situation. "Tell me the meaning of this outrage! I am the representative of the Directorate, who is in charge even here. We are required to deliver her to the airport, not to CenSeccers in charge of an Upland watchtower." I tried to put as much snap into my voice as I could, but I do not have a command presence. I have been told that in the past.

"Tell *you* the meaning?" Inoue mimicked me. "It's simple. We are the law, and we are taking charge of this girl and any reward that comes with her return."

For all I knew, Inoue would turn around and sell her back to the

Spartacists if they offered enough. After what Claire had done in shooting those two men in the shack, this would be a disaster. It also meant Sol and I would need to be dead in order for them to get away with it. I wished I were fast enough to draw my weapon and fire before he could make the slight shift in his aim to shoot me, but even if I could, he might shoot Sol. If I could make him turn his weapon on me, however, Sol might be that fast.

"What you are saying is that you are corrupt. I represent the Directorate, and I decide who is paid. I will report on what is done. You know the penalty in CenSec for corruption." I did wish that I cut a more impressive figure.

Sol mouthed the word *Don't.*

The CenSeccer remaining with Inoue laughed. "Next thing, he'll threaten us that he's from DeepSec."

"Is that it?" asked Inoue, his voice heavy with sarcasm. "You're from DeepSec, the ones who watch the watchers? The ones who have never been seen? The imaginary ones they try to frighten us with when we are recruits?"

"Of course not," I said. "There is no DeepSec beyond those stories. But I do represent the Directorate, and you would be well advised to respect what I say." He should have been impressed by the calm, level way I delivered my words. I was.

Instead, he came to a different decision. "All of you are coming to the station with us. I'm not leaving the two of you loose."

I had a feeling I knew how that visit to the station would end. Possibly, I should not have tried to impress him.

"What about this girl?" The other CenSeccer grabbed Lizzie by her upper arm and pulled her up against him. "Take her for later?"

"Get your mind off your groin, Schlansky," Inoue snapped. "We don't need another one to watch. Leave her here. They'll put her to work, and you can use her when you want. Get handties on Sol. There will be weapons under that coat. It's coming off carefully." Then he muttered, "What the fuck is taking Cameron so long?"

Schlansky released Lizzie, who shrank away from him. He took a step in Sol's direction and put his hand on his holster as he did. Except the holster was empty.

Lizzie Quickfingers had lifted the gun out when he pulled her close.

Lizzie had the gun gripped in both hands. She held it about the level of her navel as she pointed it at Schlansky. The barrel wavered back and forth.

"What the—!"

Lizzie fired before Schlansky got the third word out. At point-blank range, her aim did not need to be good nor the gun steady. The shot hit Schlansky in the gut, knocked him two steps backward, and then he toppled. The recoil propelled Lizzie back as well. She tripped and sat down heavily on the floor, still gripping the gun. Inoue spun toward Lizzie, weapon ready.

All of this took but an instant. Sometimes an instant can be as long as eternity, and that was long enough for Sol. She had weapons in both hands. Both fired at the same time. Inoue's body shook from the impact of two bullets in his chest. He crumpled.

I had my gun out by the time Inoue's body hit the floor. Sol and I scanned around the room. People were transfixed where they sat. Some had dropped to the floor, seeking the dubious protection of being under a table.

"As long as I don't see a weapon, nothing will happen to you," Sol said.

No one seemed disposed to challenge her on that. Inoue was dead. Schlansky was moaning, hands pressed to his belly. Still no sight of Cameron or Claire, but the door to the kitchen was cracked open, as though someone was peeking out. There was no sign of a gun in that opening.

"We shot gray-and-blacks," Sol said. "This is a problem."

"It was necessary," I said, "and they were corrupt."

"Okay," Sol said, "but what do we do now? They are still gray-and-blacks, CenSec."

"When the satellite window is open, I'll call my handler. They were corrupt. He will fix it."

Sol nodded. She stepped next to Schlansky and put a bullet in his head. "If he can fix this, it will be better if there are no other stories from them. Now we need this Cameron. And Claire."

The door to the kitchen swung completely closed as we walked toward it. Sol aimed one of her guns at the frozen bartender.

"You. Open that door and walk through it ahead of us."

The bartender's pants were wet long before he went through the door. No gunshot greeted him. He sagged against a cutting table and sobbed. The cook was crouched under that cutting table, hands over his head, shivering.

Cameron was at the back of the kitchen, his head in a sink. That sink was full of blood. When I lifted his head up, it almost came off. His throat had been gashed open nearly to the spine by a knife that was still stuck in one side of his neck.

"Kitchens have sharp knives as well as sticky buns." Claire was bright and cheerful. "Abigail said he was a bad man and he had bad thoughts and he wanted to put his hands in bad places. Can I have another sticky bun? This one has blood on it."

I made a mental note never to be on Abigail's bad side.

CHAPTER TWENTY-FOUR

THE SATELLITE WINDOW WAS NOT OPEN YET, BUT WE DID NOT THINK IT WAS A good idea to stick around Edge-of-the-World waiting for it. The local police were probably just as corrupt as the CenSeccers we had killed, if not more so. Their eventual appearance on the scene would be one more variable we could do without. The satellite window would open while we were on the road to the airport. I would need to forgo finding a private place to have my conversation with my handler.

I can't say I was sorry to see Edge-of-the-World drop out of sight behind us. The so-called last outpost of civilization was not worthy of the title. In fact, the place could be called civilized only in comparison to the primitive hill camps and the brutal barbarism of the farmers.

I kept my counsel to myself as Sol drove. As before, the only sound in the car was the happy nonsense humming from Claire. It was not her humming that occupied my thoughts. Perhaps it was true that we lacked the medical sophistication on Offyonder to treat her. Still, I wondered that the Director had not found a way to send her off-world for therapy, even if we were not members of the Assembly of Worlds.

Sooner or later, this "Abigail" was going to create a problem not even the Director could remedy.

A chime from my comm served notice that the satellite was available. It was also a useful reminder that Claire's future was neither my assignment nor my concern. I keyed in the codes on my comm and opened the call to my handler.

The conversation was terse. Since I was not alone, I had to keep to the main points and avoid any back-and-forth discussion. I could not afford to receive orders that might be overheard, as unlikely as that was with the roar of the IC engine, and the rush of wind past windows that did not completely close. I informed my handler of the events in Edge-of-the-World. I made clear the venality, the actual corruption, of the CenSec personnel there and the need to eliminate them in order to preserve my mission.

I omitted my concern over Sol's well-being and payment. That would have been a distraction from the point of the call. Similarly, I left out Claire's role in Cameron's death. That could not have added any insight to what my handler needed to convey to our superiors, and it might have led to a discussion I did not want to have with listeners around. I closed with the request that Willoughby at the airport be given an immediate and appropriate briefing. I emphasized that this was essential within the satellite window before our arrival. With that, I cut off the call, severing a question from my handler in mid-sentence.

"So, will Captain Willoughby bow and scrape when we arrive, or will he put us under arrest?" Sol asked.

"If he knows what is good for him, he will treat our actions as having been ordered from New Edinburgh," I said.

"That is certainly the way you sounded." Sol drummed the fingers of one hand against the dashboard. "I have taken contracts from CenSec, but they never involved another gray-and-black. You will understand that I am neither accustomed to that kind of high-level sanction nor would I expect you to be able to dictate it."

"I did not dictate anything." A bit of a growl crept into my voice. "I am, as I told you, no one. It is the people who use the tools who will do the dictating."

Sol sighed. "We'll know soon enough, I guess."

Behind us, Claire giggled at a joke she told herself.

———

As expected, Captain Willoughby was not pleased to see us. With a barked order via his comm to the guard who brought us through the door of the terminal building, he had us ushered swiftly to his second-floor office. After about a five-minute wait, he joined us. He did not sit at his desk, however. He went to the window overlooking the runway and stood there with his back to us.

I waited—we all waited—for him to turn around. That took a few minutes more. When he did, his face was flushed. I suppose that could have been caused by a collar being too tight, but it was probably due to me. Thinking of his collar made me study the rest of his uniform. His CenSec gray-and-black was still neat, all buttons tidy and decorations properly affixed. He had not succumbed to the slovenliness that this posting induced in other Serendipity CenSeccers. Yet.

"I appreciate that you have completed your assignment," he said at long last. "I do not have to be happy with the way it was done."

Standing up to CenSec officers is not what librarians are trained to do, nor would it be in the repertoire of a failed CenSec candidate. I had to do it, though. I knew I had approval from CenSec HQ in New Edinburgh, and that helped my resolve.

"Sol did what was necessary. The CenSec personnel in Edge-of-the-World were corrupt, and had Sol not acted as she did, we might be facing further problems in returning Claire. I do not think the Director would be happy about that."

"No. He would not. For certain." A mouthful of lemon juice could not have soured his words more. Referring to the Director was the card I held that could not be beat. "I am not happy, however. The loss of the three CenSec officers in Edge-of-the-World is significant.

They are not being replaced. At least, not at the present time. My personnel can stretch only so far. How do you expect me to manage the good-for-nothing local police in that excuse for a town without CenSec oversight?" With haste, he added, "Never mind that. Someone like you cannot understand the issues that need to be managed."

I could have said that, based on my extensive reading of history, it was questionable how effective corrupt officials were in handling their duties in the first place and how many other problems probably existed that those officials had only hidden from sight. I did not think he wanted to hear that from me, so I kept silent.

When I said nothing, Willoughby turned his focus to Sol. "I would suggest you take the pay you earned and either think about riding out on the next starship that comes through or find a place down in that soup where I never need to hear of you or see you again."

Sol, bless the steel in her spine that I lack, smiled at him. "I will be glad to do that, although CenSec has needed my services in the past and you may again in the future—unless your gray-and-blacks become much more efficient."

"Especially since I do not have the three officers in Edge-of-the-World. A nice way to add to the need for your *services*. People like you disgust me." My previous impression had been wrong. Willoughby's face could become sourer.

Sol's smile did not go away. "I am used to dealing with disgusting clients."

Willoughby turned away from us, back to his window.

"The crew is ready," he said in the direction of the window. "They have been ready for this return flight for days. Once the plane is fueled, Allgeier, you may take Claire Montaigne on board and accompany her back to New Edinburgh. Your bounty hunter's voucher card will be activated as soon as you board. I trust you will report that I have met your needs to the best of my ability and resources."

That was probably as close to begging a lowly assistant librarian as he could bring himself to do. I assured him I would do exactly that. It was, in fact, the truth. He had acted to the best of his ability, leaving out only my opinion that his ability was not very great. He would not be interested in my opinion, nor was I going to voice it.

"Oh, Abigail, look, the plane is out there on the runway." Claire was both pointing out the window and looking past her right shoulder.

The plane had been brought out from its hangar, although it wasn't on the airfield's single long runway. It was on a taxiway near the terminal building, below and to the right of Willoughby's window, a distinction lost in Claire's description to Abigail. A fuel truck sat next to it, attached by a wide hose. People were carrying supplies up a ramp to the cabin. This airplane was old technology, but it was what we had that could cross the wide ocean back to New Edinburgh. I was proud that we had the plane—far more than most planets in the Reach could manage—but also sad because many members of the Assembly of Worlds could do better. I fought to block away the inappropriate thoughts. I concentrated on telling myself to be glad that Claire was no longer demanding that Joshua Montaigne come in person to get her. I, Martin Allgeier, third assistant librarian, would now suffice.

"Abigail says the plane is almost ready," Claire announced. "Abigail says it's time to go."

Claire turned and walked to the office door. She stopped there, waiting for me. Instead of joining her, I turned back to the window to look at the plane. I would soon be on that plane, and the voucher card with Sol's payment would be activated. I would not see Sol again. The concept bothered me for some reason.

I was still looking at the plane when a loud crack sounded. A streak of yellow-orange fire lanced from the rocky ground beyond the airfield and struck the plane. Flame and smoke shot from the fuselage, accompanied by a blast.

"Down! Down!" Willoughby screamed. "We're under attack!"

I dropped to the floor with a lack of grace and bruised my elbows. A second later, I ceased to worry about that as the plane's fuel tanks and the fuel truck itself erupted in a secondary explosion. The windows in Willoughby's office shattered. Glass fragments flew everywhere, and I was thankful I was not standing up. I should have been shielding

Claire, but I had been looking in the wrong direction and was too far from her in any case. As soon as I realized I was intact, I swiveled around on the floor on my stomach, my eyes searching for her. Claire was lying on her back in the doorway. No glass or debris had come near her. She was giggling.

Only a few minutes separated Claire and me from being on the floor of Willoughby's office, stunned but alive, and being on that plane when the missile hit. Yes, indeed, Spartacus was pissed.

CHAPTER TWENTY-FIVE

When I was sure nothing else was flying in through the window, I levered myself up. Pieces of glass slid off my back. Willoughby and Sol were crouched below the window frame, peeking out through the opening that had been a window. Glass crunched under my boots as I moved to join them. Claire was still on the floor in the doorway, and Lizzie crawled over to her.

Crack, crack, crack went a string of sounds, along with orange flashes around the perimeter of the airfield. There were no windows left to shatter, but the impact of bullets against the building spoke of the violence being unleashed.

Willoughby was yelling orders into his comm. He may have grasped what was happening. He may have been making all the right moves. I don't know enough about it to tell. I do think he would have come across better if his voice hadn't been so high pitched.

A moment later, we were all ducking below the window frame and praying that the wall would stop bullets as a spray of buzzing ended in angry smacks against the interior wall.

"We have to pull back to the CenSec building," Willoughby said. "I don't have enough men and women to hold that and this terminal. Maybe not even enough to hold this building, as large as it is. I don't know how I'm going to get the ones who are patrolling the road back here."

"If we are all in the CenSec building and they are after Claire, doesn't that make it easier for them to surround us?" I asked.

"I don't know!" Willoughby's shout had even Sol and Lizzie staring at him. "What are you now, a battlefield tactician? Although that gun of yours came out pretty damn fast when the shooting started."

Indeed, my gun had been in my hand almost immediately.

"Martin has had weaponry training, as all Directorate officials do." Sol was virtually parroting the line I had given her.

"A librarian?" Willoughby snorted. "First I've ever heard of it."

I did not want to discuss a failed dalliance with CenSec. "This is neither the time nor the place," I said. "What's your decision?"

"I don't know!" The strain on Willoughby's face could have been the precursor to tears. "It will be hours before I can communicate again with CenSec HQ in New Edinburgh."

The prospect of making the decision on his own, at the risk of being second-guessed later, had him paralyzed.

"What's critical about the CenSec building?" Sol asked. "Is there something in it, or does it have a particular advantage in defense?"

Sol's question moved Willoughby away from dwelling on his indecision. I was thankful she thought to do that.

"It's critical to our communications," Willoughby said. "We cannot maintain constant communications with New Edinburgh, because we depend on the satellites for that. You know that. So, we store all necessary contact information there. If they take the building and get into the computer, it will expose everyone we work with in Bannion and the mines."

"That sounds like a reason to defend it," Sol said.

"Yes, yes. Exactly my thought," Willoughby said.

"Can *we* reach it?" The intermittent crackle of gunfire punctuated by an occasional scream added emphasis to Sol's question.

"If you quit pestering me with questions and let me tend to my command, I will see what we can do."

I aimed a wink at Sol while Willoughby spoke rapidly into his comm.

"On three," Willoughby said. "Everyone out the door, down the stairs, and across to the other building."

"Claire, do you understand?" I asked. She nodded. I had to take that as agreement as Willoughby started his countdown.

At zero, I heard gunfire erupt from our building. Bent low to stay below the empty windows, we ran for the door. We spilled into the hallway, where no bullets could reach us, and dashed for the staircase down.

Claire ran along with us as if we were out on a lark, clapping and chanting, "When in danger, when in doubt, run in circles, scream and shout!"

I have to say that Claire's chant was a fairly good assessment of the way Willoughby was handling the situation. For herself, Claire seemed to have no fear. Possibly, she did not fully understand the situation, but I wished I had her insouciance.

A thirty-yard dash separated us at the main building entrance from our destination. Had any of the Spartacists worked their way around the building yet? If they had, they could gun us down as we ran since there was no cover between the buildings. Willoughby's head swung back and forth, surveying the open ground to either side of the doorway we stood at. His nerve was visibly crumbling.

"Is there anyone over there who can cover us?" Sol asked. "You must have people over there by now."

"Right. Right." Willoughby spoke into his comm.

Gunshots rang out from the second floor of the CenSec building, tracers flaring across the open space.

"Now!" Sol screamed.

With nerve I would not have claimed to possess, I burst out of the door, legs pumping in a frantic race to reach the building across from us before a bullet found me. Seconds later, all of us collapsed in the relative safety of the entrance to the CenSec building.

A woman in gray and black was on one knee in the vestibule with a rifle aimed out the doorway. "C'mon! C'mon!" she shouted at us.

We scrambled, more on hands and knees than gaining our feet, and reached the shelter of the interior hallway. Moans and cries came from a CenSeccer propped against the wall, his eyes bugging out, transfixed by the shattered portion of his lower leg that remained to him, the sharp fragment of his tibia white against the bloody tissue. A female CenSeccer was securing a tourniquet.

"Captain Willoughby," she called. "What do we do?" She held out blood-soaked hands and sleeves toward him. "What do we do?"

"I can't reach headquarters yet." Willoughby was as much riveted by the wounded man's leg as the man himself was.

"Yes, but what do we do?" she asked again.

"I … I'll do something." He brushed past her and found a staircase leading up.

Sol caught my eye. "This is not good. Let me try to talk to him. Martin, can you support the woman at the door? Have you ever used an automatic rifle?" She gestured at the one lying next to the wounded man.

"Only on the CenSec range years ago. Never on automatic." I wish I could have said something else, because I wanted a better expression on Sol's face. But in some circumstances, truth is necessary.

Sol picked up the weapon and handed it to me. "This sets it for automatic fire. If they charge the door, point it at them, hold down the trigger, and spray it like a water hose. Got it?" After I nodded, she turned to Lizzie and Claire. "You two, find a room with no windows, an inside bathroom is best. This place will have indoor plumbing. Stay there until Martin or I come for you."

Claire folded her arms over her chest. "The Princess Claire should lead her troops in battle."

Lizzie tugged one of Claire's arms loose. "That would leave me alone. And we have to think about Abigail. She would be scared, even if you're not."

"You would be scared, wouldn't you?" Claire said to her right. "All right. The Princess Claire will go with my whizzy-Lizzie. For now."

CHAPTER TWENTY-SIX

T HE SPARTACISTS MADE NO ATTEMPT TO RUSH THE DOOR, FOR WHICH I WAS grateful. In the time that I waited, nerves on edge, for an attack that did not come, Willoughby managed to position his troops in and around the two-story building in a way that covered all the approaches. Whether he did that on his own or Sol told him how to do it, I can't say. Sol, when she reappeared at my position, was noncommittal about what she had done.

From that point, the battle turned into a stalemate. The Spartacists had overrun the airfield and now held the main terminal building. We held the CenSec building. We had water but no food supplies, which meant the situation could not remain stalemated forever. I wondered if the Spartacists had learned that Claire had not been on that plane. Was their ultimate objective here Claire or something more grandiose? Did they know we were in no condition to stand a siege? Of course, I did not know what constraints they had. How many were they? How much ammunition did they have? Everything CenSec thought they knew about the Spartacists on Serendipity was

turning out to be incorrect. Could CenSec find a worthwhile use for those crazy farmers?

Hours passed. The comm satellite window in the sky opened again. I was relieved of my position and retreated to an upstairs office, where I called my handler. It was an unrewarding conversation. After I made my report, all he would say was that he would speak with headquarters and see what they said. It was probably unrealistic to have expected anything else.

Logic said that since Willoughby was in command of CenSec both at the airfield and in Edge-of-the-World, whatever headquarters had in mind would go through him. What I needed to do, therefore, was find him and stay close to him.

The second floor had a larger office in one corner with an engraved plaque on the door reading CENSEC COMMANDING OFFICER. Willoughby was inside, bowed over his desk with his hands clasped across the top of his head. I have read many descriptions of great leaders confronting crises. This was not one of them.

Willoughby looked up at my entrance. His face could have passed for that of an exsanguinated corpse. I do not have that effect on people, so I asked if something had happened.

"Happened?" Willoughby asked rhetorically. "Yes, something happened. I was trying … trying to get direction … orders from headquarters. Then the comm cut out … it cut out and then Joshua Montaigne was speaking to me."

That explained the "exsanguinated corpse" appearance. Joshua Montaigne could have that effect on people, and not only figuratively.

"What did our commander say?" Strictly speaking, the library was not under Joshua Montaigne. His command, on paper, was only CenSec. However, there was no branch of the Directorate that would not defer to the Director's youngest brother. By grouping myself under that aegis, I hoped to give myself a little more stature with Willoughby.

"I need Lieutenants Margolis and Struck," he said. "Also, your bounty hunter and the girls. Now." He was already punching codes into his comm before he finished speaking.

I called Sol on her comm and asked her to bring Claire and Lizzie. Then I found a chair against an interior wall and sat down to wait. It took only a few minutes.

The two CenSec lieutenants, a man and a woman in their early twenties, looked as scared as Lizzie was. Claire was engaged in a close examination of the waving fingers of her left hand. I was surprised she did not trip. Of all the people in the office, only Sol gave off the grim determination of a warrior. I suppose that was fitting.

"I have orders," Willoughby said. "Orders directly from Joshua Montaigne. At precisely four a.m. local time, we are to launch an attack from this building and retake control of the airfield. CenSec officers from Bannion have been ordered to come up. They will be here to support our attack. Once we have control of the airfield, Joshua Montaigne will be flying in himself."

"Uncle Joshua is coming to get me!" Claire punctuated the sentence with two loud claps. "I told you he would."

"Joshua Montaigne is coming to take personal command and put an end to this Spartacist …" He fumbled for a word. "… disturbance. Orders have also gone to farmer groups that CenSec has been forming and supporting. They will be launching attacks on those cesspool hill camps. When we are done, the commander intends to have no … obstacles to civic justice and order here."

"Excuse me," I said. "What about us? You wanted all of us here, but none of this involves us. How are you going to hold this building *and* launch an attack to clear the airfield at the same time? You couldn't even hold the main terminal building before. Do you know how many CenSeccers are being sent up from Bannion? Will they be enough? You don't even know exactly what you're facing."

From Willoughby's expression, my assessment of the open questions and problems contributed almost as much to his fright as having to take direct orders from Joshua Montaigne. I supposed that if he failed at the airfield, he would probably be dead and have no reason to fear Joshua Montaigne. Saying that would have been unlikely to calm Willoughby down.

"We can't be sure of holding this building," Willoughby said, "so you will not be here. This building has an underground garage with a fueled vehicle. The ramp connects to the surface road to Bannion, about a half mile in the direction of the mountain pass. Under the cover of our attack, you will take that vehicle and take Claire to Bannion. You are to get her away from the fighting and from the Spartacists."

"If Uncle Joshua is coming here, I should be here," Claire said. "He will expect the Princess Claire to be here to meet him."

"He will not expect you to be here in the middle of a battle," Willoughby snapped. "I will not have people to keep you safe, and he was very clear that he expects you are someplace safe. After this area is secured and the … malcontents defeated, he will come get you. Understand?"

"Yes, the Princess Claire does understand. As long as I can take my dizzy-Lizzie with me."

Willoughby was shaking his head as though that would clear it. When he gave up on that, he pulled his lieutenants over to a screen mounted on his desk. From what I could see, he had a map of the airfield and its surroundings displayed. The three of them began working out their battle plan.

Claire pulled Lizzie to a seat on the floor near the office door. From the snatches of conversation I overheard, she was having a discussion with Abigail about Willoughby's orders and plans.

I am not one to give sympathy to incompetents, or even the benefit of the doubt, but I did feel sorry for Willoughby. For all the talk and all the glorious stories about fighting in the streets and saving the Directorate during the Riots, CenSeccers are glorified police, not soldiers. Even ArmedSec, which tries to train as a military unit, has never fought as one. The Peacers, on the other hand, are soldiers who fight all across the Reach in everything from high-tech combined arms operations to chasing bandits through backcountry. If Spartacus really was a Peacer, even an ex-Peacer, what might he have done with the Spartacists? I had read of how, many centuries ago on Earth, Sparta had sent one man, Gylippus, to Syracuse to help them in their war against Athens. With Gylippus in charge, Syracuse destroyed the Athenian army. I told myself the situations were not comparable in any way.

"I found a refreshment nook downstairs."

Jolted out of my reverie, I realized Sol had come to stand next to me. Right next to me. I could not understand how I had missed that.

"Would you like to get something to drink with me?" she asked.

Yes, I certainly would. It took a second thought for me to realize that I needed to say the words.

"How well do you think our side has thought this out? Willoughby is, obviously, not suited to the position he is in." I spoke after we were out of Willoughby's office and my mind was able to come up with words that related to our job rather than to having a drink together.

"Not at all," Sol said. "There are a lot of ways this could go wrong. If your HQ believes its own propaganda about the condition of the rebels, his appointment may have been a way of exiling an administrative hack, or a fuckup, to a distant post where nothing important ever happens." She went several more steps down the hall before she spoke again. "Your Joshua Montaigne may not have much choice now. The only troops he can bring from your mainland in any reasonable amount of time are ones that will fit in a transoceanic plane. And there are no armies here on Serendipity. Small units of men and women with light arms are it. For both sides. For all that Offyonder has the wealth to join the Assembly of Worlds, it does not have armies. I've been on enough planets in the Reach to see a pattern. A rapid move with a small trained force may be enough."

"If Willoughby doesn't clear the airfield, landing here will be a problem."

"Yeah. Whatever aircraft Montaigne arrives in will have the best defenses and tech on the planet. That's how the Peacers make it work."

That comment brought me back to my thoughts about the Peacers. "I'm not sure how well trained these CenSeccers are. I don't think they compare well to the ones in New Edinburgh. I think Willoughby is upset that he has to give us the car instead of being able to use it himself."

Sol grinned. "You're probably right. But I wouldn't want to be him after Montaigne gets here if he tried that."

We found the nook and sat there by ourselves to kill the time before the start of the attack and our departure. It would have been a better idea to catch a little sleep, but I had no interest in trying. For her part, Sol was willing to sit with me, which may have been the real reason I did not want the sleep I could have used. I was glad to see that she contented herself with a single small bottle of mash that we found.

This was a good setting to have, in real life, one of those conversations that I enjoyed in my mind. It could be my conversation to steer. We were together. By ourselves. No other demands on our attention existed beyond each other. Naturally, it did not happen that way.

We did discuss what we would do if we were able to reach Bannion. Sol outlined the rival gangs and the territories they controlled and how we could manage to stay hidden until we could make contact with Joshua Montaigne. It was mostly me listening and asking a question here or there. Sol knew the city inside and out. Still, the best we could do was to make a list of options. We had no idea how much of CenSec's personnel had been pulled to support Willoughby's attack and, consequently, no idea of how much order the Bannion police would preserve.

When our planning discussion became circular, Sol rambled off into stories about the Reach, different planets she had seen, hunts she had been on. I have never been off the surface of Offyonder—as indeed, nearly all humans who had gone out to the stars never left the planet they or their ancestors went to—and my reading in the library was mostly in Earth's history. It was easy to listen to Sol. I enjoyed sitting with her. I enjoyed her stories.

I should qualify that. Sol did have a tendency to dwell on Gil Mortimer's exploits at the expense of her own. I could have done without those. I also did not want to hear the way this man had treated Sol. She always found a way to excuse it or blame it somehow on herself. It induced me to concoct a variety of torments I would inflict on Mortimer should he ever put himself in a place I could reach.

Even considering those moments, our time together was comfortable. Sol talking and me listening. I think each of us subconsciously understood that we might be going to our deaths this night. The talk was good for both of us.

The time passed, swifter than I would have expected. There was still much I would have liked Sol to tell me when the alarm in my comm buzzed. It was almost 4:00 a.m.

CHAPTER TWENTY-SEVEN

"T IME TO DO THIS," SOL SAID.

"Any alternatives we haven't considered?" I knew none existed, so thoroughly had we reviewed the situation, but I felt I had to ask.

"I don't think so." Neither her voice nor her face held any sign of a question. "Even if Willoughby succeeds, trying to stay with the gray-and-blacks has a higher risk of us being killed or captured."

"Yeah. For us, being captured is probably the same as being killed except for how long it will take."

On that cheery note, we went upstairs to collect Lizzie and Claire. Throughout the building, we saw CenSeccers readying themselves: checking rifles, pistols, and ammunition and, in a couple of cases, scrawling notes on paper they stuffed into pockets of their gray-and-blacks. Presumably, those were last words for a relative or loved one in case they were killed and someone checked their bodies. It was most likely a forlorn hope. It was a bit odd, anyway, in that I doubt anyone, even me, thought of CenSeccers as having loved ones.

Lizzie and Claire were where we had left them. Lizzie was tense and shivering. Claire stretched and tried to stifle a yawn.

"I can't believe she slept almost the whole time," Lizzie said. "I tried, but all I could do was think about what could happen. Claire just went to sleep."

"Of course I went to sleep," Claire said. "The Princess Claire is never afraid. Of course, I might be," she added. "A little."

No rhymes or nonsense phrases followed. Maybe fear had pulled her back into our real world, at least for the moment. Whether that was the case or not, she followed our directions without further comment. In fact, she took Lizzie's hand and, in a reversal of their roles, it was Claire leading Lizzie and calming the younger girl.

The CenSec vehicle was in the basement garage, as Willoughby had said. It was a standard electric CenSec car in appearance, all in white with CENTRAL SECURITY in bright red across the doors. It would not have been out of place on the streets of New Edinburgh. Being easily visible was a concern, given that we were far from those peaceful streets. To myself, I had to admit that the GSG GIVES RESPECT. CENSEC PROTECTS RESPECT. that appeared under CENTRAL SECURITY was rather ironic under the circumstances.

The outer shell of the vehicle was typical Offyonder manufacture, printed from plastic polymer particles. It would stop, maybe, a rock flung from a slingshot. Protection against bullets fired from a rifle would be nonexistent. I don't know why I would have expected an armored vehicle—that would have had to be transported from off-world—to be sitting at a CenSec base where, officially, the only threats were from small bands of half-naked thieves without modern weapons. Believing your own propaganda can create dangerous illusions and lead you to ignore real dangers. I had read about enough occasions when people did that to know it for the truth. At least the battery had a full charge.

"I've had practice driving at high speed on shitty roads in the dark," Sol said. "Unless the reference material in your library has you better prepared, I should do the driving."

The corners of her mouth pulled slightly upward, which told me this was a jest between comrades going into danger. The thought warmed me. "I've got no experience at this at all. You drive; I'll shoot. But the truth is, the driving is what will get us out of here."

We put Lizzie and Claire in back, as usual. All I heard from the rear after I settled myself in the front was a brief conversation Claire had with Abigail. I think she was asking for Abigail's blessing. When I turned around, Claire had Lizzie wrapped in a tight hug.

The chrono on my comm hit the hour. Right on schedule, gunfire erupted above us. The screams of men and women entering combat were loud enough to penetrate to the basement as well. Sol clicked a release, and the garage door slid up. The shooting and screaming were suddenly louder. More important, the driveway in front of us was clear. Sol jammed the accelerator down. With a jolt that slammed us back into our seats and made the tires squeal, the car shot out of the garage.

Flashes of yellow and orange lit up the still-dark sky. They were off to the sides and remote. Nothing blocked our way. When we reached the point where the drive merged into the mountain road, a series of popping noises came from the rear of the car. We had been hit. I hoped these were only stray rounds that had hit nothing vital. Lizzie and Claire confirmed that they were okay. The car rocked, skidded, and bounced as Sol drove far faster on that road in the dark than I would have dared in daylight. No one attempted to stop us—and that was a good thing, because the way Sol drove, I doubt I would have hit any target I fired at.

It was only a few minutes, although it felt like hours, before we left the battleground behind us. We could still hear the shooting, but the human voices and the visible signs of the conflict had been absorbed into the night. The road pitched downward and Sol turned on the car's lights.

"At this point, I think the risk of us going over a cliff in the dark is greater than being shot," Sol said.

I was not disposed to argue with her. My stomach had had enough of high-speed driving without being able to see where we were going.

The mountain road to Bannion was deserted as we twisted our way down. The only dangers we faced were the sheer cliffs and the lack of guardrails. Sunrise was lighting up the sky when we passed the dip where the culvert had been blocked. I took note of what a wonderful location it was for an ambush and tensed, but no one was waiting for us. The debris, human and otherwise, from that earlier attack had been cleared away, so the only sign that remained was in my mind. We passed the hospital named for Claire as well and dipped into the smoggy soup that covered Bannion in its bowl. Quickly, the land around us blurred into grayish cloud. In places, car lights did not help. The road simply vanished into the cloud, and we crept carefully through those stretches. The smog was thick today. It was hard to believe, while swimming in gray mist, that we were returning to civilization from the barbarity of the Uplands.

At last, the road leveled off—not that driving with no visibility past the front of the car was any less nerve-racking on level ground. I could hear, but not see, the river off to our left. We had reached the bottom of the bowl, the smog here thick enough that I could imagine the particles piling up in my bronchi, blocking out the air. I would be leaving this for the clean air of New Edinburgh once this job was done. I would not have spent enough time in it, not nearly enough time, to develop the wheezes, the lung condition second only to violence as a cause of death in Bannion. Still, I was sure I could feel a little rattle with every breath I drew in and heard the whisper of a wheeze with each exhalation.

I commanded myself to stop thinking about my lungs and pay attention to my surroundings. The smog thinned enough to see the buildings of the half-built and deserted North End replace the trunks of long-dead handtrees along the sides of the road. We had gone only a short way into the North End when our headlights glinted off some obstacle in the road. Sol brought our car to a stop in front of it. We faced a barricade, rubble and trash thrown together across both sides of the road, constricting the open pavement to a single-car width in the center. That lane was blocked by sawhorses painted orange. A motley collection of men and women was ranged along the barrier.

I counted six, four men and two women, although there could easily have been others farther back in the gloom I could not see. None of them wore uniforms, neither the gray and black of CenSec nor the dull blue of the Bannion police. Instead, they had a hodgepodge of clothing, from stained worker coveralls to coarsely woven pants and shirts. All of them were armed, an assortment of pistols and bolt-action rifles that a cheap printer plant could manufacture. Of course, a round from one of those old-style, unsophisticated weapons could kill you every bit as dead as one from the latest Peacer assault rifle.

Two of the men walked over to the car. The weapons from the barricade covered us as they approached.

"Out," said one of the men.

Our odds of blasting through the blockade without casualties, if we could get past them at all, seemed poor. We got out.

"What have we here?" asked the man who had ordered us out. He had a stocky build filling out a blue coverall that had seen hard wear. The pistol in his hand shifted from aiming at Sol to me, then back again. "A C-sucker car, but you are not C-suckers."

"There's fighting in the Uplands," I said. "We got away as best we could."

"Stole a C-sucker car." He let out a harsh laugh. "Well, we're collecting tolls for Spartacus, so that C-sucker car now belongs to Spartacus. What else you got you can pay your way with?"

CHAPTER TWENTY-EIGHT

"T HESE ARE NOT SPARTACISTS," CLAIRE SAID.

I wondered again about the gun she must have kept. As on other occasions, a crisis seemed to return her to reality, but I hoped she was not thinking of trying to draw that weapon.

"How would you know that, honey?" said the man. "Spartacus himself was here and told us to collect anything valuable from people trying to go in or out. So, I'll ask one more time. What have you got to pay your way? Or maybe we should find something else to collect."

"I have money," Sol said. "Take this and let us go."

She had managed to palm an electronic voucher while she was speaking. She held it out. From the man's sharp indrawn breath, whatever the illuminated side of the card showed was a large amount.

The man reached for the voucher. Sol flicked it away. It landed in the mud between the two men who had come out to the car. Both of them lunged for it and went down to hands and knees on the muddy road, each trying to grab it away from the other. A shout of "Hey!" came from the barricade. A woman dashed out from the barrier to

where the two men were struggling over the voucher. Weapons at the barricade that had been aimed at us pointed elsewhere.

Sol's hand went under her duster, reappeared with a pistol. She fired three quick shots. I have no idea if she hit anyone, but the ones still at the barricade ducked for cover.

"Run!" Sol screamed as she was shooting.

Sol grabbed Claire's hand and dashed for a small gap between the sawhorses. Claire ran with her, and Lizzie and I were in close pursuit. I heard a shout behind us. I pulled out my gun and fired blindly into the murk. I don't know if that did any good. From the sounds that reached us, they were fighting with one another over the voucher.

I ran until my chest was on fire, then I ran some more, telling myself it was only the foul air that caused the sensation. The smog swallowed us and sheltered us. We ended our flight, panting and gasping, by the entrance to a building that had a CLOSED sign on a front door that did not look as if it had ever been open.

In truth, I was the one gasping for air, nostrils flaring. The others were a bit winded, no worse than that. Keeping my sections of history and historical fiction organized did not build running endurance.

"Now what?" I was pleased that the words came out and sounded decent, never mind that there were only two of them.

"A long walk," Sol said, "and under less-than-ideal conditions. The North End of Bannion was abandoned long before I came here. In spite of the fact that the mountain road runs through it with all the traffic to and from the Uplands, the fog and smog are the worst here. The one saving grace is that anyone we run into in this area will be pretty derelict themselves. Gangs won't have any prey, so they're not here."

"The thugs at the roadblock are here," I said.

"Because of the traffic on the road." The scowl on Sol's face was barely visible from a few feet away. "That means maybe all the gray-and-blacks were pulled out of here for the fight at the airport. Without them, the Bannion police are about as useless as you would expect. Which means we may have more trouble reaching Harborside when we are in the populated areas. What Claire said is probably right.

It will be gangs of thugs on the street, not Spartacists. Either way, I'd prefer not to do this on foot."

"There's a place I know." Lizzie stepped close, a wraith appearing out of the mists. "People go there. When they don't have money for what they need, it's a place they can trade whatever they have. Do you still have money, Solly? We can get bicycles."

"I have money," Sol said. "Solid DMs and electronic. How is it that you know about a place, this kind of place? Up here."

I could see enough of Lizzie to see her twist her fingers together. Her words came out like teeth being extracted. "I followed my ma. More than once." Tendrils of mist floated past her face before the next words came. "She said she had to do … things to get the money to protect me. I know some of what she did. But sometimes she wasn't anywhere around Harborside. I followed her. That's all. I can find my way. Okay?"

The pain in her voice told me not to ask her to say more. It would be bad enough for her, what we would see.

"Just lead us there, Lizzie," I said. "No need to talk more."

"Fine" was the curt reply. "Follow me."

"Claire, stay right next to Lizzie," Sol said. "We all need to stay together."

"Of course," said Claire. "All for one and one for all. That's what the Spartacists say. And that sounds good for all, although it could be bad if one had a fall because then all would fall and if one would stall all would be late. So, we should hurry. I'm right with you, dizzy-Lizzie." She grabbed Lizzie's hand and hustled forward so that we all had to quicken our pace.

"You know, Claire, I'm going to miss you when you go back home." Lizzie's voice was back to normal. "No matter what happens, you're the same."

"Well, naturally," said Claire. "No matter what happens, I am still the Princess Claire, so I will always be the same."

Lizzie's chuckle drifted back to me through the mist.

On my own, I would have been hopelessly lost within minutes. The fog was dense and white. It cloaked all the buildings in a dim twilight and blocked any signs of where we were. There were no lights, either in the buildings or along the streets. One block of dilapidated structures was much like any other.

Lizzie knew her way, however. She never hesitated at intersections. How many times, I wondered, had she made the trip trailing her mother, so that she knew the area even coming from a different direction than her home territory? It was not a question I intended to ask.

At last, Lizzie came to a stop and held up her free hand. "Around this corner to the left," she said. "You'll see it."

Indeed, after we made the turn, I spotted a red light shining over a doorway. There were no signs, no guards. Nothing but the single red light.

"Is there a code?" I asked. "How do we get in?"

"You just go in," Lizzie said. "Just push the door. Don't show a weapon. I'm sure that would be bad. But we just go in. I just … don't want to go first."

"I'll be first," I said.

I pushed through the door and entered hell. The interior was one large open room. It was dark. The air was a thick cloud of noisome smoke from every sort of drug that could be smoked to foul a body. It stuck to my skin as I moved through it. Dim lights scattered around the room showed little beyond a couple of feet from them. That was okay, because the little I could see was bad enough. People slumped on cushions or lay flat on the floor, insensate. Others were smoking pipes or paper joints with God-only-knows-what in them. Others were injecting themselves, seeking a faster route to oblivion than that offered by the smoke. A man and a woman were copulating on the floor, surrounded by onlookers who were placing bets on how long they would last.

I heard Claire say, "It's okay, Lizzie. I'm right here with you."

I shook my head, grateful that Claire was impervious to the horror of this world and could help with the nightmares in Lizzie's mind. Sol came to stand next to me. Her face, all hooded eyes and harsh shadows in the hollows of her cheeks, was a warning to me that we needed to leave this place as fast as we could.

"Someone sells and buys here." My voice was a harsh whisper, although I'm not sure any of the people around me would have noticed if I had shouted. "Where are they? How do I find them?"

Lizzie pointed to an interior wall at the back. "There. I don't know names."

Yes. On a low dais, a fat man sat in a huge armchair as though he were a king on a throne. Four burly men flanked him, two on each side, making no effort to conceal the weapons they carried.

"Sol, are you okay?" I asked.

"I've been in much worse. Let's take care of our business."

That was not an answer to my question—although, in a way, maybe it was.

We made our way to the dais where the fat man sat, walking around or stepping over bodies that were breathing but were totally unaware of their surroundings. The only people making purposeful movements were the ones bringing more drugs to ones that still retained some of their senses. Where the floor was not covered by mats and bodies, puddles and rivulets sat or ran, sometimes near a small mound of shit. Our boots were befouled before we were halfway to the dais.

"I can't see anything resembling transportation here." I made sideways glances at Sol as we made our way across the floor. A vise could not have been screwed tighter than her jaws. I wanted to be away from this place. I wanted her to be away from this place.

"You can buy anything here," Lizzie whispered. "Or anyone."

I had no doubt she was right.

We did not bargain at the dais. Sol stated our need. The man looked down, perhaps calculating how much money we had but otherwise showing no interest in us.

"I might have four bicycles that have not been sent into the city yet. Can you pay with solid markers? No electronics."

"Yes," Sol said.

Then he named a price that would have been exorbitant in New Edinburgh's finest jewelry shop. Sol merely stuffed a hand in one of her pockets, withdrew an amount, and handed it to one of the guards. She did not count it. Granted, the Directorate was ultimately paying whatever it cost and whatever she said it cost, but it was bothersome that she did not count.

The guard did. "More than adequate," he said to the fat man.

Beady eyes studied Sol, the first time he had disclosed an interest in any of us. "Would you like a kicker to go with it? Any way you want it. Smoke, drink, pills. Shoot it if you prefer."

Sol's features contorted.

"He can keep the change." Claire's pressured words blocked any Sol would have uttered. "We need to go home, home on the range, because otherwise we might get mange, in a place that is strange, so we should exchange. Yes, make the exchange, Solly. Let's go."

Claire had all the attention on her, the way she always did when she started shooting out words in a disjointed chant. The brief disruption gave Sol enough of an interval to regain her self-control.

"It's as she said," Sol growled. "We're done here."

The fat man grunted. He turned his head to one of the guards, and that man in turn made a gesture to the area behind the dais. "Back out the door," he said. "Four will be there."

I had the sense of a form moving and caught the sounds of feet running on the flooring, but could not make out any detail in the deep shadow. With that, the fat man's interest in us vanished. He did not care about losing an additional sale. There would always be another one.

———

WHATEVER ELSE THAT MAN WAS, HE WAS AS GOOD AS HIS WORD. WE EXITED THE building and found four electric-assisted bicycles against the wall under the red light. The cycles were unremarkable printed plastic with low-power-assist electric motors. They were scratched and dirty, the grips worn and one seat ripped, but fundamentally they were no different from numerous others on the streets of Bannion—or, for that matter, New Edinburgh. That was the point, naturally. They had been owned by ordinary people until their acquired need for drugs had reached the point that they exchanged the cycles to have the drugs.

I looked at Sol. She was nearly doubled over one of the cycles, clutching the handlebar, the combination of the cycle and the wall keeping her upright. I thought she might retch, but that did not happen. I thought of the substances she used and wondered at the memories that place might have woken in her, the needs that it called to. I started to reach for her, but she straightened up and wiped her mouth with the back of one hand.

"Let's get out of here" was all she said.

The electric motor on the cycle I chose was dead. Either that or the battery was discharged. There was no place in this dead part of Bannion to charge it. I may not put much stock in the old stereotypes of masculinity such as strength and endurance, but I was not about to ask one of the women to change cycles with me. I resolved that I would die before I did that. Fortunately, there are few hills in Bannion. It is only a shallow cup in the landscape that collects smog. We followed Lizzie to the main street.

"You knew your ma came up here?" Sol asked Lizzie.

"I told you I followed her. I knew." The bitterness could not be missed. "She'd be here sometimes two, three days at a time. She'd be a mess when she came back."

"Had you heard of this place?" I asked Sol because this seemed to be the type of place a bounty hunter would know, and the pedaling on the main street was sufficiently easier for me to spend air on talking. I was afraid to ask if she had ever gone there.

"Sure" was Sol's answer. "I know about it. I couldn't find it in soup that thick coming from that end of town, but I know about it. Plenty of people do. Obviously."

"I'm surprised they can keep going like this," I said.

"They have CenSec protection," Sol said. "CenSec is skimming off some of the money. They let the Bannion police have a small slice too. That keeps the gangs away. This is no one's territory and no one is going to piss off the gray-and-blacks. It also keeps it a monopoly, you might say."

It occurred to me that my earlier thought about having returned to civilization might need revision. It was not a matter of a single corrupt CenSec officer in Bannion, nor was it a matter of corrupt officers in a town where civic justice and order had frayed. CenSec was managing this corruption. I had come across the statement in my reading that absolute power corrupts absolutely. As the enforcement arm of the Directorate, CenSec's power was nearly absolute, subject only to the curbs Joshua Montaigne put on them. Too much of my reading connected to disturbing findings on Offyonder. This was far from the first time I had thought about it, but it would require further thought.

CHAPTER TWENTY-NINE

As we moved toward the main harbor, the ground fog and smog the locals called the soup thinned and lifted a bit, and the street traffic—pedestrians, cycles, and a few cars—thickened. It did not approach the density I had seen before, however. The streets had no life. No streetdancers entertained passersby for the few coins they would toss. No vendors hawked their roasted meat skewers. The people on the streets moved quickly. They did not tarry, and they kept their eyes averted.

What was not visible was any sign of the law: no gray-and-blacks, no local Bannion police. Word of the troubles in the Uplands had permeated the city. The CenSeccers had been pulled into the fight. The local police and most of the population were keeping their heads down, staying out of the way, waiting to hear who the winners were and what consequences would follow.

One group of people was not keeping out of the way: the local gangs. All the streets leading into one section of Bannion were barred by crude barricades. A rough-looking crew wielding a mix-and-match collection

of weapons manned each of those barricades, shaking down anyone who needed to pass for whatever valuables they could obtain. We did not need to go in there, and Sol led us on a long detour to avoid it.

To enter Harborside, though, we had no choice. We had to pass one of the roadblocks.

"Let me lead here," Sol said. "Whatever happens, do what I say, follow what I do. Claire, do you understand?"

"Yes, Solly, I do."

That was the best assurance we were going to get. Sol wheeled her cycle in front of the three of us and led us directly to the roadblock ahead.

This barricade had been thrown together hastily. In fact, many of its components appeared to have been literally thrown into their places. There were cans and boards and wooden planking, bricks and paving stones, and a pile of concrete blocks. A narrow gap at one side allowed foot and two-wheeled traffic. It was a barrier that a man on foot could have easily scrambled over. What prevented people from doing that were two men and two women with holstered pistols. One of the men also carried a shotgun.

"Ho, Solly," called out the man with the shotgun. "You doin' business on the streets today?"

Sol wheeled right up to the man. She ignored the shotgun, which he pointed in her general direction, as she closed in.

"Whatever business I'm doing is my business, Cimino," Sol said. "You're not about to get in the way of it, are you?"

"No, no," said the man she had called Cimino. "We're just taking a collection, you see."

"Who are you taking a collection for?" Sol asked. "For the sick and needy?"

A wide grin split Cimino's face, revealing more gaps than teeth in his mouth. "I'd say we're pretty needy. We're collecting for us."

"You sure of that?" Sol asked. "Just for you?"

"That's all I'm saying, Solly. I've seen you around Harborside a long time; I know who you are, but you and your friends want to pass, I need something. That's the way it is today."

"Which means you are collecting for someone and if you won't say, that's okay with me. Not my business. How about four cycles? Will that serve as the price of entry?"

Cimino relaxed, glad to have an easy acquiescence from Sol. "That will do fine," he said. "I'll give you a tip as well. If you're headed to the docks, pick your way carefully. Some have guards, some don't. Some of the guards might shoot first even if you're willing to pay. Might not be able to tell which until one of them shoots. It's that kind of day."

Sol thanked Cimino and we all stacked our cycles against the barrier, where I could see a substantial collection of loot. After we did that, we were allowed through the passage in the roadblock.

Sol walked far enough down the street to be out of earshot before she spoke. "My guess is that the people who can are taking advantage of the situation to grab whatever they can get their hands on. I doubt it's any single gang, and since they don't know who's going to win, they would prefer that people not know where the money is going."

"All of which makes sense," I said, "but it doesn't tell us where to put Claire. Are there any people you can be sure are not Spartacist sympathizers, or simply ones you can be sure would not sell us out?"

Sol grinned. "This is Bannion. The one thing you can be sure of is that if the price is high enough, anyone will sell you out. The best place, of the options we discussed at the airport, is Grandma Toby's. She owes me enough for past favors when I wasn't paid in full, and she is set up to hide people for a while."

"With what we are seeing, do you think past favors are enough to buy security now?" I asked.

Sol's face hardened. "She also knows me well enough to know not to cross me unless I'm dead afterward, and I don't think she's ready to bet on that."

By the time we reached the main harbor on foot, the light was dimming. This was a function of the soup thickening again, as it was not late enough in the day for the sun to be going down. Penetrating into the normal fog, white layers of smog touched down to the wavelets in the harbor. The murk was not thick enough or low enough to hide the garbage in the water. Even where it did obscure the sight of the trash, it could not hide the stench of innumerable rotting lumps.

Grandma Toby's place was a ramshackle building on a pier where the main harbor narrowed down into the mouth of the river. It loomed above the pier as though floating in the fog, two stories of wood construction with gaps between planks and broken glass in some of the windows. The wood itself was stained with rust that flowed from nails and fastenings, and all of it was bleached by the omnipresent smog. The building showed no evidence of paint. Four small boats were tied up along the pier. Their paint was chipped and faded, but they bobbed at their moorings and, at a quick glance, appeared watertight.

The building, in fact, was elevated over most of the pier's length on stilts. Hatches in the underside of the building suggested convenient ways to haul cargo up or lower it down, ways that could allow boats to be loaded and unloaded without the process being apparent to observers away from the pier. By the time we crossed the rough wooden planking, the world outside the pier was hidden behind walls of light gray. The cloud flowed across the pier to conceal even those planks underfoot. I worried about where to put my feet.

A wall loomed up out of the fog ahead of us. The structure did come down to the pier at its end. A metal door was set into the wet wooden planks of the wall. Locked. Of course. Sol beat on it with her fist for half a minute. No response.

Sol pulled out her comm. "Dammit, Toby. I know you're not out in this weather, and I also know you've got a comm!"

The dry answering chuckle was audible from where Sol held the comm in front of her face. "Solly, it's good to hear from you. An old woman has to be careful who she opens her door to, you know. Give me a moment. I don't take the stairs as fast as I used to."

It was more than a moment before we heard multiple latches being released from the other side. The door creaked open to reveal Toby in a dimly lit vestibule. She wore gray twill pants and a loosely woven shirt that might have been the same clothes I had seen her wear in the Wormhole. Over top of that ensemble was an open robe of battered wool that came down to her ankles. One of her hands was deep in a pocket. I could guess what it held.

Toby's face was impassive. Only her eyes moved, flicking from one of us to another. "So, Solly, you are bringing the librarian who met you the other day. I would never have thought you took an interest in books. And Lizzie Quickfingers. And, I assume, the job you were hired for." Toby's eyes rested on Claire, who kept herself still. "If you have a need, Solly, I have a price."

"Same as me," Sol said. "I can pay."

Toby stood back from the door to allow us entry. Then she led us through a small and empty room to a staircase built against the back wall. We went up one creaking step at a time, constrained by Toby's slow pace.

The landing on the second floor opened onto a long undivided room. It was sparsely furnished near the landing with kitchen facilities, a table, and a half dozen straight-backed chairs. More prominent than the furniture were stacks of crates spread out along the length of the room above the pier we had just crossed. Toby caught me appraising those crates as well as the hatches above the pier, which I was now seeing from the other side.

"I make a modest living facilitating trade," Toby said.

"Smuggling," I said.

Toby sighed. "That is a harsh word, although I am sure you have read it in the books of your library. You could also learn it easily in Harborside, so I do not care to deny it."

"I take it you don't particularly care if CenSec hears it either."

Toby's brown eyes were steady on mine. "CenSec takes their slice of the trade. They are no different from the Bannion police or any gang in its territory, except for the fact that they wear pretty uniforms."

"And when the replacement for Captain Campbell arrives, you

expect that person to, shall we say, accommodate to this way of doing business?"

"Hah!" That was somewhere between a laugh and a snort. "I came across the sea to Bannion fifty years ago. In all that time, I cannot remember any C-suckers who did not arrive fully imbued with that way of doing business. I can understand that a library would not run that way—there is no money to be made in books—but that is the way all of CenSec operates, the way all of Offyonder operates."

The Directorate had made Offyonder a rare society in the vastness of humanity's expansion across the Reach, a near utopia, we were fond of saying. CenSec was the foundation of the Directorate's power on Offyonder. They were the only power on Offyonder. An absolute power. Again, the duality of power and corruption. I had read much in my history section that was consistent with that. Our description of what we had created on Offyonder might need revision.

"Why don't we have tea and consider what you want?" Toby asked when I made no further comment. "And it will be tea for you and no mash, Solly."

Sol's face flushed red, but she said nothing. She simply took a seat at the table while Toby busied herself with a pot on the small stove. One of Sol's hands dug into a pocket, then put a stack of DMs on the table. She waved at the three of us to seat ourselves as well.

The pot whistled after a few minutes. Toby fussed around the stove, then placed a cup of tea in identical white plastic cups in front of each of us. She made another trip to the stove and returned with a cup cradled in one of her hands. She made a show out of lowering herself into a chair. Smiling, she swept the markers off the table with her free hand. A clink sounded as they dropped into a pocket of the robe. She smiled some more. Waited.

"What is the situation in Bannion?" Sol asked. "In Harborside, at least. We saw gang checkpoints on the streets coming here, and a group of thugs claiming to be working for Spartacus had a roadblock on the route down from the Uplands."

"Then you probably know as much as anyone here could tell you,"

Toby said. "There is fighting in the Uplands, Spartacists and CenSec. That much people know—that, and the C-suckers from here have been pulled up there to fight. More than that, no one knows. The gangs will take as much advantage as they can, which makes it a good time to stay off the streets if you don't need to be on them."

"Where do the sympathies of the people here lie?" I asked. My tea was cooling. I had no interest in drinking it, and not from any fear it was doped. "We need to … make a delivery, and whoever has control here matters."

Toby tapped her teacup with one fingernail. "What you will discover, librarian, is that if the Spartacists win the fight up there, you will see a swarm of self-proclaimed Spartacists and their partisans here. Contrariwise, if the C-suckers win, everyone here will have been a loyal supporter of the Directorate, and some will settle old, unrelated scores by murdering a few so-called Spartacists. Do you blame them?"

I did not, in fact, blame the populace for having no convictions beyond a pragmatic desire to be on the winning side. What did concern me was that if we had to deal with a mob of suddenly rabid Spartacists, it would make my job of returning Claire to New Edinburgh via the airport a near impossibility. I remembered the Riots of a decade ago, when protests turned into mobs and the mobs ruled the streets even in New Edinburgh. That chaos had been brief, but the bloodletting when CenSec reestablished control had been almost as indiscriminate as the destruction unleashed by the rioters. I could not have Claire caught in the middle of such a scene, not again. I did not want Sol in the middle of one either.

"You have connections to smugglers—and, yes, a librarian is familiar with the word. If the situation here becomes … difficult, could you get us out to a transoceanic ship?" I did not like the idea of three and a half weeks tossing in waves across the ocean—I was certain I would be seasick the whole way—but if that were my only option, I would take it. I had little faith in Willoughby as a battlefield commander. My one regret would be that Sol would want to be paid off here and would not leave Bannion. A far corner of my mind created a daydream in which

Sol said she would accompany us to provide security and would take her pay when Claire disembarked.

Toby sipped her tea. "There are two transoceanic ships in harbor. It would be expensive, but possible."

"The expense is not a problem," I said. "That will not affect my agreement with you." I said the words hastily to Sol in case she would worry that taking Claire by ship would let me claim that Sol had not fulfilled her bargain by putting her on a plane at the airport. I immediately regretted the words. I had been caught up in emotion, wanting to show that I would be honest with her, would never cheat her. Instead, the words came out sounding as though my only connection to her was a business contract. Of course, that was the truth.

"I do not want to go on a boat," Claire said. "A boat is as good as a jail. Actually, a jail is not good, unless bad people are in it, but I am not bad, so a jail would be bad, which would make me mad, and a boat would be sad because a boat can sink in the water. Water should be for drinking, not sinking. Can I have a glass of water to drink?" She turned her wide blue eyes on Toby.

Toby almost dropped her teacup. Hot liquid sloshed over the rim and dripped from her fingertips. She put the cup down hurriedly, wiped her fingers on her robe, and sucked on one of them. When Claire said nothing else, Toby walked to the sink and filled a glass with water.

"Three weeks at sea with a secret and a boatful of sailors who might be disposed to take advantage of it poses its own problems." Sol availed herself of the break in conversation Claire had caused. "I could take your pay and say it would be your problem, but I would suggest seeing how this conflict is going to play out before trying that route. You have a spare room upstairs from here." That was to Toby. "Let us use that while we collect some information about what is happening."

I should have figured that someone in Toby's business would have a hideaway for people who wanted a place for a short, discreet stay. I told myself that only my urgent need for success in my job had driven me to think first of a boat. But I must admit, if only to myself, that the little fantasy of Sol accompanying us for three weeks to secure her pay before I never saw her again had played a role.

Safely behind the firewall of my face, I enjoyed her company in that scene, even though I doubted she would ever go on board in the real world, and I had promised to pay her off anyway. Hiding at Toby's, though, would give me a little more time in her company. This was a parody of rational decision-making. I could not allow a hint of its existence to reach Sol. Or anybody else. I should not have such thoughts.

While I was having thoughts I could not have, we climbed another set of stairs to a second landing. Toby had her living quarters at the head of those stairs. A glimpse through a door left partly open showed a suite far more lushly appointed than the nearly barren room below. Toby lived well off her trade. I suspected she had a far better kitchen tucked in that suite as well.

A door led to a long room similar to the one below holding the crates, but this one had only piles of junk ranging from worn and cast-off clothing to torn fishing nets. At the far end of the room, an empty set of shelves that would have made a nice case for printed books slid aside at the push of a button and a gentle shove.

Beyond the bookcase was a small windowless apartment. It wasn't much. A tiny desk with one chair and six pallets on the floor took up most of the space. Spartan as they were, the living conditions my employment at the library provided were better.

"Help yourself to the food in the kitchen where we sat," Toby said. "I'll tell you the extra charge afterward, Solly. All of you sleep up here, and if you're in the kitchen and I give you a signal, you get here fast. There is a toilet built into the wall of the long room out over the harbor. Use that to relieve yourselves."

After those instructions, Toby was gone. The claustrophobic nature of the room said these were definitely short-term accommodations. We inspected the pallets. They had been stuffed with hay. We made a careful check to be sure the mechanism for the sliding shelf worked from our side. Then we closed the door and dropped onto the pallets.

CHAPTER THIRTY

"Let's see if I can reach Willoughby," I said. I keyed in the code but received nothing more than a standard request to leave a message. Three calls obtained the same result. "Do you want to try?" I asked Sol. "He may respect you more than me."

Sol had no better luck with her comm.

I checked the time and the information for the satellites. The window was open. I made a call to my handler in New Edinburgh, reported our situation, and emphasized that Willoughby was not responding to my calls. Fifteen minutes after I clicked off, my comm buzzed.

"I am in the middle of a goddamn battle!" Willoughby's voice exploded out of the speaker as soon as I clicked on the connection.

Well, if he was in the middle of a battle, then he hadn't lost it yet. "We need to know what the situation is so that we can make decisions."

"Yes, you need to make decisions. You had them threaten my family—"

"I did nothing of the sort." I cut him off as sharply as I could. "I merely reported the situation. If they chose to take that step, it shows

the importance they put on this call. Now, can you tell me the situation, which was the purpose of this call in the first place?" I did my best to sound like someone other than the third assistant librarian. I believe I succeeded.

If nothing else, my comments gave Willoughby the opportunity to realize that I would report on this call as well. His tone and wording made a profound change. "We are winning here. We have pushed them out of the terminal and cleared the airfield. I have been able to establish a perimeter around the airfield that will allow an aircraft to land. I have notified CenSec HQ of this accomplishment. Joshua Montaigne personally told me to hold the position we have taken or die doing it. He is on his way to take charge."

Willoughby's intake of breath was audible. "Not everything is good. Those idiot farmers. Some fool named Calhoun led a whole troop of them into a trap outside one of the hill camps. I don't know exactly, but it sounds like there was a massacre. What the town police in Edge-of-the-World are reporting to me is that Spartacus led the attack himself and executed everyone they captured, but we're also hearing that Spartacus is personally leading the rebels here, so I don't know about that.

"What I do know is they are shitting their pants in Edge-of-the-World that the Spartacists are going to show up on the streets. I also know that it is my troops under *my* leadership that are winning, and when Joshua Montaigne arrives, I'm sure his gratitude will extend to doing something about what you did. Now, is that enough of a report for you?"

I tried to make clear that whatever might have been said as a result of my previous calls, I personally was sincerely grateful for his information and his success. He clicked off before I was halfway through.

"Do you think Willoughby is better than you expected or is it that the Spartacists are much worse fighters than we thought?" Sol asked.

"I don't know," I said. "I don't suppose it matters. What does matter is that Joshua is coming. It's a thirteen-hour flight, so figure he lands early tomorrow morning. Even if Willoughby has it all under control at the airfield, Joshua is going to need to make some arrangements to fix the mess Calhoun and those idiots created. My guess, if the executions were real, is that this Commander Marco is in the hill camps and Spartacus is outside the airfield, but that also probably doesn't matter to us. We don't know how bad it is in Edge-of-the-World."

I ran my fingers through my hair, then kneaded my temples. The evolution of campaigns like this always unfolded so logically in the texts of my favorite histories. It was clear which commander had made the critical error, and which one had planned properly. Having to work this out myself without knowing the final result was difficult.

"I figure Joshua will spend all the next day dealing with those problems," I said when I realized I would never be able to add it up more clearly. "That means he won't try to get Claire out of here before the day after, and that's assuming nothing goes wrong. Do you think Spartacus has enough fighters to attack Edge-of-the-World?"

"No." Sol rubbed at her scar. "Even if they wiped out those farmers, I don't think they have the force to assault the town. If it is defended. I would think Montaigne would make sure of their defenses. So, what you've said about timing makes sense. I don't see any better way to figure it."

Her assessment and approval made me feel very warm inside. It was worth the effort of grappling with the problem to hear that. I had to make certain none of those feelings showed on my face.

"That means we're here tonight, all day tomorrow, and tomorrow night," Sol said.

We both looked over at the other pallets. Claire was stretched out on her back, smiling and looking at the ceiling. Her lips were moving, but whether she was having a conversation with Abigail or the ceiling I couldn't tell, because whatever she was saying was too soft to hear. Lizzie sat next to her and held one of her hands. Lizzie looked scared, which meant that she understood the situation.

"I'm going downstairs to see if there's any mash in that kitchen," Sol said. "I know the people Toby deals with. There has to be mash down there." She dug her hands into the pockets of her duster and, after some searching, came out with a single blue pill. She regarded it sorrowfully. "There has to be some mash there."

I suspected she was right while I hoped she was not.

———

A NIGHT, A DAY, AND THEN THE FOLLOWING NIGHT COOPED UP IN THE SMALL interior room promised to be a boring stretch of time made worse by the underlying tension. Claire was happy enough, possibly because she lived in a different world, and Lizzie stayed next to Claire. In a way, the two of them took care of each other. Sol said little but was up to pace often. I took this as irritability and suspected the cause was either finding no mash in the kitchen or having finished what was there and finding that Toby did not replace it. For myself, I could manage periods of boredom—the library had many of them. But here I lacked my books. I resigned myself to endure it. At least I could think about Sol.

That next day was headed toward evening when the nothingness I had allowed myself to sink into was broken. Our door of shelving suddenly slid back. Toby stood in the opening. From her posture and hard face, this was an unhappy Toby.

"I've learned that I am going to have visitors this evening," she said. "I can't imagine you could have been seen coming here in the soup we had yesterday, but it is possible."

"One of the men at the checkpoint we passed knew Sol," I said. "Could they have connected her to you?"

"Most people who do business in Harborside are connected to me in one way or another, and Solly's business is one most people try to stay out of. For all I know, this is nothing more than wanting an extra score before some authority reasserts itself. It doesn't matter. I always pay the right people for my business and I will do that again. What I do not want is for you to be found here." She pointed at me and Claire. "That would complicate any dealings I need to have."

"You need us to leave, we'll go," Sol said.

Toby nodded. "What are you going to do about her?" She pointed at Lizzie.

"She'll come with us for now," Sol said.

Toby's expression shifted between uncaring and concern. Concern won out. "And after now? After you do what you are going to do?"

"I'm not going back to the Uplands!" Lizzie sprang off the pallet, defiance in her voice. "My ma always paid protection for me. I'll find a way to take care of it for myself."

Toby's face changed to pity. "You still haven't told her. Have you?"

"Toby …" There was warning in Sol's voice.

"Solly's not one for truth. We all know that. But you"—Toby faced Lizzie—"how do you think your ma was paying protection?"

"I don't know. What she had to do. Things she didn't want to talk about. Things I won't do." Lizzie had her fists on her hips, her chin thrust forward.

"Goddammit! Enough!" Toby was angry now and that anger was mostly directed at Sol, but she was talking to Lizzie. "Your ma was an addict. A drug-head. Any money she got fed that addiction with little enough left to feed your bellies, because that's the way an addict is. Solly gave your ma the money for protection and Solly made sure she used it to pay the right people and not feed her habit with it. Until the last half year, when your ma was so far gone she wasn't even scared of Solly. Then Solly gave me the money and I made it look like it came from your ma, which is how I know about all of this."

"What … no." Lizzie's legs gave out. She sat down hard on the pallet.

"Yes." Toby's voice had the finality of a judge's gavel. She turned to Sol. "Solly, you spent years watching out for this girl, now you figure out what to do next. Don't ask me again to send her to the Uplands."

"Solly?" Lizzie's voice could barely be heard. "If that's true about my ma, why did you do it?"

"You remind me of a girl I used to know." The identical line she had given me.

"Then why didn't you just pay for me? Why let me think my ma cared?"

"Because if people knew I was paying for you, it would be leverage they'd use on me. You would always be in danger from what I do. And then I put you in danger just as bad when your ma died and certain people thought there would be no more money. Dammit, Toby, I didn't need you doing this now."

"No. But *she* did."

Sol kicked the nearest pallet. Some of the stuffing flew out. "First things first. We need to get out of here."

I noticed that it was Claire who took Lizzie's hand when we left.

CHAPTER THIRTY-ONE

THE DAMNED SMOG HAD LIFTED AND THINNED IN THE TIME WE HAD STAYED AT Grandma Toby's. The lower stories of the buildings around us were easily visible, and a whitish blotch in the cloud layer gave away the position of the sun. By agreement between me and Sol, we were headed for her apartment. To be exact, she had said that was where we ought to go and I, a man of little experience in these affairs, had agreed.

The distance was short, but that did not mean we walked easily. To me, any of the people on the street could be a lurking Spartacist, or simply a robber seeking to take advantage of the more-lawless-than-usual climate. We made certain not to be seen as easy pickings. Sol walked in front, gun in hand. I had the rear, also with my gun out and turning to walk backward every now and then. That was enough for others on the street to leave a large buffer zone around us. What those people thought, I didn't care. Claire and Lizzie were sandwiched between us. Claire had one arm around Lizzie and was speaking into Lizzie's ear too softly for me to know what she said.

We arrived at Sol's building without incident. Whether that was because of our precautions or because they were unnecessary, I could not tell. The three-tail kit greeted Sol with an aggrieved growl, probably as chastisement for having to catch her own food or be fed by someone else. Then it spat and scampered for cover as soon as it spotted the rest of us. Sol slipped her pistol into a holster under her duster, then stood aside, arms akimbo, as Claire and Lizzie entered that front room.

"Oh, wow!" Lizzie turned around in place, taking in the pieces of Sol's life that were scattered all over the room.

"It's a museum!" Claire clapped her hands together, then hopped up and down twice.

"I do not have people here." Sol's voice lacked its usual certainty. "Only Martin has been here. And the person who feeds Midnight when I'm gone. You two will take the bedroom. It's less … cluttered."

Sol led Claire and Lizzie into the hallway at the back of the room. She returned with a cup of mash in her hand, tossed it down in one swallow, and went back for a refill. She returned to stand by the couch.

"As long as we can contact CenSec tomorrow, we should be fine for the one night. I can't think of a better alternative." She sounded apologetic.

I was thinking that if we did not hear from Joshua Montaigne by tomorrow, our problems would go beyond the indefensible nature of her apartment. "If they do not call me, I will contact my handler when the satellite window is open," I assured her. "They will reach us."

Any further conversation about Joshua Montaigne and CenSec was cut off by the reappearance of Lizzie and Claire.

"Solly," Lizzie began, "Claire told me that I need to be thankful for what you did, and I can't be angry at you because it means my ma didn't take care of me." Lizzie stopped and chewed on her lip.

"*Claire* said that to you?" I had my eyes on Claire, but she was staring at a patch of ceiling through gaps in her interlaced fingers.

"Well, Claire said that Abigail said that, and she said that it's best to listen to Abigail," Lizzie said. "I knew about my ma. I did. I just didn't like to think—"

"It's okay, Lizzie," Sol said. Then her shoulders slumped and a long breath came out. "No, it's not okay and maybe we should talk more. Maybe when you're older. We'll figure something to deal with … things for now." Sol sounded even more uncomfortable than she looked. She finished what was in her cup, pushed past Lizzie to go to the kitchen, and returned with yet another full cup.

The interlude allowed Lizzie's gaze to find the statuette on the shelf. She crossed the room to pick it up and turned it around in her hands.

"Solly! The girl you said I remind you of. It's you!"

"A little. A bit. In a way." Sol turned her head and fastened her eyes on that bottle of pills she had taken when we rescued Lizzie.

Meanwhile, Lizzie moved on to the picture of Sol and Gil Mortimer. She plucked it from the shelf and held it up to her face. "Oh, Solly, this was you! You were so beautiful!"

"No!" Sol's hand had started for the pills, but she pulled it back. She dropped heavily onto the couch. "I was never all that pretty. I wasn't. I knew it. Even my mother told me that. I remember how she showed me about makeup and what I could do to be attractive and said that would be the best I could be."

The pain in her voice caught me. Misery marked her face with lines and hollows, but under that misery and the strain of the years past, I could still see the beauty that glowed in the old picture.

"Lizzie is right, Sol," I said. "You were stunning then, and you are still stunning now."

"And you became famous," Lizzie added. "You became a famous interstellar bounty hunter who came here to get rich and you're the most famous person in the Reach who's ever come to Offyonder, and I can't believe I remind you of you."

Sol gulped down whatever mash was left in her cup. Her hand shook. The cup fell to the floor. Sol's armor fractured.

"No!" It burst out as a scream. "You don't understand. None of you understand anything!" Tears flowed over the darkness beneath her eyes and dripped off her cheeks.

"What don't we understand, Sol?" I tried to keep my voice quiet, which is usually not a problem, but to my ears I sounded like an interrogator.

"I didn't come here to get rich! I came here to die!" Her voice cut through me. "I ran here because Offyonder was the farthest planet in the Reach I could get to and all I wanted to do was die. I just haven't managed that yet. I ought to be put to death for what I've done."

"Sol, you're a bounty hunter," I said. "Of course, you've done … things." I noticed Lizzie still holding the picture. I made a connection. "This is about Gil, isn't it? This is something else he did. I'm right, am I not?" My anger about Gil Mortimer flared. For all my effort to be careful about my emotions with Sol, they broke through then.

"Yes!" That one word was a wail. "We were on Oberon. I remember the planet, the town, the case. We took down a gang of three. Gil brought in two partners for it. We all celebrated, got drunk, got high. Gil said we would all have sex. Together. All of them with me. I told him no. I told them no.

"I remember what Gil said. 'Solange doesn't mean what she's saying. She knows it's fun. She only says she doesn't want to, but that's not what she's really thinking. You are thinking this will be fun, Solange. I know it and you know it and we're going to do it.' And something snapped. And I went for my gun. I was always faster. Gil always told me he was the best shot, but I was better. I was always better. I was. I killed all of them. I murdered Gil!"

"That's not murder, Sol," I said. "That's self-defense. He earned that. More than that."

"It was murder! I should die for that! Gil always told me I loved him, and I did and I murdered him."

"What you did was right." Claire's voice was sharp, a laser cutting through fog. "He deserved to die, and you were right to kill him."

Again I wondered about Claire, about what had happened to her and what it was that could bring out this other Claire. I had no time to dwell on that, however. Sol let out a sob and curled up on her side on the couch. I put a hand on her shoulder, the one time I touched her intentionally. She did not notice. I pulled the blanket from the back of the couch and spread it over her.

By the time I turned around, Claire's eyes had gone vacant again. She was humming a soft tune and twirling her thumbs. Lizzie put the picture back on the shelf, spread her hands wide.

I hoped Joshua Montaigne would call early in the morning.

CHAPTER THIRTY-TWO

MY COMM BUZZED AS I WAS WAKING UP. IT WAS MY HANDLER.

"I have been told to give you specific orders." The tremulousness in his voice told me who had given those orders. "Joshua Montaigne will be coming to meet you and to take Claire Montaigne for her return to New Edinburgh. Be at Donovan Black's Wormhole in five hours from the time of this call. That is all." The comm clicked immediately after the last word, leaving me no opportunity for questions.

That was typical of Joshua. He gave an order; you followed it without questions. However, I would have liked more information. Why pick the Wormhole? CenSec knew of the place; I had been told I could find Sol there. Presumably, they knew enough about it to judge it defensible for anything involving the second most important man in the Directorate. Was that enough reason since they did not know where we were? It would be easy for us to reach it, but they would not know that. There was also the matter of the time Joshua had set. The Wormhole would not be filled for lunch, not yet, but it

would have plenty of customers. That did not make sense.

There would be reasons, I told myself. Joshua Montaigne did nothing without a reason. It was not for someone such as me to question him.

I sat upright in the chair and tried to ignore the sensation in my lower back. Across from me, Sol was still curled on the couch under the blanket. She might not have moved an inch from where she fell asleep. Midnight perched on an arm of the couch, three tails twined around one another, and regarded me with baleful eyes.

This would be the last day I would have with Sol. I would be headed back to New Edinburgh, my mission accomplished and all the benefits that would bring awaiting me. The prospect did not make me happy, although it should have. I wished the previous night had not gone the way it did. I wished I could do something for Sol to ease that pain, paint a different vision of life for her. I wished I were a different man.

Wishing for the impossible did not make it happen. I forced myself to stand, twisted my torso in an attempt to loosen it. We had five hours. Waking the other three now was pointless. I managed to work my way to the kitchen without causing a clatter. I found a pot of tea that had been sitting there since I was last in the apartment with Sol. I heated it, wiped out a cup that was in the sink, and went to the table.

The chairs were straight-backed and uncomfortable, but it was a different discomfort from the armchair I had slept in and, so, was welcome. I sat and tried to imagine how the day would unfold.

Sol joined me after I had worked my way through the tea. She kept one hand to the side of her head, possibly as a consequence of a headache but also possibly in conjunction with keeping her eyes averted. She poured herself a cup of mash. Drank it. Sat down with a groan. I offered to fry her some eggs, which she accepted with a grumble. I am not much of a cook, but I have no one to do it for me, so I can handle the basics. While I was working on the eggs, I told her about the order to meet Joshua Montaigne at Donovan Black's Wormhole. She digested both silently while looking at a patch of the floor.

"It's best that we have this done and over," she said long after I had given up on any conversation. "After you and Claire have gone, I will talk to Toby about Lizzie. Toby can use help these days and that's a trade that will always be in demand."

"What about you?"

"I said far too much last night and I have no interest in saying any more." The edge in her voice was easy to pick up.

I did not want this to be the end of our last private conversation, but I was afraid that whatever I said would only make the situation worse. I might wish I could change history, but all I could do with history was read about it and learn it. Even if I had been able to say comforting words, Claire and Lizzie picked that moment to appear. I relayed the information from my handler to them as well.

Claire brightened immediately with a clap of her hands. "Since the Princess Claire is finally going to be rescued by Uncle Joshua, *she* needs to be prepared. I will need the bathroom."

Claire vanished in that direction. Lizzie rolled her eyes and put her hands up.

After half an hour, Claire reappeared. "Don't I look suitable for the occasion?" She ran her hands over her body from chest to hips, patting down the same lumpy overalls on top of coverall that she had been wearing and, indeed, sleeping in. The only change was that her loose blond hair had been pulled into a tight braid. Lizzie told her she looked wonderful, and that satisfied Claire.

We set out for the Wormhole well in advance because if one has an appointment with Joshua Montaigne, it is essential to be early so that you are waiting for him. Anyone at any level of the Directorate knew that. Even the third assistant librarian.

Outside, the soup was dripping, as they say in Bannion. I would say the smog was drizzling, a wash that added more grime to the buildings than it removed. Sol turned up the collar of her duster. Claire wiped her newly braided hair over and over. Lizzie ignored it. I tried to copy Lizzie's attitude and focus on what would happen at the Wormhole, but something about the dampness seeping through my hair and running down the back of my neck interfered with my concentration. What the miserable weather did for us positively was reduce the number of people on the street. If anyone intended to obstruct our progress, we would see them coming.

At Donovan Black's Wormhole, we found the metal shutters rolled down over the windows as though it were still the very early morning. The sign on the door read CLOSED.

I turned to Sol. "What do you think is going on?"

She pointed down. A line of light was visible through a gap between the bottom of the door and the paved street. "Try the door."

I did. It was unlocked.

We stepped into a brightly lit barroom, brighter than I remembered because this time no smoke clouded the air. The place was empty. No, not empty. Donovan stood behind his bar, polishing a glass.

"Opening late today, are you, Donovan?" Sol asked.

"Was told not to open at all." Donovan put both his glass and his rag down on the bar. He turned, lifted the shotgun off its rack, and put it under the bar in front of him. "I'm only here because somebody has to keep an eye on my place and I live upstairs anyway."

It didn't matter who had told Donovan not to open. That order could only have originated from one person.

Sol walked over to the bar. "Are you taking money from CenSec, Donovan?"

He shrugged. "Yeah. You work for CenSec too. Money is money."

"You give CenSec information on me?"

"Yeah. It's that kind of business, Solly. You know that. Sorry." Donovan took a bottle from the top of the bar and poured a full glass. "This one's on the house." He pushed the glass toward Sol.

She took it, walked over to the same table I had seen her at the day I arrived, and sat by herself. So, Donovan Black was the source of our information on Sol. No one had told me that.

We waited in silence for about half an hour until multiple footsteps sounded outside the door. The bang on the door that followed was more suggestive of a rifle butt than a fist knocking.

"It's open!" Donovan yelled. "You can come in. There's no need to break it down."

The door flew open and slammed against the wall as two figures burst into the barroom. Both carried automatic rifles, the latest version of the ones the Peacers carried, and they swept the room with the barrels. Only when they saw no one but us and Donovan did they relax. Both were men in the triple-black—black turtleneck, black pants, and black jacket—of the Specials, the personal guard of the Montaigne brothers. Even the body armor over their torsos was a matching black. They whipped through the room, passed into the kitchen, returned, and went up the stairs to Donovan's living space. They were back quickly.

One of them called out through the doorway. "One extra teenage female. It's secure."

They took positions that allowed them to cover all of the barroom and us. More came through the door. Six Specials, each carrying a holstered pistol, one man in gray and black also armed with a pistol, and in their midst, Joshua Montaigne.

I studied Joshua as they walked in. He rarely appeared in public, but I had seen him on several occasions at CenSec headquarters when there were reference questions I had to address. He stood ramrod straight, clad in the same triple-black as his Specials, with the black body armor and a battle helmet. He removed his helmet and placed it on top of the bar, then looked around. His face was all harsh angles, not a bit of softness anywhere. His high forehead extended back deeply on either side of a promontory of dark hair that had begun to thin and streak with gray. Deep-set dark eyes smoldered when they rested on me briefly. Every part of him exuded menace and said this was a man to be feared, as indeed he was. This was Joshua Montaigne, the Dark Musketeer.

I spent a brief moment on the gray-and-black. He was a young man, good-looking, with unruly brown hair and a cleft chin—all that I was not. This had to be Gregr, Claire's favorite guard. From the long look that went between them, I wondered at the nature of their relationship. It was Joshua who commanded my attention, though, and that was where my focus returned.

In the time I took to check Gregr, Joshua had surveyed the room and its occupants. He inclined his head a fraction toward Sol.

"She will be heavily armed. You," he said to Sol, "take that coat off and do it very carefully." Sol complied slowly, making sure her hands stayed in view save for the brief time it took for arms to come out of sleeves. "Good. Search her and the coat." That command went to the two Specials nearest her.

One of them was one of the riflemen. He slung the rifle and began going through her duster. The other checked Sol, groping her thoroughly as he did. Not a trace of emotion crossed her face. When they were done, three handguns, four knives, three shuriken, and a spike lay on the table on top of her coat.

"That's all of it," said the one with the slung rifle.

"It is good to have accurate information." Joshua made the slightest tip of his head to Donovan. His focus moved to Claire and Lizzie. "What is this, Claire, my delusional gambit pawn? A new pet?"

I was thankful that Lizzie was canny enough to say nothing and keep her face blank.

"Lizzie is my friend, Uncle Joshua," Claire said. "This is my dizzy-whizzy-Lizzie. We talk together all the time."

A faint grimace passed across Joshua's face. "Gregr, it will be for you to take care of this."

"Yes, sir," said the young man in gray and black. A side-eye look passed between him and Claire, which I noticed even if no one else did.

Joshua turned then to me with eyes of cold enjoyment. "When I dangled Claire in front of Spartacus, he snapped her up as I expected, and I thought that would lead us to him. Your mission did not go quite as I intended—not that you knew exactly what was expected—and the plan needed modifications, as plans often do, but in the end, he has shown himself and his force and been crushed."

From outside the building came a series of pops. Gunfire. The initial shots were followed by the sustained chatter of automatic weapons along with three blasts that had to be grenades. The shooting was nearby and from more than one location.

The lower half of Joshua's face pulled into a deep V, a wicked smile. "The last try of a desperate man. I knew Spartacus would take the bait of me coming here, and he has walked into a trap, one final trap. Spartacus is a fool." His air of self-satisfaction was obvious. "Some people play chess better than others. We will need to wait only a few minutes before we can leave."

"While we are waiting, there is my payment to be made," Sol said. "The agreed-upon amount plus my expenses."

"I have the voucher," I said. "It is activated."

"Yes, yes, she does need to be paid off." Joshua's voice was quiet. His eyes bored into mine. "Shoot her. Do it now."

One of Joshua Montaigne's infamous loyalty tests, despite how dirty my hands were already. My gun was out of its holster almost of its own accord. I did not raise the weapon, however. He did not know me quite so well as he thought.

"No," I said.

Joshua raised one eyebrow, flicked his eyes to the rifleman whose weapon was still at the ready. The man grinned. I knew what was coming next.

"No!" Claire screamed. "No! Solly should not be harmed. Abigail says not to hurt Solly. Oh, whizzy-Lizzie, help me!" Claire grabbed Lizzie, spun around with her, and planted a kiss full on the startled girl's mouth.

Joshua stared at Claire. His face twisted in disgust.

And then all our lies fell away.

ACT III

Finale

All changed, changed utterly:
A terrible beauty is born.

William Butler Yeats, "Easter, 1916"

CHAPTER THIRTY-THREE

Claire gives Lizzie an abrupt shove that sends the girl to the floor. Then she pivots. There is a gun in her hand.

Joshua Montaigne has only enough time for his expression to change from disgust to surprise before Claire shoots. A small round hole appears in Joshua's forehead between his eyes. The back of his head explodes outward in a spray of blood and brain tissue.

The Specials are all experienced and highly trained bodyguards. Nothing has prepared them for *this* assassin. They are caught flat-footed. In their hesitation, Claire is firing again. The one with the rifle that is not ready enough falls. Gregr shoots at almost the same instant, and the other rifleman crumples. My gun is already out, my mind already made up. I fire, swift and deadly as I have always been, and claim two more of the Specials. At this range, the body armor does not stop the rounds we are firing.

Claire's third shot takes down another while these are falling.

In synchrony with these killings, Donovan pulls his shotgun from beneath the bar. One Special has freed his pistol from its holster, but

the blast from Donovan's shotgun takes him in the chest. The body armor probably stops the shotgun bullet, however, the impact knocks him into one of his fellows. The shot from the second barrel obliterates his face. The last two Specials start to raise their hands. There is no mercy in this room. Gregr kills one. I kill the other.

All of this takes scant seconds. I turn to find Claire's weapon leveled at my heart. She should shoot me right then, but she does not.

"Drop your gun, Colonel," Claire says.

I drop it.

Outside, the firing dwindles. I hear one more blast, then a last single shot. Then silence.

There is a knock on the door and a voice calls out, "All for one."

"And one for all," Gregr replies.

The door opens. A man wearing a standard blue coverall steps in. He wears a white brassard on his left arm with a red *S* on it. He scans the room and says, "It is all clear. They were overconfident and walked into our trap. It helped that they were operating on incorrect information." He tips his head to Donovan, who reloads the shotgun and covers Sol as she picks herself up from the floor where she had dropped when the shooting started.

"Tell Marco to start the counterattack in the Uplands," Gregr says. "We'll need a few more minutes here." He is checking the fallen Specials as he talks. Two of them are still alive. He dispatches them with a bullet each.

I use the opportunity to ask Donovan, "You are taking money from the Spartacists too?"

"It's a business," Donovan says. "Although, given a choice, I like the Spartacists better." His lips twitch in a smile of sorts. "If you had aimed at Gregr or Claire, the first barrel would have been for you."

No doubt. By force of habit, my mind makes a note that Donovan's role explains Lizzie's so-coincidental connection to Claire and to us in Edge-of-the-World, although I doubt I have a future in which that knowledge will be useful.

I regard Claire. Those blue eyes are narrow and cold, her face dispassionate and hard. She has not said anything since ordering me to drop my gun. I am still alive, so I decide to satisfy my curiosity.

"You are Claire. The real Claire. What were you doing before—what have you been doing? Was it all an act?"

"An act, yes. Maybe the performance of a lifetime." Her voice is as hard as her eyes. "Call it a big lie, if you wish, and there have been times I thought I was turning into her, but an act it was."

"And Abigail? Do you have an invisible friend?"

She gives me a harsh laugh that carries no humor. Again, her eyes do not change. "'Abigail says' is an alert code for those listening to my prattle over a one-way, always-on comm. That part was easy. After all, no one from CenSec is going to search the Princess Claire."

I have nothing to lose, so I ask the question. "Why? Why the act?"

Claire is accommodating. "It's simple, really. Joshua wanted to succeed the Director, be the future absolute ruler of the Directorate. He desperately wanted to be publicly named heir. He would never make a move against the Director as long as the Director was alive because he feared the reach of the Director's DeepSec."

She pauses and examines me for a reaction, which I do not give. "When the protests began to escalate, ten years ago, Joshua had my father murdered to clear the path for him to succeed the Director. He blamed the assassination on the rioters and used that pretext to call out ArmedSec and crush what we call the Riots.

"If I had my wits about me, I would be dangerous to him, and he would get rid of me also. So, Claire had such a breakdown. She would never be of sound mind again. Demented old Claire would never be a threat, and protecting me made Joshua look good to the Director, who actually felt sorry for me since he had acquiesced in my father's murder."

"That explains the act." She has not shot me yet. In general, people do not engage in lengthy conversation with those they intend to kill. They simply shoot them. If she is going to let me talk, however, I might as well continue. "But the 'kidnapping' was also an act. Obviously. Why and how does that fit with what Joshua said about dangling you in front of Spartacus?"

Claire smiles, and not one of those vacuous smiles. I see cunning in those eyes. "Yes, Joshua had a plan. And Spartacus had a simple plan, a way to get Joshua out from behind his layers of protection in New Edinburgh, out where Spartacus would have a shot at him. I get kidnapped, as Joshua planned. Joshua would come with a strike force because he expects that a trail leading to me will also lead to Spartacus. Joshua saw himself, in a single stroke, eliminating Spartacus, being in at the kill, rescuing me, and becoming the hero for the public.

"In reality, Spartacus would snap the trap shut. But then the two of you got in the way, and Spartacus needed to improvise. To give Joshua a more *compelling* reason to lead a force out here. You almost caught on at the transmission tower. I was supposed to lead you to the hill camp so you would believe the story about my *recapture* and escape, all of which was to buy time, but you got there first and the plan had to change."

"Sol is very good at what she does, and Lizzie is a good thief. The scene at the shack in the hill camp was staged," I say. "No one was killed in that shack."

"Correct. It all worked out, as you see, the way Spartacus planned. Some people, as Joshua said, play chess better than others."

I am incredulous. It is almost enough for me to forget she has a gun trained on me. "You are telling me you let yourself be a tool for the Spartacists, the bait to lure Joshua out. You could have been killed yourself quite a few times, even if the Spartacists were not actually after you."

"Well, all for one and one for all, as Spartacus likes to say. Yes, there was risk, but it had to be done—and not only because I could not play that role for the rest of Joshua's natural life. Our precious civic justice and order and the whole Directorate may have started as an honest desire to have everyone equal, to avoid putting any individual or group down by word or deed. But when the rulers are allowed to dictate what you can say, what you can think, what you are not permitted to say or think, what you have is despotism, an absolutism of the worst kind.

"Our Director is a tyrant. My uncle Joshua"—her free hand

indicates his corpse—"was an evil man who reveled in his power. It is going to end."

"When you say it is going to end," I tell her, "you must know that will mean more fighting, even more bloodshed."

"We all have some blood on our hands. I'm not afraid of it."

"You should be."

"I suppose you would know." Claire sounds like she has scored a point in debate.

"Yes." That is the only response I can make to that statement. "And in the end, do you believe Spartacus will do better? That you will not go back to one group of people trying to put down any group other than their own, clawing their way on top of others, making scapegoats where they need them? How do you know Spartacus won't go back to everything our ancestors came to Offyonder to escape?" It is unwise to argue with someone holding a gun on you, but I am sure how this will end, so I do not care.

"Freedom includes the freedom to screw it up," Claire says. "We'll do the best we can."

"You said 'we.' You're actually a Spartacist," I say. "You are, in fact, one of them."

This time her eyes light up, although the gun does not waver in the slightest. "Guilty as charged," she says, "except I became one of *them* long before Spartacus appeared. It was at the time of the Riots. You remember them, I'm sure. They started as a youth and student campaign against the GSG, against the requirement that speech and thought had to conform to what was acceptable as judged by the Directorate. It went from campaign to protest to riot. It was more than the young rebelling against having their thinking regimented through school drills. It spread faster than a blaze in a grainfield.

"Joshua crushed it with ArmedSec and the Specials. The young men who were the student leaders were brought to Monument Center and drawn and quartered. One of the leaders was a young woman, a schoolgirl really, only a year older than me. They gang-raped her, dragged her naked to Monument Center, lashed her ankles together and pulled them up behind her back tied to a noose around her neck, so she strangled herself. Slowly. Her name, like the others, has been deleted from all our records, but I remember it and you know it too. Her name was Abigail Rose."

"I do know it."

"That was when I learned that Joshua had had my father killed, when I knew Joshua for what he was. Being out-of-my-mind crazy and simpleminded kept me safe from him. That worked for Joshua, for what he wanted. It gave me an opportunity to disappear from time to time, to learn and train and to read widely. There is no check on what I can read out of that library."

Claire sighs. "But enough about me. Let's talk about you." She tosses the words off the way she might if we were making small talk at a garden party in New Edinburgh. But in the next sentence, her voice is harsh. "You are Ronald Dupuis, Colonel Ronald Dupuis of DeepSec, the rumored but officially nonexistent Deep Security Service, those who watch the watchers and who do whatever needs to be done. The only people Joshua really feared. You were a young man, a CenSec trainee who infiltrated and betrayed the leaders of the protests. You gave Joshua the histories with those … punishments. Then you disappeared into DeepSec and, outwardly, became the carefully constructed Martin Allgeier. So carefully constructed that even Spartacus did not learn who Martin Allgeier really was until recently."

"Also guilty as charged," I say. I now see the reason why I am still alive. Claire, the Spartacists, want something from me. This is why Claire has talked instead of pulling the trigger. I am a man of few scruples and fewer illusions, but I see the chance for a deal. "I will make a full confession of my crimes and all my actions. All I ask is that you spare Sol. I accept whatever you will do to me."

I am watching Claire, but I hear Sol gasp. Claire shakes her head, just a little. "I thought you heard. Abigail said Solly would not be harmed. That is the truth. As for a listing of your activities and your crimes, that is not what interests us about you. What we do find interesting is the cover you adopted: third assistant librarian at the

Directorate library. You have maintained that cover for many years. It has allowed you to read freely, like me in a way. You have read John Locke, Thomas Paine, Ben Franklin, Jean-Jacques Rousseau, Aleksandr Solzhenitsyn, Ayn Rand, and many others from Earth's history, not to mention more modern ones, like Ezra Hankins from the Reach. Spartacus has many sources. You have become a deeply disaffected man, Colonel Dupuis. Is that not true?"

How did all of that get exposed? If this is one of Joshua's Specials holding the pistol, I will be dead as soon as I answer. But it is Claire, and what is her objective? "It is true," I say. "Many years of dangerous words and even more dangerous thoughts. That is why those books, those thoughts, are banned."

"Thank you." Claire's tone says she has scored a point in some game she is playing, but nothing about this is a game. "So, Sol, you said you came to Offyonder to die, but you did not. And this man is actually willing to die so that you live. Can we offer you a job? Join us and help change this world."

"You have not mentioned pay." Sol being Sol, she says that first.

"There is none," Claire answers. "Only the chance to spend your life doing something worthwhile. Because as much as you may protest otherwise, we know you care what happens to people."

Claire's words find their mark. I watch Sol's eyes go to Lizzie.

"If Spartacus will take someone like me, I'll take the job," Sol says.

"And what about you, Colonel?" Claire asks. "Will you work with Sol—will you work for us? The terms are the same. A chance to die in a good cause. And a chance to be with Sol. With Joshua dead, we are going to come out of the shadows and fight. You can be valuable to us, and you know it."

Which is the answer to why I am still alive and why Claire spent so much time talking. And why not? I know the Directorate. I have known for years that it is rotten to the core, and I did my job even as my reading informed me of the monstrosity I worked for. I don't know if I have a soul, and if I do, I don't know if there is anything I can do to save it. I am what I have been. It cannot be erased.

"I would accept," I say, "but I am DeepSec, and it appears that Spartacus knows what I am guilty of. Bring me in front of Spartacus and we will see what he says, but do not be surprised if he simply puts a bullet in my head."

Claire's smile has nothing of the angelic about it.

She says, "I am Spartacus."

ABOUT THE AUTHOR

Colin Alexander is a writer of science fiction and fantasy. He has had a career as a physician, biochemist, and medical researcher. He now lives in Maine with his wife, where he also studies and teaches taekwondo.

The Case of the Princess and the Interstellar Bounty Hunter takes place in the universe of the Interstellar Reach of Humanity (the Reach). This universe is also the setting for *Complicated: The Interstellar Life and Times of Saoirse Kenneally*, a story that provides a detailed look at the Peacers and at an antihero in need of redemption. More stories of the Reach will come in the future, but next up is a return to the universe of Leif the Lucky. It will not be about Leif, but about some of the people he met and impacted on one of his journeys and their kids.

Bricks and stones will hide the bones™

Find Colin Alexander on the web at:
www.afictionado.com
www.facebook.com/ColinAlexanderAuthor
www.goodreads.com/colinalexander